Make You MINE

BOOK ONE IN THE ALLISTER COLLEGE SERIES

KC MATTHEWS

ISBN: 979-8-9947184-0-7 (Paperback)

Character Art by Samantha Kling

Background Art by K. Kennedy

Cover Design by KC Matthews

❀ Formatted with Vellum

To anyone who has ever felt love, then pain and heartbreak, and came back from it. You are strong. You are amazing. You are beautiful.

CONTENT WARNING

"Make You Mine" was written from a place in my life where I was dealing with the complexities of adult emotions and reactions to things that were going on around me. Because of this, please know that this book is not just another soft, fun summer romance. It deals with incredibly mature themes and is not recommended for readers under 17. These themes are:

- Sexual Content (on page) between two consenting adults
- Dissociative Amnesia of a repressed event.
- Death of a family member (not on page, but discussed by character)
- Sexual Assault of a minor (not on page, but discussed by character)
- Severe Anxiety Disorders

SONGS THAT INSPIRED
MAKE YOU MINE

Whenever I write, I listen to music, and the music influences what is happening on the page. It always has. Here are some of the songs that had a big influence on Allie and Teddy's story:

The 1 by Taylor Swift
Thanks For The Memories by Fall Out Boy
Fire Burning by Sean Kingston
Bad Idea, Right? By Olivia Rodrigo
Dirty Little Secret by Nocturn
The Fate of Ophelia by Taylor Swift
Disturbia by Rihanna
Siren Sounds by Tate McRae
Make You Mine by Madison Beer
Lighting The Flame by Lauren Spencer Smith
Cardiac Arrest by Bad Suns
Stained by Selena Gomez
Creatures In Heaven by Glass Animals

ALLISTER SHARKS

Although hockey doesn't come up much in the book as it takes place during the summer between school years, the dynamics of the Allister College hockey team are incredibly important to this book and any future books:

Teddy Novak - Center Forward
Luke Dermont - Left Forward
Ezra Bennett - Right Forward
Logan Finlay - Left Defense
Patrick Evans - Right Defense
Nik Rohjan - Goalie
etc.

Coach - Jesse Hennings

CHAPTER 1
ALLIE HENNINGS

I hate moving day.

Not because I'm sentimental about my sophomore-year dorm. No, the place smelled like a mix of ramen, *Febreze*, and whatever weed drifted in from the guys down the hall, but because moving meant chaos. And chaos always attracted Teddy Novak.

I kicked my suitcase closed with more force than necessary, wincing when the zipper protested. "Ana!" I shouted over the mountain of boxes and bags in our tiny room. "Please tell me you're not still trying to fit all of your stuff into two suitcases."

From her side of the room, Ana Flores popped her head out, curls tied up in a messy bun, face flushed with effort. "I don't think it's that bad," she said, sheepishly, "I'm just… strategizing."

"Strategizing?" I laughed, "Ana, you have double the amount of stuff you started the school year with. Double the books, double the clothes. You need at least a couple of boxes."

Her cheeks went pink, "Well, I ran out of options."

"Options are fine," I muttered, yanking my backpack onto

my shoulder, "but a U-Haul isn't included in my tuition, so I'm sure it's not included in yours either."

The hallway outside was alive with the sound of slamming doors, rolling carts, and parents calling instructions. Across the hall, Logan Finlay's door was propped open. Logan was busy packing his things up, while Teddy was leaning against the wooden dresser as though he's propping it up.

Of course.

The devil himself, perfectly relaxed while the rest of us drowned in cardboard boxes.

"Don't look now," I told Ana, lowering my voice, "but your boyfriend is supervising the world's laziest man."

Ana glanced out the door and smiled, "Logan's just waiting for his ride. His parents are coming soon."

I didn't miss the way her face softened. Logan had that effect on girls, but only one of them truly mattered to him. *Her.* He and Ana had grown up together, started dating in high school, then broke up again before college. They got back together around Christmas break, after dancing around the obvious fact that they are soulmates.

Teddy smugly looks up from his phone, looking toward our room. I swore the guy was allergic to shirts with sleeves. Even now, he was in a cut-off tee that showed off biceps he knew he had. His brown hair was a little too long, curling at the ends, and his smile, when it appeared, was the kind of thing that could melt common sense.

As if summoned by my glare, he exits his room and saunters over to our doorway, standing in place with that stupid grin. His muscular frame leans against the doorway, "Hennings. Didn't know you could lift something heavier than a vodka cran."

My blood pressure spiked instantly, "Didn't know you could stand upright without your ego propping you up."

"Ouch," He clutched his chest dramatically, "You wound me."

"You'll live."

"Only because your dad hasn't kicked me off the team yet," he shot back, grinning like the cat who'd eaten the canary.

There it was. The jab that always came. Coach's daughter. Daddy's favorite. The implication that I got some kind of special treatment because my dad happened to coach Allister College's hockey team. Even if my Dad wasn't the coach, I would've gotten into Allister. I had the grades. I had the scholarships from dance. I just so happen to go to the college that my dad works at. Big deal.

"You know what, Novak?" I stepped into the hall, hands on my hips. "The only reason my dad hasn't kicked you off the team is because he actually believes in second chances. Too bad you burn through them like lighters at frat parties."

Logan groaned from the bed, "You two are gonna kill each other one day."

"Or hook up," Ana muttered under her breath as she tapes a box.

I whip around, "Excuse me?"

Ana raised her hands innocently. "I said or shut up. You two bicker so much, it's like foreplay."

Teddy's grin widened, wicked and knowing, "Hear that, Hennings? Even your roommate thinks you want me."

I glared so hard I hoped he combusted, "I'd rather drown in the lake."

"Careful," he said. "I might hold you to that."

I turned away from him, pretending as though he isn't just standing there, watching. The worst part was, my heart was pounding. Not with rage, well, not entirely rage. There was something else under it, something I refused to name.

By the time my mom showed up to help me load the car, I'd plastered a smile back on. She swept into the dorm like she owned the place, bright sundress swishing, hair pulled back in her signature messy ponytail. Where my dad was all structured schedules and gruff pep talks, Mom was warmth and chatter and the smell of vanilla lotion.

"There's my girl," she said, pulling me into a hug that smelled like home. "You're all packed? Ana, Teddy, Logan! How are you three? Did you survive finals week?"

Ana beamed, Logan gave a polite nod, and Teddy shrugged. After making some small talk with my roommate and the boys, we begin taking stuff down to Mom's black range rover. The boys of course helped carry stuff down, making it so we only had to do two trips from Buchannan 226 to the parking lot.

By the time we'd loaded my stuff into the car, I was exhausted from holding back my irritation. Mom hummed as she adjusted the boxes, already talking about the summer plans at the lake house. My dad would join us in a few days once hockey stuff wrapped up. I nodded along, picturing a quiet summer with my mom, the water, and peace.

No Teddy. No chaos.

———

The drive out of campus was quieter than I expected. Mom hummed along to the radio, tapping her fingers on the steering wheel. I leaned my head against the window, watching the familiar buildings roll past. The library where I'd pulled all-nighters, the quad where the dance team had done an impromptu performance during Homecoming week, the sorority house with its ridiculous string lights and overflowing flower boxes.

Between school and the dance team, my life had been full. *Chaotic*, but full.

And yet...there was still this nagging part of me that wondered if I was doing enough. If I was enough. My dad thrived on discipline and achievement, my mom radiated warmth and effortless connection. Where did that leave me? Somewhere in between, I guessed, constantly trying to prove I wasn't just "Coach's daughter," but also terrified of letting anyone see how much that label weighed on me.

Summer was supposed to be my reset button. Lake Michigan. Early morning swims, late-night bonfires, the smell of sunscreen and the sound of birds overhead. I'd spent every summer of my life there. It was tradition, comfort, escape.

I pictured myself stretched out on the dock with a book, the water sparkling around me, my phone buried at the bottom of my bag. No schedules. No pressure. Just me and the lake.

The thought made my chest loosen for the first time all day.

"You're smiling," Mom said.

I blinked. "What?"

"You were smiling," she teased. "Thinking about something good?"

"Just summer," I admitted.

Her smile matched mine. "It's going to be a good one. I can feel it."

I let myself believe her. For now.

We didn't get far before Mom pulled off at a gas station to grab snacks. I stayed in the car, scrolling half-heartedly through my phone.

This summer was supposed to be mine. *Peaceful. Simple.*

But a voice in the back of my head whispered that nothing in my life had ever been that simple.

CHAPTER 2
TEDDY NOVAK

When I first met Logan Finlay, he was the mopey roommate they'd randomly assigned to me because we both played hockey. We'd only met twice before move-in day; once, when they had all of us come in and showcase our skills, and a second time at a Meet the Team barbecue that coach had hosted. We never so much as said more than three words to each other. For the first three weeks of the semester, he wandered around campus like a wounded puppy, shoulders slumped, headphones glued to his ears, eyes set on the ground like the world had personally offended him. Everyone assumed he was shy. I later learned he wasn't shy so much as heartbroken.

Ana had done that to him.

I have tried to keep track of their relationship status and have failed every time. "On-again/off-again" is giving it too much credit; it's somewhere between a soap opera and a badly plotted rom-com. Logan is, unquestionably, down bad for her though. I'm not here to judge him. *Okay,* maybe a little, but only because it's comical how much he suffers for her.

Logan is finishing packing the last of his things while his

parents ferry boxes back and forth from the car. I call his father Mr. Finlay because he's told me a million times to call him Dean, and I keep calling him Mr. Finlay just to annoy him. He says it makes him feel older than he really is, or something pretentious like that.

Dean is a former college football star. Apparently he was nearly drafted to the pros, but a knee injury and a surprise pregnancy ended his career early. Nine months after finishing college, he and his girlfriend at the time, had Logan, then got married. He didn't even hesitate in making a choice between football and being a dad, and honestly, that's admirable.

"Teddy, when are you moving out, bud?" he asks as he hoists the final box into the trunk.

"Uh— I might be staying here for the summer. Because my mom moved to Paris after Christmas break. Coach is trying to figure something out with housing," I say and he pockets my phone like he's making a habit of collecting my possessions.

He looks at Logan, then back at me with actual concern. "Well, if you need anything, don't hesitate to call us. We're only an hour or so away."

I nod thanks. It's the kind of offer people make when they're not sure what else to say but mean it anyway. His smile is easy and real; if I'd been less stubborn, I'd have accepted his initial offer to stay with them this summer.

Logan swings his hockey bag over his shoulder and turns to me. "Wherever you end up, man, I'll visit. Promise."

"See you then, Logan," I answer, and we do the thing boys in dorms do — a quick, awkward bro-hug like we're trying to measure how much distance friendship can actually bear without snapping. He leaves. The elevator dings. Their car rolls away. Logan Finlay is gone.

The hallway feels different without him. It's weird how people can neutralize the ache of a place just by existing in it. Buchanan 225 — west hallway, first floor — used to be chaotic in the most livable way. Forty people sharing a stretch of corrugated plaster and bad carpet; the walls were paper thin and conversation, music, laughter, and the occasional breaking heart traveled through them like wind. There were pre-gaming sessions in the stairwell, loud arguments in the laundry room that ended in beer-smeared apologies, and midnight runs to the party store where we all pretended we were more mature than we actually were.

Now the doors are all wide open. Boxes stacked like small fortresses at thresholds, trash bags bulging with poster tubes and bad decisions. Luke Dermont left first. He's heading over-seas for some humanitarian internship for the summer. Doing medical work in a third-world country. Luke was not only the hall's residence hall assistant, but also on the hockey team with me and Logan. He moved like a man with too many contacts and not enough patience. Allie left soon after. Both years I've been at Allister, Allie has lived in close proximity to me. Coach likes to keep an eye on the team, probably as much for convenience as for spite. She's not a snitch, though, she's just Allie. The type of girl who laughs at things that are supposed to be serious and then has the audacity to look offended when you call her on it.

She's only snitched twice in my time here: once for Ezra Bennett when he'd drunk himself into a bathroom coma, sprawled like a used dunce in a puddle of his own puke and piss, then had to be hospitalized; the other time was to get back at me. I had spilled beer on her at a party, harmless enough, except she'd been furious and when she found out Ana said it wasn't an accident. She ratted me out for smoking in the dorm. I just did it to get her riled up. I like that look on her face when she gets riled up by something I say or do. My punishment? Team laundry duty for two weeks. The stripes on the laundry bag never looked so shameful.

After Allie, Patrick Evans and Nik Rohajn moved out at the same time, both sets of their parents weaving in and out of the room next door to the girl's. Those two families got out the fastest. Like a perfectly coordinated dance. The boys lived together freshman year too, so it seems that they got it down into a routine.

Ana left right after Allie. Her sister and brother-in-law swooped in and had her out of Buchanan in ten minutes, like they were the organizers of a very delicate extraction mission. Ana always moved like a carefully planned event: quick, efficient, pretty. She smiled in that way that made men rewrite the dictionary. Shit, I know Logan has been rewriting his since he learned how to speak.

Now it's just me. Sitting in a room that still smells faintly of body spray and pretzel crumbs and detergent, surrounded by empty sockets where laughter used to live. The silence presses in. It's not the good kind of quiet that settles in after everyone's gone to bed, when you can hear your own breath and the world feels like a private club. This quiet is hollow, like the hall swallowed its heart and the organ forgot how to beat. It's a silence that makes me feel sick to my stomach. A silence that makes me feel incredibly isolated from the outside world.

I've got a problem we all have but don't want to talk about: nowhere to go.

Back in January, just after I had returned to Allister after Christmas break, my Mom called me with this news that should have sounded like an adventure and instead made my chest hollow out: she was moving to Paris to get married. She'd met a French baker named Pierre at some culinary conference in November. They'd spent a weekend together and apparently, one baguette later, she was infatuated. My mom's been a romantic catastrophe most of my life — the type of person who treats every relationship like an epic film and every date like a scene that will save her. I'm not surprised she fell for someone who can write love letters in pastry, but surprise and relief are different things, and I had neither. But she also gets bored of these men faster than flies hit shit. Most of her relationships haven't lasted beyond a few months.

She suggested moving in with my dad for the summer. My dad agreed — begrudgingly. I assume she guilt-tripped him into saying yes. My Dad lives in a Hell's Kitchen high-rise with his new wife and his two new children. My sisters. I've met them twice their lifetime, and I dunno if they even know I'm their brother. Whatever. It's not like I have a rela-tionship with him anyway. He just said yes out of pity for the fact that he upped and left me when I was a kid to start a new family with a new woman.

So now I'm shit out of luck.

Scholarship money covers tuition and the essentials. Anything outside of that requires an up-charge. Summer housing is one of those fees that sound small on paper but look large when you're staring at a ledger that insists you are not the hero of your own bank account. I cannot afford to pay extra. So, I sit on my bed, stare at the ceiling, and do what I always do when the future becomes a math problem I didn't study for: I catalogue everything that could go wrong until it all starts to feel inevitable. My own panic spiral consuming every ounce of thought.

I linger in my own anxiety for four hours before I finally hear anything from coach. It's a simple message that is telling me to come to his office.

I change out of the tank and athletic shorts I've been living in since yesterday. I throw on jeans and a t-shirt. Nothing flashy, nothing to make me stand out. Morrey Arena sits on the edge of campus like a well-kept secret: all glass and metal, its name adorned in plaques that reek of glory years. The arena is named after Jim Morrey, the man who started Allister College's hockey program, then went on to join the NHL and bounce between teams across North America for twenty-years, before finally returning to his hometown of Allister, Virginia.

I knock on the doorframe out of habit before entering. Coach Hennings' office is a museum of wins: walls decked with trophies, framed jerseys, team photos from eras that still smell faintly like sweat and triumph. Coach himself sits behind his desk — late forties, early fifties, the kind of man who still has a decent amount of muscle because coaching is exercise by another name. His hair is mostly dark but flecked with grey, and his beard keeps the two colors in a constant negotiation.

"Novak, come in," he says without looking up.

I close the door behind me and take the chair opposite him. He doesn't waste time with small talk.

"Did you talk to housing? Am I shit out of luck or staying on campus?" I jump straight to the question that has probably aged me five years in the last six months. My voice might be too eager. I don't care.

"Neither, actually," he says. "Housing didn't have enough space to squeeze you in this late, but you're not shit out of luck."

Huh?

I lean forward. "I'm listening."

Coach takes a slow breath, the kind that means he's already turned this over in his head. "It might be unconventional, but I spoke with my wife, and we've agreed that you can stay with us for the summer."

No. Let me emphasize the *no*. The image that pops into my mind is Allie folding her arms across her chest, every inch of her saying she will resist like she's made of brick. Allie's idea of "hospitality" hovers somewhere between a five-alarm insult and a passive-aggressive note.

"A summer with spoiled princess Allie?" I try not to let the word "spoiled" sound like it's incredibly passive aggressive, "Sounds like a disaster in the making."

Coach throws his head back a little and laughs, the low laugh that I've heard on the sidelines after a ridiculous goal, after a stupid play, after life being itself, "Don't be dramatic, Teddy. Your situation is a unique one. Never in my fifteen years have I had to scramble like I did for you. Besides, I think a summer away from life in Allister could do you good."

"Is your daughter okay with it? Last time I checked she wanted to cut me into pieces and feed me to a pack of lions."

"Don't worry about Allie. She's all bark, no bite. She'll throw a fit, but she'll get over it." He smiles like he's already rehearsed the conversation, "I'll talk to her beforehand."

I picture the conversation. Coach Hennings in his all of his earnestness, rabbit ears perked, telling Allie that her personal space is being invaded by me, Teddy Novak — human chaos and supposed arsonist at parties. The next thing I can see is Allie with a list of infractions the size of a grocery receipt, each item checked off with an eye-roll sharp enough to carve granite.

My practical brain tries to calculate the cost: free housing, a roof, a fridge, some semblance of stability. My pride and Allie's inevitable displeasure jostle for attention and win. The weird familiarity of being under Coach's roof. Of being within earshot of actual family dynamics instead of in the dorms is strangely appealing.

He stands as I do, the conversation winding down like the last fifteen seconds of a game. "Be packed by five," Coach says, "I'll swing by, load your stuff, and we'll drop it off at our place."

For the first time all day I feel two things at once: supported and trapped. Support is a warm thing a blanket thrown over me just because someone wants me to keep warm. But there's also the bear-trap feeling, like I've stepped into an arrangement that will clamp down on my freedom just when I thought I could breathe. A summer under the same roof as Allie and my coach sounds like a recipe for a disaster.

"Thanks, Coach," I say, because gratitude is something I can offer even if my internal monologue is loudly composing a list of grievances.

He claps a hand on my shoulder in a way that's equal parts fatherly and coachy, "You're part of this family, Teddy. We take care of our own."

The word "family" is heavy with implication. Coach's family is a different animal than mine — more organized, less messy, probably smells better. I'm part of the team, yes, but here's the thing teams do: they impose obligations. They call for sweat and loyalty and sometimes, for a summer, spending an obscene amount of time with Allison Hennings.

Back in Buchanan, the place is quieter now than when I left it. I stand in the doorway, looking at the empty space Logan once occupied.

I start packing. It's slow and methodical. I fold each shirt with a ritual precision that feels ridiculous, like I'm preparing artifacts for a museum of my own life. I fold my jersey last, smoothing the creases like they are things that will keep their shape while I'm gone. Photos from home don't come out of drawers; they go straight into a small box. The box is heavy not because of the paper but because of the memory that seals with each photograph.

At three-thirty, with the sun slanting gold across the quad like it owns the semester's final hours, my phone buzzes. It's Mom from Paris. A picture of some cobblestone street I've never seen and a message that says, in French, "Mon petit — I miss you." I reply with something that sounds like an adult and then pocket the phone. Distance does strange things. It turns love into postcards and forgets the in-between.

Though, it's not like I truly miss her very much. I miss the idea of having a mom who cares so deeply about me, not the mom I've been given who has spent more time chasing men than acting like a parent.

By four-fifty-eight I'm downstairs with two duffel bags and two cardboard boxes. Coach pulls up in his truck. It smells faintly of pine air freshener and old coffee domestic and normal. He helps me load the trunk with an efficiency borne of raising athletes and careers. There's a rhythm to it. Him, me, each thing finding a place, the imminent summer folding itself into the space between the rear seats.

It's a short ride to the Hennings' house, the kind that should feel small and ordinary but hums in my veins like a goddamn cliff. I keep replaying the empty dorm, the echo of laughter that's no longer there, the image of my mom on some foreign street. I tuck all of it somewhere in my chest, like a bandage, and look out the window as Allister recedes. I bury it deep, never wanting to take the lid off the box that I conceal it in.

If this summer is a bear trap, at least it's a house with air conditioning and real food on a schedule. And, if nothing else, it's a place to be.

CHAPTER 3
ALLIE HENNINGS

Eldridge Bay is a sleepy lakeside town. Not just a coastal town, but my mom's hometown. It sits on the coast of Lake Michigan, just south of Traverse City, a postcard-perfect mix of cottages, docks, and pine trees bending toward the water. Tourists flock here every summer to rent cabins or lake houses, drawn by the promise of swimming in clear water, boating at sunset, and quiet nights around fire pits.

Is it worth the nearly fifteen-hour drive from Virginia? Not a chance in hell. But we always make it.

Usually when I mention a beach house, people assume I'm heading to Myrtle Beach or Wrightsville, maybe somewhere with palm trees and boardwalks. They're always surprised when I explain that my family's summer house is in the middle of Michigan, tucked into a small town barely large enough to sustain a single stoplight.

My mom was born and raised here. She grew up in Eldridge Bay before leaving for a small liberal arts college in Detroit, where she studied business and joined every volunteer club on campus. She met my dad at a hockey game during his senior year. She was only a sophomore, a hopeful twenty-year-old who thought he was cute and decided to take her chance.

That's her version of the story, at least. My dad tells it differently. His version has more banter, more games of hard-to-get, more "I knew she was it but she didn't know yet." They've been happily telling conflicting versions of the same story for twenty years, and I've heard both so many times I could recite them in my sleep.

The drive up feels endless. Fourteen hours in total, stretched across two days, seven-ish hours each. Mom handles most of the driving since she trusts herself more on the highways, though I took over for a few stretches when she needed a break. We spent the night in a hotel just outside Columbus, the kind of place that's so nice you immediately know it cost too much. Plush pillows, a lobby that smelled like lemon water, and a bathroom bigger than mine and Ana's dorm room.

The familiar streets of Eldridge Bay roll into view, I'm more restless than tired. The houses appear like old friends, each one marking our progress closer to the water. I lean my head against the window, watching as the lake peeks through gaps between trees and rooftops. It glimmers in the distance, silver and blue under the early summer sun.

And then I see it.

The Summer House.

My heartbeat stutters the way it always does when we pull into the dirt driveway, like I've been holding my breath for months and can finally exhale. The house itself isn't big or flashy—no wraparound decks or private docks like the tourists rent—but it's ours. Light blue siding, a grey tiled roof, a cobblestone path up to the door. It has quirks and creaks, rooms that smell faintly of cedar and lake air, and a backyard that slopes down toward the beach. It's the place I've spent every summer of my life.

This house means so much to me, it always has. The fresh,

lake side air and the blue sky with a soft breeze is always a reminder that I am home.

In Eldridge Bay, I'm not the sorority PR manager at Allister College, or the treasurer of the dance team, or the coach's perfect, sometimes spoiled daughter. Here, I'm just Allie Hennings. I'm the girl who bartends part-time at the country club, the one who knows every lifeguard by name, who buys ice cream from Carla's on Main Street three nights a week, and who everyone in town remembers as "Martie's daughter."

Because here, my mom isn't just Martie Hennings—she's *the* Martie Hennings.

She was Eldridge Bay's golden girl. Cheer captain, fundraiser organizer, homecoming queen. The reason the Lakeside Park gazebo still exists is because she rallied the whole town to save it from developers. That gazebo became a landmark. It's where she and my dad got married at twenty-two, where she hosted dozens of charity events, where she mourned her parents when they passed.

I was six when Grandma Maeve died of cancer, eight when Grandpa William had a stroke. I don't remember much about them, but I remember enough. The smell of my grandma's perfume. The way my grandpa whittled little animal figurines and slipped them into my pockets when Mom wasn't looking. Losing them hurt more than I could ever explain, even with time dulling the memories. They were the extent of loss that I have experienced in my life, and they've hung over me as a haunting reminder than life is so short. It's so precious.

When they passed, the Summer House went to Mom. None of her siblings wanted it—except Uncle Mitchell, who only wanted to gut it and turn it into an Airbnb. Mom refused, and with Dad's NHL money, she bought out her five siblings' shares. She was determined to keep the house exactly as it was meant to be: a family place, not a business.

As Mom parks the SUV, I glance at her. She has the same expression she always wears when we arrive—eyes glinting with unshed tears, a small, nostalgic smile tugging at her lips. I can't help but smile too. Seeing her so sentimental makes me wish I had been raised here instead of in Allister. I imagine what it would've been like to grow up in a town where everybody knew my name, where summers meant the lake and friends and the kind of memories that stick like bubblegum on shoes.

Instead, I grew up fifteen minutes from Allister College, destined from childhood to attend the place where my dad coaches hockey. Not that it was ever really in question. With or without his influence, I had the grades and the SAT scores. But it didn't hurt that financial aid gave me a full ride— tuition, room, board, everything. The only thing I pay for myself are textbooks, which I cover with money from my summer job here in Eldridge Bay. People assume I'm rich because my parents are, but that doesn't mean I walk around with their credit card and buy whatever the hell I want. They raised me better than that.

I climb out of the car, stretch my legs, and breathe in the scent of the lake. It's sharp and clean, a mix of water and pine and sand. The sun warms my skin as Mom pulls her purse and an overnight bag from the backseat. I wrestle my suitcase out and follow her up the cobblestone path.

The house feels exactly the same as it always has. No stale, shut-up smell thanks to our neighbor, Mrs. Callahan, who comes by during the year to air things out and dust. Mom drops her bag in the entryway and spins slowly, taking it all in. "Allie-cat," she says softly, "we're home."

I throw my arms around her in a tight embrace and for a quiet moment, we linger together in the doorway and just hold each other, glad to finally be *home.*

We part ways to unpack, though I make two more trips to the car before finally retreating to my bedroom.

My room hasn't changed since childhood. Pale yellow walls, the same full-sized bed, the same mismatched picture frames on the dresser. I remember when I finally moved to the upstairs bedroom from the basement bedroom. I felt like I was finally a grown up.

The same posters from when I was fourteen line the walls. Most of them are from concerts that had happened that year, or new album releases.

There's even a movie poster from the *Marvel* movie that had come out that year.

I unpack quickly, earbuds in, humming along to music as I line up my toiletries and stack my folded clothes into drawers.

From one bag, I pull out a photo frame. It's a picture of me, Ana, and Logan—Teddy grinning in the background, photobombing with his tongue out. Of course. I roll my eyes at his face before setting the photo on my nightstand. My gaze lingers a little too long, though.

That had been taken at the first frat party after Logan and Ana had finally gotten back together. Patrick had taken it and Teddy had photobombed at the last minute.

A knock at my door pulls me out of the moment. Mom leans against the frame, changed into jean shorts and a tank top, her hair clipped back. "Your dad's almost here. Will you be ready to help him unload?"

"Unload what?" I ask, frowning. "We already brought everything. Isn't he only supposed to have a backpack?"

Mom gives me a smile that makes my stomach twist. It's the smile she uses when she knows she's about to drop a bomb. She leads me back to the living room, sits on the couch, and watches me like she's bracing for impact.

"Mom," I say slowly, "what happened?"

She sighs. "You know how your father would do anything for his players?"

No.

She cannot be serious.

I already know where this is leading, though, I'm hoping it's someone tolerable like Brian or Patrick or even Nik, for fuck sakes.

But I know that I'm not that lucky.

The front door opens downstairs. "Honey, I'm home!" Dad's voice booms through the house. I hear another set of footsteps behind him. The front door opens. My dad's voice is booming—always the kind of entrance he makes—and the house fills with footsteps that mean something is about to change. I hear another set behind his; someone lighter in tempo, someone I recognize on instinct from the footprints he leaves at parties and sideways stares.

I know exactly who is coming up the stairs behind my dad before I even see his face. I can just feel it in my bones.

Teddy Novak. Six-foot-three. Curly hair that will never behave. A grin that makes him dangerous and infuriating in equal measure.

And just like that, my entire body betrays me. My pulse kicks up. My palms sweat. My face feels hot. My heart does the idiotic thing it always does when he's near: stutters, speeds up, becomes something portable and ugly. I feel heat under my skin and a ridiculous urge to punch him or smile at him or both. Part of me wants to hold up my hands and curse the world because what the fuck is he doing here?

"Hey, Hennings," he says, grinning like he owns the place.

And just like that, my perfect Eldridge Bay summer goes up in flames.

I make sure my scowl is locked in place because the world does not need my smile hijacked by his brazen charm. He meets my scowl with a tilt of his head, a grin that says sorry-not-sorry, and the sort of unapologetic glee that would ruin a saint. "You never mentioned that the your infamous summer house is this nice?"

"Because I didn't want you contaminating it," I reply putting my hands into my pockets.

The problem isn't that my dad likes Teddy—he does and I don't fault him—but that the idea of us sharing the same summers feels like a negotiation I hadn't signed up for. If Teddy is here, that means our routines will be different. It means chances of small, private spaces becoming public shrink. It means I will not be able to stomp down to Carla's with a hoodie and sunglasses and pretend I don't know anyone. For better or worse, my summer just became the kind of complicated someone writes about for a reason.

CHAPTER 4
TEDDY NOVAK

So this is the summer house.

It's nice, sure, but not the paradise Coach made it sound like on the drive up. The way he kept hyping it, you'd think he owned a private villa on the Amalfi Coast instead of a cottage on Lake Michigan. In reality, I'm standing in front of a one-and-a-half story place with yellow siding, a garden that looks like it belongs in a Better Homes magazine, and a driveway just big enough for two SUVs. One of which is already here.

Translation: Hennings beat me to her own damn beach house.

Of course she did. She always has to win.

I step out of Coach's SUV and stretch my legs. Four hours in the car is a lot. We arrived this morning in Michigan by plane, I can't imagine driving here. I grab my suitcase and duffle, the only bags I brought. The rest of my stuff? Left back in Allister at Coach's house, because he insisted I wouldn't need it here. Guess we'll see.

I follow him up the dirt driveway, my sneakers crunching against the gravel. "So, uh… does your wife and Allie know I'm with you?"

Coach grips the sunflower-yellow door handle and flashes me that infuriating half-grin of his. "Martie knows. Allie does not."

"Oh, great." I drag the words out as dramatically as possible, because what the hell else am I supposed to do?

He gives me that sharp Dad-look, the one that's supposed to cut through sarcasm and shut me up. "I know you and Allie don't get along, but I also know she can play nice. And I expect you to do the same."

"Aye aye, Captain." I snap off a lazy salute.

Coach chuckles under his breath, shaking his head like I'm a hopeless case. He opens the door, calling out in some sing-songy tone I don't catch because my brain is too busy cataloguing every detail of the house.

And wow. The inside hits different.

The walls are painted this soft, bluish-gray color that makes the whole place feel cool and calm. The air smells faintly sweet, like sugar cookies or vanilla candles, and the central air practically kisses my skin after being baked alive in the car.

It feels like a proper home. Not a rental. Not an apartment you're just crashing in until the next eviction notice comes. A real home, with years of memories etched into the walls.

For a second, it almost knocks the wind out of me.

There's a moment of silence after Coach calls out that he's arrived and I follow him up the stairs with my duffel bag haphazardly slung over my shoulder.

My eyes land on her and a weird feeling kicks in. I've never saw Allie outside of Allister. She has a glow to her, one that she doesn't have back at school.

Allie and I exchange snarky comments, right on schedule, and Martie approaches with a soft, motherly grin.

"Welcome to Eldridge Bay, Teddy."

Martie pulls me into a hug before I can even adjust to the

house. She smells like citrus and sunscreen, and she squeezes me with the kind of warmth only moms seem capable of.

"Thank you, Mrs. Hennings for letting me stay with you guys this summer," I manage, stepping back.

"It's no problem, truly." She smiles, her eyes soft. "Jesse told me what happened with your mom. I am so sorry."

Allie scoffs at the words. Figures.

I shake my head quickly, brushing off Martie's apology. "No, no, don't be sorry. My mom's always been that way. Unfortunately."

Coach returns inside with my suitcase, closing the door behind him.

He clears his throat and gestures toward Allie, clearly trying to cut through the tension. "Allie-cat, can you show Teddy to the spare bedroom?"

The look she shoots him could kill a man. Unfortunately for me, Coach just raises his eyebrows until she caves.

"Alright, spawn of Satan, let's go," she mutters, pushing off the wall. She's clearly not thrilled about my invasion of her summer house, but what else was I supposed to do? Live on the streets?

I drag my suitcase behind me, following her down to the lower level, "Are you always this rude to guests, or am I just special?"

"Nope. Just you, Theodore." She spits the name like it's poison, stopping in front of a door.

"It's Teddy. Not Theodore. You know that."

"Yes, I do." She smirks, opening the door. "But guess what? I don't care. Stay out of my way, and I'll stay out of yours."

I grin, leaning casually against the doorframe. "That's gonna be a little tricky, Allie-cat. We're living together. For three whole months."

"Not really. You've got the whole lower level to yourself. Only thing you'll need upstairs is the kitchen."

She spins on her heel and slams the door on her way out.

I stand in the middle of the room, taking it all in. Light blue walls. A full-sized bed covered in crisp white bedding. A painting of a freighter ship hanging above the headboard. It's nicer than any place I've stayed long-term. Certainly beats the thought of another summer in a dorm or, worse, Logan's couch.

Dean Finlay was kind enough to offer, but the guy's already got three sons, two of which still share a room. No way was I going to wedge myself into that chaos.

This, though? This works.

I flop down onto the bed, staring up at the popcorn ceiling, its jagged dips and shadows staring back like they know I'm in way over my head.

What the fuck have I gotten myself into?

Three hours later, after unpacking, more snide comments traded with Hennings, and a whole lot of me silently wondering if I should've just stayed in Allister, I find myself sitting at their dining table.

Coach and Martie sit across from each other. Allie's across from me, because apparently the universe likes its drama symmetrical. We're eating pizza, and the tension between me and Hennings is thicker than the crust.

"So, I was thinking about heading down to the beach tonight," Allie says, like it's no big deal. "We don't have anything else planned, right?"

"Just your usual Bay friends?" Coach asks. She nods, chewing.

Martie brightens. "Oh! You should take Teddy with you!"

"Not a chance." Allie doesn't even blink.

I clutch my chest dramatically. "Ouch. Shot through the heart."

"Allie, be nice," Martie scolds, wiping her mouth with a napkin and setting it down.

"Well, Mom, nice went out the window when Dad showed up with Satan's reincarnate."

I set my slice down and lean forward, "Hold up. Am I the spawn of Satan or his reincarnate? Because I can't be both. Pick one."

"You're the living embodiment of evil, Theodore."

Coach sighs, pinching the bridge of his nose. "Allie, enough. Teddy, ignore her."

"Dad—"

"Allie." His tone is final, the kind of voice that silences locker rooms. "No. Teddy had nowhere else to go. Your mother and I agreed he could stay with us. Can you be mature about it?"

"Whatever." She shoves her plate away, stomping off toward her room. The door slams shut seconds later and a silence rings through the air as Coach and Martie look between me, each other, and Allie's closed door.

"Well," Martie says lightly, "someone's dramatic."

I finish my slice, setting the crust down carefully. "Are you sure I'm not imposing? This is her house too. I don't want to make her summer worse."

Martie shakes her head firmly. "What happened with your mom was awful, Teddy. You've been dealt an unfair hand, and you deserve better. This is your home now too."

Coach nods. "I've seen fifteen years of players come and go. You boys are like my own kids after everything we go through together. You're not the first player we've opened our home to, and you probably won't be the last."

Something catches in my chest. Tight. Sharp. I swallow it down, nodding. "Thank you. Really. For everything."

I polish off my second slice, pushing back from the table. "But I think I'm gonna take a walk. Clear my head."

Coach nods. "Understandable. If we're in bed when you get back, just make sure you lock up."

"What about Allie?"

"She's got keys. You don't."

Fair enough.

I toss my plate, grab my earbuds, and slip out the front door.

———

The sky is melting into pinks and oranges, the lake reflecting every color like a painting. Classic rock booms in my ears, but after a few minutes I pause the music because the world itself feels too alive to drown out.

I've never been to a beach like this. The only ones I went to were all gray and brown sand, trash cans, cigarette butts and busted beer bottles. This? The sand here is pale and soft, almost white. The water stretches endlessly, the horizon a straight line you could balance on. If I didn't know any better, I would assume that I'm staring out at the ocean, but I'm not.

I kick off my flip-flops, picking them up by the throngs, and step onto the wooden path that leads down to the beach. The sand molds around my feet, warm but not scorching. The kind of warmth you want to sink into.

I walk until I find a clear patch near the waterline, then drop into the sand, leaning back on my palms, ankles crossed. The waves roll in quietly, brushing the shore in rhythm with my heartbeat.

For the first time in days, maybe weeks, my chest loosens. My head clears.

This town might not be the heaven Coach made it sound like, but staring out at this lake with the sun dipping beneath the horizon…

Yeah. I could get used to this.

CHAPTER 5
ALLIE HENNINGS

The sun has set, the tiki torches are out, the bonfire is roaring and it can only mean one thing. Summer has officially started in Eldridge Bay.

I scanned the crowd, taking it all in. Most of the faces were strangers—tourists who had rented cottages for the season—but there was one face that made my chest lift in recognition. Misha Copperwaith. She was perched on the edge of a folding chair near the fire, her curly black hair tied into a messy bun, a few rebellious tendrils escaping to frame her face. Her skin glowed under the torchlight, and her jean shorts and thin bathing suit top made her look like she belonged in a summer ad campaign.

I first met Misha when her family had bought a timeshare in Eldridge Bay, a small three bedroom house down the road from mine. We were six or seven and had been sent to a children's day camp, hosted by the local school. Neither of us are locals, but we both have spent every summer here. We both come from similar backgrounds. Her father had grown up here, then moved to Chicago and met her Mom. When she's not here, she's in Chicago, studying Dance (and sports medicine) at the University of Chicago, where her Mom is a professor. Yet, somehow, we both end up here every summer, destined to collide and collide again, year after year. We became summer sisters in the truest sense: inseparable during the day, sneaking into trouble, plotting beach raids, swapping secrets under the stars. During the school year, we'd keep in touch, texting about homework or boys or absolutely nothing of consequence. But summer? Summer was our realm and we were the rulers of this kingdom.

I approach her quietly, sneaking up behind her, then wrapping my arms quickly around her. She turns quickly and lets out a squeal that you could probably hear in Allister.

"Allison Marie Hennings! You're here!" She throws her arms around my neck, spilling some of her drink on me, but whatever, it's summer. If a summer night didn't involve sand in uncomfortable places and a little sticky beer on my skin, then it wasn't a summer night well-spent.

"Mish!" I hug her back, but my joy is quickly interrupted when I see the sculpted chest and broad shoulders of Satan himself. He's lost his shirt, of course, a usual from Teddy Novak at parties. And of course he beat me here. Because why wouldn't he.

Misha releases from the hug and follows my gaze over to Teddy, "Heard a rumor he's staying with you guys. What's his story?"

"He's an ass."

"Well, you say that about most guys, Allie. Which, I won't disagree, Men suck, but do all of them suck as much as you say they do?" She takes a drink from her red solo cup, a party cliche, for sure.

"Trust me on this one. He goes to Allister, is on my Dad's team, lived across the hall from me both Freshman and Sophomore year," I look to her, "Remember the story I told you about my neighbor who would stay up until the asscrack of dawn hooking up with girls or watching porn at a very high volume?"

She nods, recalling a story I told her last summer, "Yeah, the serial jerker."

"Ha-ha, yeah, that's Teddy Novak. Who just so happens to now be homeless. You know how much my Dad likes taking in strays."

"Strays? Well, make sure your Dad gets him neutered before he gets half the girls in this town pregnant." She nods her head in the direction of him, point her cup in that direction as well.

"What?"

I follow her gaze to where Teddy is now making out with some blonde girl I've never saw before. Probably a tourist. Her arms are around his neck, his tongue is shoved halfway down her throat. They're not just kissing, they're sucking each other's faces as if there is no oxygen left in the world. One of her hands moves to his abs, then slides down into his shorts.

Lovely.

I've saw worse at Allister, but being here in Eldridge Bay makes it feel different somehow. Almost as though I want to protect my town from his reckless behavior.

At this rate, by the end of summer, Teddy is going to have slept his way through the entire town and I don't even doubt that.

"I'm going to need a drink, then we need to dance, Mish."

———

Four drinks later, straight from Cameron Kavanaugh's Keg, I don't even feel buzzed, but my stomach begs to differ. One more drink and I'll be puking up pizza and cheap beer on the beach.

I'm sitting on the sand and watching Misha attempt to drunkenly flirt with some unrecognizable girl. Misha came out to me as gay the summer before we went to high school. Obviously I support her. I love that girl like a sister.

That's what our parents used to call us. *Summer Sisters*. I mean, it's an accurate description of what we are.

My eyes wander over to Cameron Kavanaugh, a local to Eldridge Bay. He was my first kiss when we were eleven. He's a flirt, but I don't reciprocate it. Personality wise, he's just like Teddy. Cocky, arrogant, flirty, kinda *sexy*.

No. Teddy is not sexy. There's nothing sexy about Teddy Novak. I've saw him so drunk that he couldn't move, found him lying in a puddle of his own vomit and had to carry him back to the dorms with Logan and Luke. There's nothing sexy about Teddy Novak.

Not his emerald green eyes. Not his light brown, nearly blonde curls. Not his well defined six pack, or the small tattoo on the back of his muscular bicep.

I stand up quickly, black spots fill my vision. Okay, maybe I am drunker than I thought? I move my way through the people, to where a group of people is dancing and jumping with the beat to an older frat party song by *Pitbull*.

I put my dancing skills to the test, removing article of clothing in the process. First, the baggy black zip up, then the tight, white camisole underneath.

I let myself give up control as the music takes over, feeling louder and louder, the bass growing heavier. The crowd chants with the song.

A hand snakes around my front, wrapping around me. I turn my head and see Cam. He's also shirtless, my back pressed to his chest as we grind into each other. The worst part is, I don't even mind. It's summer, I'm a thousand something miles from my hometown, and I've known him since I was a child.

The entire time, my eyes are glued elsewhere. The place I don't want them to be.

They're locked on Teddy. The blonde still has her hand in

his shorts, which is classy, saying we're at a public party. He seems focused on her, smiling even as they dance. Her arm moving up and down in his shorts tells me one thing: she's giving him a hand job… on a public beach. That's enough to get her put on a list of some kind, I think?

The song changes to yet another song I hear frequently at the frat parties of Allister. With the song change, a set of eyes is locked on me. The green of his eyes seeming lighting up the night all around of us. As though there is no one else at the party but the two of us. Everything feels hazy, as though I'm floating through a dream.

Or a nightmare.

Our gazes now locked to each other.

I feel a masculine hand move to my thighs. The minute Cameron's hand wanders, Teddy peels away from the girl, sight set right on us. *Motherfucker.* He storms across the sand, rounding the roaring fire and he yanks me away from Cameron, then shoves Cameron so hard he lands flat on his ass in the sand.

"Dude, what the fuck?" Cameron stands quickly, shoving Teddy back like two immature children on an elementary school playground.

"You were fondling her! She's clearly drunk!" Teddy shouts

"I've known Allie since we were kids. Who the fuck do you think you are?" Cameron countered, and suddenly the two were in each other's space, chest to chest, shouting over the music.

I tried to intervene. "Cameron, this is Satan. He's staying with me this summer."

Holy shit, I am drunk. I did not just call him that out loud. His confusion begs to differ. Wait, what's his name?

Teddy blinked, while Cameron's eyes went from me to Satan. "This tool your boyfriend or something, Allie?"

"No. He's my Dad's player." I stammered. Shit, I am drunk. Definitely drunk.

Misha comes over, her hands tugging the girl along, "Allie, what's going on?"

"She was dancing with me, then this dickbag marched over and shoved me away like I was doing something wrong." Cameron shouts angrily.

"I asked Allie, nuts for brains." Misha's tone was sharp, protective.

"I—um—" My head spun. And then, mercifully, my stomach revolted and the alcohol and stale pizza lurched into my throat. I fall to my knees.

And I vomit into the sand, bile burning the back of my throat, tears stinging my eyes. The party around us blurred into muted chaos as I dropped to my knees.

A hand landed on my shoulder, another grabbed my hair, holding it back. Misha muttered something, but I couldn't hear through the ringing in my ears. Cameron tried to help, but Teddy shoved him aside, his long arms steadying me. *Teddy*. Yes. Not Satan. I'm too fucking drunk right now.

"I've got her," he said, voice low, calm, commanding. He lifted me, bridal style, against his chest. My limbs were lead, my head spinning, my ears ringing.

"Call me in the morning, Allie," Misha said quietly as Teddy walked toward the car.

I nodded, exhausted beyond coherence. My head rested against Teddy's shoulder, the smell of him, the sand, the fire mingling into a strange comfort.

"Close your eyes, Hennings. I've got you."

I obeyed, too drained to argue. Oh, how the tables have turned.

CHAPTER 6
TEDDY NOVAK

I n movies, they always make it look so easy, the guy carrying the girl in distress. It is nowhere easy as it is in real life. Then again, these guys in movies usually only carry the girl through the door and to the bed before a director shouts cut.

I'm carrying the deadweight of Allie six blocks back to the Hennings' place. She passed out pretty quickly after we left the beach, eyes fluttering closed as she looked dazed, completely out of it.

I've saw Allie Hennings drunk before, but never that drunk. She's never, ever gotten that drunk. At least not that I have seen.

I probably look like a bad guy, carrying a passed out girl who's in no more than a bra and skimpy shorts down the road while I'm wearing nothing but shorts. At least I tucked my t-shirt into the space between a trashcan and a recycling bin. I can go back for it tomorrow.

But, we're both half naked.

Go figure. The moment I see the house in the distance, I wake her up. She's out of it, completely gone, not a thought behind those pretty blue eyes. I slowly lower her to the ground, her feet hitting the pavement shakily, like a baby deer learning to walk for the first time.

"Can you walk, Allie?"

She nods, mumbling something incoherently. I hold her side as we walk up to the front steps of the house. The lights are off, well, all of them except for the porch light.

Allie and I quietly enter the house, "Where's your room?"

"I am not going to fuck you, Theodore." She proclaims, rather loudly. I shush her, shaking my head.

"I don't want to fuck you, Allie. Not like this, at least. I just want to make sure you get to your room safely." Fuck. Did I really just say that? Whatever, we're both drunk and she won't remember in the morning and I'll pretend it never was said.

"Not like this? Theodore, are you trying to seduce me?" She starts giggling like a school girl. Fuck. Jesse and Martie are going to wake up and see me and their daughter, drunk, half-naked and slurring words as we try to make it up stairs.

"No Allison, I just don't want you to wake up your parents."

I guide her up the steps, toward the living room. She stumbles over to a door, slowly cracking it open. She peaks inside, then turns back to me and nods.

"Thank you, Theodore."

"You're welcome Allison." She gives me a sly, knowing smile, then slips into her room, closing the door behind her.

———

I wake up to the smell of pancakes. I love pancakes. I love all breakfast foods, really, but pancakes are my weak spot. I roll over and grab my phone from the nightstand.

Out of the very little I unpacked, my phone charger was a

must. We got back from the beach party and my phone had five percent left. Along with a handful of missed calls from my Mom and a couple texts from Logan and Ana, teasing me about being careful around Allie.

I can still feel the sweat, the smell of bonfire, and alcohol lingering on my body, so I opt to shower before making any public appearances in front of the Hennings family.

I don't know how I smell like alcohol, maybe Allie? I didn't even drink last night.

After unpacking a few more things, such as fresh clothes and my bathroom stuff, I head to the downstairs bathroom and take the quickest shower ever, then get dressed and brush my teeth.

When I make my way up to the kitchen, Allie is sitting at a barstool silently, just staring at the breakfast food in front of her as if it's going to kill her.

Martie and Coach are in the kitchen with Coach making food and Martie cleaning up the dishes as he finishes using them.

"Teddy! How'd you sleep?" Martie asks as I take a seat next to Allie. I look at her.

"Better than she did, I think?"

Allie looks to me, clearly not amused, "I think I'm coming down with something."

Coach turns quickly to face us, sliding me a mug with coffee, "Yeah, it's called you got drunk on your first night back. It's not contagious though, so you'll be fine."

She rolls her eyes at her Dad's snarky comment and I add cream and sugar to the coffee, then take a sip from the mug which has an Allister Hockey logo on it. Of course.

They finish getting breakfast around and the four of us move over from the kitchen to the dining room table. While the rest of the house is all pale blues and pale yellows, the dining room table looks like an absolute relic. It's old, stained a dark, deep brown. It looks as though it's much older than me and Allie.

We dig into breakfast, though, there's not much digging on Allie's part. She's been swirling the same piece of pancake around in syrup for about five minutes. It looks sad, honestly. The piece of pancake is just begging to be consumed and she's waterboarding it in syrup.

I doubt she would find that very amusing, so I keep the comment to myself.

"So, Allie, where'd you go? What'd you do?" Martie pipes up as she takes a sip of orange juice.

Allie shrugs, "Just the beach with a couple of friends."

"And you got wasted? Allie, how the hell did you get home?" Her Dad asks sternly, the bad cop parent swings into action.

"Teddy."

Martie and Coach look at me, confused and wanting an answer.

"I was just walking the beach and I found Allie and her friends. Allie threw up, so I walked her home. I didn't drink anything. All they had was some shitty keg." I didn't drink more than a sip, this is true. I took a sip of the blonde's drink when we started talking; it was the shittiest beer I've ever had a sip of.

"Let me guess, Kavanaugh?" Martie asks?

Allie nods, "Yep. The usual."

I look confused and Martie must pick up on this because she adds "The Kavanaugh's own a bar downtown. Cameron is about Allie's age. His Dad used to do the same thing when we had beach parties, take a keg from the bar and bring it down to the party. The beer was absolutely disgusting, but it's all we had access to."

I nod, then set my fork down, "So have the Kavanaugh's always been assholes?"

Martie sighs, "They've always been a little cocky, arrogant. They're related to the police chief and have gotten away with a lot. Why do you ask?"

"This Cameron kid was just getting a little too friendly with Allie last night."

Allie drops her own fork, hard, "Okay? He's hot and maybe I wanted to have sex with him, Teddy. Did you think about that?"

"Really? Because not even two minutes later you were puking in the sand and he was pouting like a little bitch."

Coach stops both of us, "Woah, woah, woah. What happened?"

"He was getting handsy with Allie so I went over there and called him on it. She was too drunk to coherently make a choice like that." I explain, looking to Allie as she bows her head, thoughts racing on what to say next. She lifts her head quickly, an anger-filled glare taking over her expression.

"You don't get to decide that, Teddy."

"Allie, you barely remembered my name. We've been in the same circle of friends for two years. I would say that you were pretty drunk."

"And you haven't gotten drunk? Who helped your team-mates carry you back to your dorm from a frat after you puked all over yourself?"

"The difference was, I wasn't actively being fondled by some girl I didn't know. And I at least remembered your names." I argue back. Allie sighs, trying to compose herself.

"Dad, this was a bad idea. Why is he here?" She quickly turns to her father.

"Allison!" Her Dad says angrily, Martie looks to me, frowning.

"Teddy is one of my best players. He is my family too, might not be blood, but family takes care of each other. He is here because your Mom and me invited him. I under-stand that you two have some weird rivalry going on, but it's got to stop." Coach says, then pinches his brown in frustration.

Allie huffs, eyes looking to me, "I can't stand you, Novak."

I clutch my chest, "Oh, I'm wounded. I'll remember that next time you're drunk and puking your guts up on the beach."

"Good! Remember it. Next time, just leave me there and keep making out with some random blonde girl you had met what, an hour before? Fuck you."

Jesse and Martie look to me apologetically and I shake my head, bowing it and focusing on the breakfast in front of me.

With that final remark, the table goes silent as we all slowly, quietly eat. For the remainder of breakfast, no one says a word. Not Coach or Martie, not Allie, and certainly not me. Then again, what is there to say. She's made herself very clear. She doesn't want me here, intruding on her life outside of Allister.

Maybe I should just go stay with Logan and the Finlay's? Maybe Patrick or Nik might have space, too?

We finish breakfast and I offer to do the dishes. I mind as well do something here, since I'm living here rent free and all.

I haven't really thought about it, but what the hell am I going to do this summer? Usually, back in Philly, I would go home, take two weeks off, then get back to the job that I've been working since high school. I worked as an assistant to the city, making sure the public parks stayed safe and clean. I've been doing it since sixteen, but truthfully, I haven't even considered what I would do without that job. Should I find a job in Eldridge Bay? This is probably the only summer I'm going to spend here, so there's really no point, but I also can't just sit on my ass all day and do absolutely nothing. That's just not me.

Martie approaches with a few more dishes and I turn to face her, "So Mrs. Hennings, I've been thinking about maybe trying to find a job this summer, just to keep myself busy? Do you think that is possible?"

She smiles, "Yes, of course Teddy. It's Martie, though, not Mrs. Hennings. That's reserved for my mother. I can help you find something. There's a big business boom in the summers in the area, so a lot of places are probably hiring right now. How about we go hunting for something after lunch?"

I smile, "Sure, that works. Thank you, again."

She nods with a warm, maternal smile, "You're very welcome."

Before she walks away, I stop her again, "I feel like I'm intruding, Allie is all upset about it-"

"Allie truly can and *will* get over. She's just not one to love big changes. She never has liked change very much."

I truly hope that Martie is telling the truth, because I don't know if I can spend the summer listening to Allie's hyperbolic threats and consistent shaming and bickering.

After lunch, Martie and I drive toward the downtown area of Eldridge Bay. It's a small, cozy downtown. Something straight out of an old *WB show*. Like *Dawson's Creek* or *Gilmore Girls*.

"I spoke to some friends, found some people who needed some extra help this summer, first thing is first though, Carla's." Martie tells me as she parks the car in front of an old fashioned ice cream shop. It has a brick exterior, a swirled, plastic cone out front and attached to the sign. A large, neon sign hangs in the window.

I get out and follow Martie inside. The small ice cream parlor looks as though it was taken straight out of the fifties. I half expect a douchey biker gang to march in like they own the place and make all the girls swoon. There's pink and blue booths lining the wall, with a few matching tables and chairs in the middle. There's an old-fashion jukebox against the wall and it plays some old song I don't know.

Girls being Martie, the woman behind the counter who I am assuming is Carla, Allie's friend from the beach last night, and a blonde girl who sits across from her.

"Well if it isn't the Martie Hennings!" The woman behind the counter says with a big grin. She's an older woman, 70's or so. She's a bigger woman with dark brown, nearly black hair. I assume she's known Martie since she was a little girl.

Martie leans over the counter, hugging the woman. After their embrace, Carla's eyes drift to me, taking in my presence.

I don't mean to sound cocky, but I get that a lot. Especially from women who are significantly older than me.

"Now who is this hunk?" She leans on the counter, chin resting on her hand.

Admittedly, she's a sweet old lady. I give her a million dollar grin.

Martie also smiles, "This is Teddy! He's one of Jesse's players and he's staying with us for the summer!"

"Well aren't you just a sweetheart!" She leans against the wood counter, "What can I get for ya?"

Martie puts a hand on my shoulder, "Actually, Teddy is looking for a job! Just for the summer. I was hoping you needed some extra help this summer?"

Carla's smile doesn't falter "Well, well, well. You ever work in food service before Teddy?"

"Does being water-boy for two weeks count?"

Carla laughs, it's a loud, homey laugh. One that reminds of one of the few times we visited my grandparents as a kid. At least, my Dad's parents. My Mom's parents suck.

"Well, I am looking for extra help, it's a super easy position to learn," Carla tells me, reaching under the counter and pulling out paperwork.

I take it, looking down at the employee paperwork. Martie

is beaming. She found me a job at her first stop of the day, she's bursting with success.

"When can you start?"

"Whenever you need me to, ma'am." I reply.

"How about Monday? It's a slower day, perfect time to train you."

"That sounds great, ma'am."

She laughs, "Don't call me ma'am. Call me Carla. Ma'am makes me sound twenty years older."

At that same instance, the bell on the front door chimes and someone enters. Martie, Carla and I turn and see Allie entering. She's wearing a baggy black hoodie, sunglasses and denim shorts that barely peak out from under the hoodie.

"Well if it isn't the Allie Hennings." Carla says excitedly.

She takes off her glasses, eyes locked on me.

"What are you doing here, Theodore?"

"Starting a job."

Allie's hungover eyes widen in shock. She looks between me, Carla, then her mother.

"You can't be serious." She pouts. That pout, her tired eyes. Even in this state, I think she's incredibly hot.

Martie scowls, "Allison, I understand that this is a change, but that doesn't give you the right to be mean. Your father and I raised you better than that."

Allie's eyes move to me, looking me up and down. Her face flushes, as if her mind has wandered somewhere she doesn't want it to.

Oh, she's so thinking something inappropriate right now.

She mumbles something angrily under her breath and marches over to Mish's table, interrupting whatever her friend had been talking about with the preppy looking blonde.

Martie looks to me with a shrug and small smile, Carla shakes her head, mirroring the same smile. I look between them.

"What?"

"Nothing, just I remember being twenty-something once." Carla replies, leaving me with Martie.

I follow Martie out of the ice cream parlor and to the car. We sit in silence for a moment as she starts her SUV and we buckle up.

Things will be good here. *This is good for me.*

CHAPTER 7
ALLIE HENNINGS

Turns out, when I sat down with Mish and the random blonde at Carla's, I had been interrupting Mish's date with some tourist who is visiting her grandparents who recently moved to Eldridge Bay. *Whoops.*

It's been two weeks since we arrived in Eldridge Bay and every single day is worse than the last. First, Teddy wakes up around the same time as me every morning and will hog the bathroom for twenty minutes to get ready, belting out Britney Spears songs like he's at some drunken karaoke night. Then, he usually finishes off the pot of coffee without making more, leaving me with none. On top of it all, he now works at the one place that I would go to get away from home and work and life. Carla's. Every single time I've gone in there, he's been working.

Admittedly, he is good at his job, but I cannot stand seeing his face as he scoops ice cream for me, or seeing how his muscles tense under the light blue polo shirt as he digs a scoop into the tub of rocky road.

Fuck me.

I fear I have fallen under the spell of Theodore Novak, something that pretty much every girl at Allister has fallen for. The first time I noticed something blooming, was the night he carried me home from the beach party. Our very first night in Eldridge Bay. Though, I don't remember most of it, Teddy jogged my memory one time when we were cleaning up after dinner.

"Close your eyes, Hennings. I've got you."

That is the only thing I remember. That moment, my head against his shoulder, the smell of bonfire and beach and his musky cologne. Our warm skin pressed against each other and his tense chest against the side of my body. Even now, whenever my mind wanders to those words, my heartbeat increases, my chest becomes tight.

What is this feeling?

I know exactly what this feeling is, I just don't want to succumb to it. The last time I felt this, I was seventeen. I had been a junior in high school and had fallen for the most talented, most charming, most intelligent boy.

Adam Crushem. He was not only the star quarterback at East Allister High, but he was also incredibly smart. Four-point-oh GPA, honor's student, going to study family law. We had dated for about four months, but he decided that his future came first. It broke my heart.

Maybe that is why I've become a stone-cold bitch when it comes to men?

No, I'm not a stone-cold bitch to men. I get along well with Logan and Luke and Nik, it's just Teddy.

Though, in the case of Adam. My parents never liked him. They always seemed on edge whenever he came around. They're not like that with Teddy, and we're not even dating. It's weird.

My phone alarm brings me out of my thoughts and back to present day.

I don't work today at the country club, thank fuck, which meant I got to sleep in.

I drag myself out of my bed and to the kitchen. Mom must

have already left for her volunteering, as I only see my Dad sitting on the back porch.

I grab a cup of coffee, adding way too much sugar and very little cream, then step out and join him.

He's finally started to settle into summer. Those first few days after we arrive, he spends most of his time at the dining table, working on hockey stuff. Usually wearing the same pajamas and having messy hair.

But today? He's wearing his casual khaki shorts, Allister tee and boat shoes. I look like shit in comparison.

"Morning, Als." He says, not looking up from his book.

"Morning, old guy." This causes him to look up.

He fake gasps, "Old? You better watch it, honey. I'm only thirty."

He's obviously not thirty, but him and my Mom do this thing, even on birthdays, where they claim to be much younger than they are.

"Yeah, if you're thirty, then you're childless." His face falls in defeat.

That dampened the joke and he shakes his head, "What are you doing up so early? I thought you didn't work today."

"I don't, but Mish and I were going to head up to Traverse City to visit this bookstore that's going viral online."

He nods, "So, I heard from your Mom that you're still giving Teddy problems?"

"I'm not-" I pause, "It's just that we don't get along."

"Really? Because every time I've saw you together, it seems to be more so that you want nothing to do with him, yet he just wants to be respectful to you." He retorts, closing his book and leaning back in the deck chair.

I nurse my cup of coffee in my hands, "He just gets on my nerves, Dad. You know that."

"But why, Allison?"

Ladies and gentlemen, my father, the former psychology major who gave it all up to play hockey. He could, if he truly wanted, work in a therapist office, seeing clients 9-5, but it turns out, being a hockey coach for a team that is way past it's glory is more his style.

"Dad, you're doing that thing again."

"What thing?" He asks innocently.

"Playing armchair psychologist."

"No, I'm just speaking to you, as my daughter, about a player who I have spent significantly more time with than you have,"

"Dad, he lives across the hall from me. You see him once a day for a few hours at practice. I see him numerous times from walking to class, to going to my dorm. He's a pest."

"Allison, be mindful. He's gone through a lot and I doubt you're making it any easier for him."

As if he was summoned by my words alone, a very shirtless, very sweaty Teddy approaches the back porch. He's wearing athletic shorts and running shoes, his muscles taught.

"How was the run, kid?" Dad asks and Teddy nods.

"Good, I didn't expect it to be as hot here as it is."

I roll my eyes, "It's eighty, not a hundred and two."

"Could've fooled me." He uses the banisters of the porch to stretch. He makes his way up the porch and stands next to my dad, directly across from me.

My eyes wander to his chest as he has mindless small talk with my dad. The carved abs that line his stomach. His pecs, muscular, well-built, with dark hair lining the nipples. The rest of his bare chest is clean-shaven, or maybe he just doesn't grow much hair on his chest. A small trail of hair climbs up to his belly button from beneath his shorts. The hair is darker than the hair on his head, looking black as it's soaked with sweat.

An egregious thought enters my mind, one that doesn't deserve to be there at all. It's not even a question, as I've saw it and I know the answer, but to be up close and personal-

"Allison?" Dad's voice interrupts me from my trance and I shake my head quickly, flustered. Did he see me checking Teddy out?

Based on the cocky smirk coming over Teddy's face, I would safely assume that he saw me checking him out. That's why I can't even object when his gaze drops to my chest.

"What?"

"You and Mish should take Teddy up to Traverse City with you." Dad suggests. I shake my head quickly. Absolutely not.

"I doubt Teddy would want to go to a bookstore, that requires too much reading." I retort and Teddy's gaze lifts from my chest to meet my eyes.

"You know Allie, I do read books occasionally." He shrugs, taking a seat across from me.

"Business textbooks for class don't count."

"I know. Try me."

Oh, so he wants me, someone who enjoys reading, to come at him. Okay, I can play this game. I lean forward competitively.

"The Hunger Games?"

"Read that in elementary school."

"American Psycho?"

"Read it, preferred the movie though. Christian Bale is hot."

Okay, I think of something more difficult, something that Ana would have on her shelf, "Pride and Prejudice?"

"The distance is nothing when one has a motive." He fully recites a quote from the book. My Dad looks at him for a moment.

"You holding out on me with how smart you are?" A laugh escaping his throat as he looks between me and his prodigal player. Well fuck, maybe Teddy is more than just a pretty face and a killer slap-shot?

"We all have subjects we're more interested in than others.

I just so happened to like English in high school." Teddy shrugs.

"Fine, you can go with me. I'm leaving to pick Mish up in thirty minutes though, so you better be ready." I grab my mug and head back into the house and to my bedroom. I get changed and head to the kitchen to take care of my coffee mug. I set it on the counter and as I do, Teddy trudges into the house, carrying his shoes with his fingers, the socks tucked into them. He looks at me for a moment, setting his shoes down on a stool and he approaches slowly.

He's close enough that I can feel the heat emanating off his body. He leans in, his sweaty body is nearly touching me, "I saw how you were looking at me Hennings."

I shake my head quickly, "How was that, Theodore?"

He smirks, looking down at me quickly, then back in my eyes.

"You want to touch me so fucking bad, don't you?" His fingers reach out and slowly move to my stomach. My body slowly moves into his touch. His fingers skimming the small part of my stomach that shows through my t-shirt. My breath hitches in my throat and we slowly move closer and closer into each other's orbit. We're so close to kissing, but I stop myself, his face inches from mine.

"Not at all, actually. I was just imagining how bad you probably smelled and oh- Look at that, you smell horrendous." I reply quietly, then slap him on the stomach. My hand makes contact with his well-defined body and part of me wants to do it again.

He laughs quietly, "If it makes any difference, I want to touch you too."

My stomach drops and in this moment, have I truly realized how complicated this summer will be with Teddy in the picture. He saunters off, leaving me standing in the kitchen in complete and utter shock.

————

The drive from Eldridge Bay to Traverse City is only an hour, but with Mish and Teddy talking to each other, it feels like an eternity. Mish sits in the passenger seat, legs up on the dashboard as she sips from a 7/11 cup.

The silence is the car is… overwhelming. If it wasn't for *Taylor Swift* playing in the background, you would be able to hear a pin drop.

Teddy leans forward from the middle seat, to the center console, "So where are we going?"

I roll my eyes, he knows exactly where we're going. Why is he playing dumb.

"It's this bookstore in Traverse City called Horizon Books. It's been getting a lot of attention online from Michiganders recently," Mish explains to Teddy. He nods.

"So we're driving an hour to just a bookstore?"

"If you're going to bitch, I'm not going to even consider letting you tag along with us anymore, Theodore."

Mish eyes me, then Teddy silently. She takes a sip of her cherry slurpee, "So, Als, I thought you said you two weren't together?"

In sync, Teddy and I both respond, "We're not."

"Really? Because you bicker like my ex and I did."

I gasp, "Oh, we're so not friends anymore."

Mish laughs and shakes her head, "All I'm saying is, you could've fooled me."

I scowl, my gaze looking to Teddy's in the mirror. He's smiling, as if he's taunting me. From his comments earlier, to Mish's comment now, I feel as if my world is closing in on me and my worst nightmare is coming true. It's horrifying.

Slowly, I turn up the radio, sending the signal to Mish that I really do not want to talk about whatever the hell is going on between Teddy and me. Do I find him attractive? Sure. Objectively speaking, Teddy is attractive. He's got the charm, the body, the deep gaze in his sparkling green eyes and a grin that could make someone weak in the knees.

The song changes to one from her newer album, it's incredibly romantic and I go to change it, but Mish swats my hand away.

"Don't be a hater, Allie."

Teddy pipes in, "Yeah, don't be a hater, Allison."

"I'm not a hater, Theodore."

Mish turns to face Teddy, "Is your name actually Theodore? Like Theodore Roosevelt?"

"That's a funny story actually," He starts but I interrupt him, turning off the radio.

"Wait, so Theodore is actually your name?"

"Yes and no."

"How come I never knew this?" I retort and he shrugs.

"Because Teddy is my legal first name, now, at least." He leans forward, between Mish and me.

Mish sets her slurpee into the cup holder, "Tell me more? Did you originally have an old man first name? My Dad's first name is actually Ezekiel, but he goes by EJ."

"At birth, my Mom named me after her Dad, who eventually went to prison. My name was originally Theodore. We changed it when he went to prison and I don't like using it anymore."

This fact distracts me enough that I nearly run a red light, abruptly breaking in order to not break the law out of pure shock. Teddy is thrusted forward, Mish as well. They both look at me.

"You're that shocked, Allison?"

"Yeah, kind of, Theodore." I say flatly and he sighs.

"Don't call me that." His voice is stern. There's a painful memory there. I can tell. It's the same voice my Mom uses when she talks about her childhood. Especially her other older brother, Markus, who went to jail at fourteen for getting in a fight that paralyzed another student. We hardly talk about it, but the times she has mentioned it, she has that same look in her eye, her voice comes out incredibly similarly to Teddy's at this moment.

I make a mental note to stop calling him Theodore if it truly bothers him that much.

"Why'd he go to prison?" Mish asks nosily and I swat at her, sensing he doesn't want to talk about it.

"Uh, he did some really shitty things. I don't know the details, my Mom never told me. It happened when I was six or so." Teddy replies.

"Do you know how bad?" Mish continues to pry.

"Enough to where he hung himself after only serving two years."

My heart sinks to my feet and I feel all the color drain from my face.

What the hell?

So we spend the next hour of the car ride in complete silence, only the quiet hum of my music playing over the bluetooth. Every few minutes, I catch Mish looking through the mirror to see Teddy in the back. He's staring down at his phone, completely engrossed by whatever is on the screen.

I feel as though Teddy just peeled back a layer that he has never peeled back for anyone else, and I don't know if I should be honored that he did that for me, or if I should be worried about what could come next.

We arrive at the bookstore and I park the car in the lot behind the building. None of us have even spoken a word since Teddy's confession. As we approach the large, two story building, Mish walks at my side while Teddy walks a few feet behind us. She leans towards me, bumping into my shoulder with her shoulder.

"That was awkward. Did you know that info?"

I shake my head, "No. He never has ever talked about his family, at least not on that level. I knew his Mom is a serial dater and his Dad jumped ship at some point, but not that."

Mish nods as she grabs the door handle, "Talk more later?"

I nod and enter, followed by Teddy, then Mish.

"I'm going to check out what they have for romance, where are you going?" I ask, turning to my friend.

"Probably horror. I want to find a good summer slasher," She walks off in one direction. I turn to Teddy.

"Oh, I'll probably just stick with you, if that's okay?"

He's gonna stick with me? While I look at smut books? Okay, then.

I head off in the other direction, reading the signs above the tall bookshelves until I find Western and Romance. Teddy's eyes comb over the shelves quickly and he grabs a book with a broken heart on the front cover, big pink font scrawled across it.

"This sounds interesting," He flips it over, the white paperback in his hands tightly. My gaze lingers on his strong hands. I don't know what comes over me, but now, I'm imagining those hands on my body, finger tips tracing delicately over my skin, my hips between both hands as he pulls me closer to him.

My skin flushes and I brush a loose strand of hair behind my ear.

"So, um," I clear my throat, "What's it about?"

"True love, facing addiction, and family. I think." He replies. He holds it out to me and I take it.

Admittedly, it does sound interesting. I spent my sophomore year taking a couple of psychology classes about addiction, so I wonder if the author did it justice?

I tuck it under my arm and continue to scan the shelves. Teddy pulls out another book, it has a hockey stick on the cover and some cliche title.

"Oh look, Allison. It's hockey porn."

I roll my eyes at him, "No it isn't. It's a romance novel. Not all romance novels are smutty."

"No, but this one is."

He flips to a random page and starts reading it out loud, "His throbbing cock-"

I throw my hand over his mouth, silencing him, "Teddy. We are in public."

Instead of moving my hand away, he fully sticks out his tongue and drags it along my palm like a dog. I jerk it back in response and he bursts out laughing.

"You're a child." I push his shoulder.

"And you're a prude."

I cock an eye brow as I wipe my hand off on my denim shorts, "I'm a prude? I just don't want to get kicked out because you're reading porn in public, out loud."

"Oh, so it would be okay if I did it behind closed doors? I think we could arrange that." He replies, shelving the book. I grab his wrist and pull him away from the romance section and into a more secluded part of the bookstore in the far, right corner.

"Teddy, what the hell are you doing? Whatever it is that you're trying to achieve, it's not working-"

He slowly saunters toward me, backing me into the shelf of textbooks, "Oh really? It's not working?"

I nod, but my body reacts differently. My breathing hitches, my skin becomes clammy and my face reddens as he inches closer toward me. Our bodies are practically touching.

"Your reactions beg to differ, Allison."

Everything grows tense. One touch would push me over the edge right now.

So I'm completely taken aback when his hand reaches forward, slowly tilting my chin up to him, our eyes locked.

What is he doing to me?

CHAPTER 8
TEDDY NOVAK

What am I doing to her?

I know that I shouldn't have feelings for Allie.

We've been in Eldridge Bay for two-ish weeks now. Two weeks away from normalcy at campus and we're already caving into this untapped desire between the two of us.

I slowly lean forward, drawing her closer and closer. She does the same, I can feel the heat of her breath against my mouth, I can practically taste the way her mouth tastes. My hands cup her cheeks and slowly, I lean forward.

What the hell am I doing? Coach would crucify me if he found out I kissed his daughter.

I drop my hands and take a step back, "We shouldn't do this, Allie."

I stare at her and she's attempting to catch her breath. I want nothing more than to just kiss her right now. She looks hot as fuck in her tight, pale yellow baby-tee and her denim shorts. Her blonde hair is held up in the back by a hair clip, loose strands falling forward into her face.

"Your dad would kill me if I kissed you. I can't. I respect Coach too much to do something like that to him." I reply and she quickly nods, moving past the situation even quicker than it occurred.

"No, no, no. I understand. That was a horrible idea, Novak."

"Agreed, Hennings." I tell her and she fixes her hair, pulling the loose strands back into the clip.

"Let's find Mish and go get lunch."

I follow her, leaving the intensely intimate moment we shared in the corner of the bookstore.

I lie in my bed, staring at the ceiling as I playback the day. It's now ten p.m. and Allie and I have already moved to our respective rooms. It's odd.

Just two weeks ago, we would've probably still been at practice or the library studying or at practice, but now we're in our respective rooms under the same roof. I can't help but imagine what would happen if I had kissed her.

Allie is absolutely gorgeous. I've always found her to be annoyingly attractive, since we met during Freshman Orientation.

Well, no. It wasn't orientation. It was the Hockey Team Barbecue for the new players to meet the older players. It was at Coach's house, the week before classes had started.

It was also the first time I had met Logan, my roommate who had been randomly assigned to me a month earlier. Though, seeing as we're on the same team, it doesn't exactly seem random.

Logan and I sat on the back porch, talking with Coach when a blonde-haired girl with bangs stepped out wearing nothing but a little black dress and a black, lace choker.

That was the first time I had met Allison Hennings. Coach was quick to introduce Logan and me to his daughter, but it wasn't in the way that some parents do to try and hype their kids up, it was in a way that he was setting a boundary. Never, ever try to get with her or he would cut you into pieces using your own skates.

Those first few weeks of Freshman year had been hard. I had a massive crush on Allie, Logan was drowning in his heartbreak for Ana, and I had learned what adulthood really felt like.

To keep myself distracted, I drowned myself in activities on campus. I had signed up for rush the minute it had opened, joined multiple clubs including weightlifting and ice skating.

Both clubs, I eventually dropped after I had gotten a bid from Alpha Beta Nu. I know I only got it because a couple of my teammates were also a part of the fraternity. I immediately got as involved as I could. The time spent in my dorm room was limited, but that was on purpose. There was only so much of Logan's sulking and Allie living right across the hall that I could take.

It's like the housing department on campus was out to get me. They were purposely throwing Allie in my face, taunting me with her, knowing that whatever happened, there would never, ever be a romantic connection between the two of us.

I think I had known all along that those thoughts were a bunch of shit anyway. From day one, I've been drawn to her like a moth drawn to flame. I so badly wanted to just collide, for her to brand me with her scorching hot touch.

I close my eyes and imagine that Allie is lying next to me, wearing my Allister Hockey tee, her head on my chest as she quietly snores. My arm is wrapped around her and holding her close to my body. It's really all that I want right now. I want her to be next to me. The idea makes my cock stir in my boxers. The very concept of her being so close to me, is enough to nearly give me a boner. That's embarrassing as fuck.

The way she makes me feel is complicated. Part of me is

turned on by the idea of having her touching my skin, being so close that she could touch it if she wanted. Another part of me just wants to be in her orbit, circling her like she is my sun and I am her earth.

But I also just want to respect her parents. They're letting me live with them for the summer, rent-free.

I saw the way Martie was looking at Allie and me during dinner tonight. As though she knows that something is going on between the two of us.

Would she voice these concerns to Coach? What if she does and they're just trying to come up with a solution to get rid of me? Ship me off with another family friend? Another player from the team? What if coach had already called Dean Finlay or someone else to see if they'll take me instead?

My feelings for Allie aren't worth the risk of becoming homeless this summer. Being here is testing every ounce of strength and self-restraint in my body. I so desperately want to kiss her. To hold her. Though, I know what will happen if that happens, and it's not a risk I want to take.

I'm catastrophizing again, as my former therapist said. I know it's not a real word, I'm not stupid. But there are a lot of things that people don't know about me. Allie and Mish are the first people to learn why I don't like going by Theodore. Why my name is legally Teddy.

There's a list of things that people don't know about me. Things I keep close to my chest and don't tell anyone unless I must. My name, for example. Or that I was in therapy from ages seven to eighteen to deal with the anxiety and the stress of even being alive. We were never exactly able to learn the cause, but it was something I learned to manage.

I haven't had a slip like this since I was seventeen. Where everything feels like one wrong step could cause life to spiral out of control.

It's hard because my heart wants one thing, but my brain is ruining my chances.

Hockey was a good outlet for this problem, so was medication, which I haven't taken since I started at Allister. I've felt stable. Life has felt relatively okay.

But now? Now, my mom has moved to Paris to date some French baker she met, and my feelings for Allie are taking over, even though I know it can't happen. It's becoming more than just playful banter and bickering just to get a rise out of her. It's beginning to consume me.

The only reason I went on a run as early as I did this morning was because I was seconds away from jerking off, imagining her in that tight bikini top from the beach. The feeling of her tits against me as I carried her. It's like every time I closed my eyes, all I could fucking imagine was her.

My heartbeat increases, my body begins to tremble and shake as everything feels like it's spinning. I recognize this as a panic attack. I used to have them a lot in elementary school, usually about things that were completely out of my control.

I close my eyes and curl into a ball, bringing my knees to my chest and wrapping my arms around them tightly, attempting to control my breathing as I let the panic spiral take over. The trembling quickens and I shake the same way that I did as a small child. I clench my eyes shut and do everything I can to control my breathing, but it's a battle. It truly is a fucking battle. It's a battle that I've pretty much been fighting on my own since I was a child. My mom was never truly there to help me through a panic attack like this. She was never there to run a hand through my hair or rub her hand up and down my back. I never had the comfort of my mother in a moment like this. It has and always be something I have to work through on my own.

But I don't want to do it on my own. It's just too much to handle all on my own. My legs kick away the sheet and carry me up towards Allie's bedroom door. I knock once.

"Come in!" She shouts. I slowly open the door and stand

there like a child who just had a nightmare. The room is dark, illuminated by her laptop screen on her bed.

"What do you want, Novak?" She mumbles. Not looking up. I don't respond. I stand there in silence, the tremble of anxiety growing. Her eyes flit up and she notices the tremble. She closes her laptop and turns on her bedroom lamp, kicking back her blanket and approaching me.

"Is everything okay?" There is a genuine concern in her eyes. One that I've never, ever saw before, at least not for me, "Did something happen?"

"Nothing specifically." I shake my head quickly, I feel so fucking dizzy. Like I could fall over onto her carpeted floor. Her hand reaches up and presses against my forehead, but she's met with the cold, clammy skin.

"Okay, then what's wrong? You're trembling and you're pale as hell." She walks me over to a bean bag chair in the corner, sitting me down and she sits on her bed, facing me.

I let out a deep, pent-up sigh, and the words just start shakily spilling out, "When I was seven or eight. I was diagnosed with a severe anxiety disorder. The doctor said he usually doesn't see the type of anxiety I had without there being an underlying event causing it, but the thing is, my parents and me, had no idea what could've caused it. My mom and dad aren't diagnosed with anxiety or depression or anything, but-"

I see her soak in the words I'm saying. I'm being incredibly vulnerable in this moment. In the two years I've known her, I've never been this vulnerable with anyone. Not Logan or Luke, not Coach, not even my mom over the phone. I've never laid my problems out like this for anyone.

I rub my eyes as tears prick in the corners.

"I'm having a panic attack, Allie. I haven't had a panic attack like this since high school." I continue. Confusion and a sense of fear fill her face, as though she doesn't know what to do to help me. She moves to the floor, sitting on the carpet, her back to the metal bed frame as she holds a hand out towards me, taking one of my clammy hands in hers. She squeezes it.

"It'll be okay Teddy. I promise. It'll pass." She mutters quietly, squeezing every few seconds, "Does anyone else know?"

I shake my head quickly, "No, God. No one else except my parents and the campus health clinic."

She nods slowly, releasing my hand and working her way up to her knees. Allie brushes her hair behind her shoulder as she leans towards me and throws her arms around my neck, pulling me towards her into a tight embrace. One hand moves to the back of my head, while the other moves to my back and subconsciously works its way up and down.

I feel as though, in this moment, everything has changed between me and Allie. Something has shifted between me and her. It's a big, dramatic shift. One that could have big consequences, and the very concept of that makes me feel sicker than before. But there's one thing that has shifted. It's the feeling of anxiety in my chest. In my muscles. It feels lighter, looser. My heartbeat begins to slow. My breathing doing the same. She's done it. Allie just got me through a fucking panic attack in seconds.

I used to have to take sleeping medication to knock myself out and just ride the panic attack into sleep, but Allie just single-handedly ended it in the span of a few minutes.

"Do you want to talk to someone about it?" She releases from the hug momentarily.

"I dunno. Who are you thinking?" Wiping my eyes again. She reaches for a tissue box and hands one to me.

"Who do you think, Novak?" she giggles and sits back, but continues to hold me hand. I let out a chuckle at this. She's not wrong. Who else would we go to about this?

"Your dad?"

"Would you be up for it?"

Then I nod in response, "Yeah. I would."

CHAPTER 9
ALLIE HENNINGS

"My mom is picking you up, right?" I ask as I park in front of a small brick building. Teddy looks over to me from the passenger seat and nods.

"Yeah, in an hour." He unbuckles his seatbelt and grabs his phone.

After sitting down with my Dad and talking about his anxiety, my Dad decided to get in contact with a friend of his here in Eldridge Bay who is runs a private practice. He's agreed to meet Teddy an hour before his office opens, completely for free. Well, not for free so to speak.

He has family coming for Thanksgiving and they're going to stay in our house. It's odd, sure, but it's a sacrifice my parents were willing to make for Teddy which is saying a lot. My Dad must care for Teddy more than any other player he has had before. He would've never done something like that for anyone else.

I also haven't bickered with Teddy in the last three days, so progress. I guess.

"See ya, Hennings."

"You too, Novak."

He rolls his eyes and my eyes follow him as he gets out, "Have fun getting ogled by old dudes, Allison."

"Oh I will! Have fun talking about your feelings."

The bickering is back, I guess. Just after I was thinking about how we haven't been bickering back and forth with each other. I make note that if we're going to bicker, to aim above the belt. We can still have playful bicker without making each other feel like shit about it.

He gets out and slams the door closed. I don't leave until I fully see he has entered the office. Yet, as he stands on the porch, shaking hands with Dr. Faber, I can't help but feel as if I've been the one on that porch, shaking his hand before.

That's odd, though. I have never gone to therapy. Not that I can remember. Maybe Mom and Dad brought me here to talk to him when Grandma or Grandpa died? That would make sense. I was young. I had never experienced death before. I wouldn't be surprised if they brought me to talk to him for a couple sessions.

To be completely honest with myself, there is a lot about my childhood that I don't recall. I remember growing up with Mish in the summers. I remember when I started dance. I can remember the hockey games I went to with my Dad, but it feels like, especially in this moment, there's a piece missing.

I've pondered this before, what could I possibly be missing from my childhood, but I never am able to remember. It's like a blank slate.

It's probably just that I was young and my brain wasn't fully developed.

Elizabeth Loftus was a psychologist we studied last year in my Early Childhood Development class. She had a theory of childhood amnesia. That the brain isn't fully developed in childhood for one to be able to recall memories as adults.

It's probably just that.

Except for the fact that Grandma and Grandpa both died

in the winter. We wouldn't have been spending a prolonged amount of time in Eldridge Bay.

I turn up my music, hoping to drown the mental whiplash I just experienced.

———

The end of June and going into July is the busiest time of the year for Plutarch Country Club. It's a small country club and golf course just north of city limits. It's on a hill that overlooks Lake Michigan, mainly the two large, bean shaped pools, the golf course is inland.

I stop my golf car near a group of older men, maybe around my Dad's age.

"Can I get you gentleman anything to drink?" I say in my best customer service voice.

On these busy days, the bar becomes a traveling bar, and it just so happens that today was my day to drive around the property in a golf cart, serving drinks to the people enjoying the amenities of the club.

One of the guys, who I recognize as Cam's dad, nods, setting his club against his cart.

"Hello, Mr. Kavanaugh! What can I get for you?" I ask, opening the cooler.

"Well, Hennings, you got an Ultra?"

I take out some shitty beer, handing it to him. I'm sure that if the country club allowed people to bring their own coolers, he'd probably just bring drinks from his bar.

His eyes flit to my light blue polo shirt, then my white skirt and long legs.

Charming.

I keep my composure, smiling, despite the fact that every alarm is going off in my head. As it usually does when I have to serve the skeeze-balls on the green.

"It sucks that you and my son never worked out." His

condescending glare makes me feel even more uncomfortable.

You mean Cameron who I kissed a couple times in Elementary and Middle school? Yeah, that was never going to happen. Especially on Martie's watch.

"Well, the universe has other plans for us both, I'm sure." I bite back any rude thing that I want to say to him, keeping my composure.

"Not the universe, Darling. The lord."

Well. Not only do the Kavanaugh's own the most successful bar in town, they also are the heads of the church and come from an incredibly religious, incredibly racist and misogynistic background.

It seems like an oxymoron, owning a successful bar and also being incredibly religious and also running the local church.

My Mom once told me a story that when she was in high school, Mr. Kavanaugh here, was trying to get with her and make her into his stay-at-home wife.

Martie Hennings is many things, but she is not, and would never be a stay at home mom. She owns two successful businesses in Allister and can barely escape from them for the summer.

She does all her work remotely, usually in the mornings, but her phone will also ring at any given time from one of her two locations.

"Well, I apologize sir. The lord just had different plans for Cameron and me." I correct myself and he nods with a smile.

"Maybe one day, you'll return to the Bay and realize how great of a guy he is. I'm sure you would make beautiful children." The thought makes me vomit a little in my mouth. Kids? With a Kavanaugh? I don't think so.

Admittedly, Cameron is probably the best of all his family members. But that's not saying much. That's like saying he's Cameron has some controversial opinions about some very controversial topics, but at least he isn't a sexist pig like his Dad.

A few of Kavanaugh's buddies get drinks, one of them tips me forty dollars. Because of course he does.

Buddy, you don't even have a chance with me.

I pocket the tips, then put the money for the drinks in the cash drawer.

I'm so going to ask Phoebe to move me to the bar after my lunch break.

I drive to the next few groups, giving them different beers and mixed drinks. Most of them are older men and their sons, all of them tip pretty well. Flashing their cocky grins and making creepy remarks about "how pretty of a girl I am."

By the time I head back to the clubhouse for my lunch break, I've already made two-hundred dollars in tips.

I might hate it with every ounce of my soul, but I can't even deny it. The tips make it worth it.

Sort of.

I head into the office where there are numerous Chinese food take out boxes set out. Phoebe returns with a clipboard and she smiles.

"Take whatever one you want. Mrs. Plutarch is actually feeding us today."

I grab the fried rice and chicken.

"How's it going on the green today, Hennings?" She takes a seat at her desk, leaving the door to her small office open.

Phoebe Briggs is not only a close friend of mine, but she's also my boss. She's was promoted to manager last summer when our old boss, Edith, retired. She's young, fit, and always doing something. Her light blonde, rose gold tinted hair is pulled back into a tight, high ponytail. She wears the same blue polo shirt and high rise white shorts.

"The green is still green." I laugh and lean against the door. This gets a quiet laugh from her, "But the men are extra sleazy today. I had one guy, had to be in his eighties, suggest that I drop a button."

Phoebe rolls her eyes, taking a bite of her own food, "But he tipped good, didn't he?"

"Forty bucks, but he bought drinks for everyone, so he tipped what would be normal for an order that size."

Phoebe groans, mumbling a few choice words, "Well of course he did. Do you know what time Mish is coming in today? She was originally going to come in the same time as you and couldn't because she had an appointment."

"I don't. She's been pretty wrapped up with her new summer girl. We've only hung out a couple of times."

"Lame. I think she said she'd be in to close instead, so two to eight. Do you want her to be out on the green and I can put you on the bar?"

She must be a mind-reader because that is exactly what I want. While I tolerate the men being sleazy on the green, Mish plays into it. She knows what will get her good tips. She said it never bothered her like it bothers me.

"I was actually going to ask you about that. You read my mind."

Phoebe shrugs with a small smirk, "Nah, I've just worked with you since you were sixteen. I know your preferences."

I nod understandingly.

"What are you working on?"

Phoebe smiles excitedly, jumping in her spinning chair and setting her take out box down, "Well, Allison Marie, thank you for asking! I am working on an End of Summer party at the club. I'm thinking, a swim-in theater. Like a drive-in, but the projector screen is at the end of the pool and we light the patio up and watch a movie in the pool. I also want to get some food trucks in, to limit the number of staff members on shift. I just have to get all the details straightened out, then I'm taking it to the Plutarch's.

Our bosses, the Plutarch's, were like the devil's reincarnation. They were incredibly critical of your every move. So, while I know Phoebe has great intentions, and it sounds incredibly exciting, I highly doubt that they'll let her do it.

They run things in a very traditional manner. The girls are working as bartenders and waitresses, the men working in janitorial roles. They knew what their *clientele* liked to see, and they truly did not give a fuck about how badly it affects their employees.

My phone vibrates just as I go to respond to Phoebe and I take it out.

A text from my Dad.

> Your mother, Teddy and I are stopping by for lunch. She is insistent that you wait on us.

> Thanks for the warning lol. I'll see what I can do.

I reply back quickly to my Dad, then pocket my phone.

"Looks like my parents are stopping by with Teddy for lunch. They want me to be their server." I tell Phoebe and she nods, taking a bite.

"I can make that happen. One of our waitresses called in sick today," She takes another bite, "Who's Teddy?"

"Remember how I told you that my Dad brought one of his players to stay with us for the summer?"

Phoebe nods, "Yeah, the asshole."

"That's Teddy." I reply.

We continue chit-chatting for the next twenty or so minutes. Phoebe tells me about how her boyfriend proposed to her on Christmas, which I already knew, but I definitely wanted to see that ring. He makes a crap ton of money and the ring definitely shows that. She also tells me about how she was moved to a first grade classroom this school year.

Phoebe had been teaching fourth graders. She got her degree in Elementary Education from the University of

Michigan. She teaches in Grand Rapids, then returns to her hometown in the summer to work at the country club and make extra money.

I tell her about Dance, about how Ana and Logan are coming to stay in the next week or so. She's excited to meet my roommate, yet I'm shitting bricks.

Ana might come off shy at first, but the minute you move the curtain, she's non-stop. Though, she has said the same thing about me. I shrug.

My break ends and Phoebe moves me up to the dining area and just as she does, my parents enter, followed by Teddy. My parents wear their usual country club attire, and Teddy wears khaki shorts, loafers and a loose-fit stripped button up, the top two or three buttons undone, exposing the top of his chest.

He smirks at me as I grab menus and silverware, "What a surprise!"

Mom rolls her eyes, "I already know your Dad warned you, Allison."

I laugh, "Yeah, he did."

I lead them to an open table. My parents take their seats, but Teddy doesn't. He turns to face me.

"Where's the bathroom?"

"Uh, around the corner from where you entered."

He looks at me, then heads in that direction. I lean down toward my parents, "So, how are things going?"

"Teddy said therapy went good. Nothing to report. He seems to be in a good mood right now." Mom tells me and Dad nods in agreement as he looks over the menu. He's been here so many times, there's no reason for him to even look at it.

"What can I get everyone to drink?" I ask, taking out my handheld device to enter their order.

"Just waters for now." Dad says and Mom gives me a solid nod in agreement. I leave them at the table and head for the kitchen, but I find Teddy wandering around as if he's lost. Like a lost little animal.

"What are you doing back here?" I cross my arms across my chest and stand only inches from him, taking in his frame. The way the button up hugs his arms, the shorts hug his thighs. He could wear a burlap sack and still fill it out perfectly, looking hot as fuck.

"I can't find it." He jokingly pouts.

I cock an eyebrow at him, "So are you five?"

He counts on his fingers, "Last time I checked, I'm twenty-one."

I gasp over dramatically, "No way!"

I drop the act and motion for him to follow me. He follows closely behind me as I walk him over to the bathroom. He gives me a small smile.

"Thanks, Allie." He mutters, going to open the door, but he stops me. His eyes drift over my body for a second, working their way up my legs, then my chest and ending at my eyes, "You look hot in that skirt."

He goes into the bathroom, his comment hanging in the air between us. Oh my god.

What the fuck?

My face heats, reddening at the remark. These last few weeks with Teddy have been... overwhelming to say the least. Being around him all the time has awoken something in me that I didn't even realize was there in the first place. A need. An ever-consuming hunger.

And it scares the hell out of me.

———

Two'o clock arrives and Mish finally comes rushing in. Phoebe and I are sitting in the break room, waiting for the front bell door to chime so we can help someone. The lunch rush has ended and it's quiet in the dining area.

"What are you two doing this Friday?" Mish asks as she clocks in, then fixes her hair.

"Um, I work until four?" I reply and Phoebe nods.

"Until six."

Mish nods quickly, "I'm having a party at my house. My parents are heading up to Mackinaw for the weekend. Allie, bring your hunky hockey player with you. I'm sure the girlies will love him."

"Teddy? Teddy is not hunky." I retort far too quickly.

Phoebe scoffs, "Girl, do not even play. He's like a walking Men's Health magazine cover."

"Aren't you engaged?" I turn to face her quickly. She sits on the edge of the desk, crossing one leg over the other and swinging them back and forth.

"Yes, but I can still appreciate the beauty of individuals. Just like how I think Mish is absolutely beautiful today." Phoebe replies and Mish rolls her eyes.

"Oh, don't play, Pheebs. You know I'll get turned on."

Phoebe winks. I missed this. Even though I have friends just like Mish and Phoebe at school, no one can replace them. I've known Mish since I was a kid, Phoebe since I was sixteen. We've always been close friends. These two are some of my favorite people in the world.

"Can I bring Lucas?" Phoebe asks, referring to her fiancé. Mish nods, getting her cash box together to be out on the green.

"Yeah." Mish shrugs.

I sigh, and motion for them both to come closer, "So, I do have to say something, but you can not make a big deal out of it."

Phoebe and Mish lean in as if I'm telling them where secret treasure is buried.

"Oooh, do tell." Phoebe tucks a strand of her rose gold hair behind her ear.

"So Teddy and I have been kind of flirting with each other.

I mean, we always have bickered, but the bickering here is so much more than it is back in Allister. Earlier when they came in for lunch, when I was showing him where the bathroom was, he told me I looked hot in my skirt." I explain quickly, trying to stay nonchalant about it, but there is absolutely no way that I can.

Mish claps, jumping up and down, "I knew it! I knew you two had the hots for each other!"

"I don't know if that's what I would call it, but I do hate him significantly less than I did when we got here."

Phoebe nods, "But how would your Dad feel?"

"What?"

"How would Jesse feel if he found out his daughter was hooking up with his player?" Phoebe replies.

Mish nods, "When you say it like that, it sounds like the plot of a shitty drama series."

Phoebe shrugs quickly, "Well, it's true! Jesse would probably be pissed."

I nod. I know my Dad would be fucking irate if Teddy and I started seeing each other. I mean, what if Teddy doesn't even want to date? What if he just wants us to fuck around with each other?

Would the risk be worth it?

"If I'm going to be completely honest," I start, "The other night I had a very interesting dream that involved Teddy and the beach."

"You had a sex dream! You freak!" Mish shouts, Phoebe and I both shush her.

She's not wrong. It was a sex dream. The two of us had been at the beach, swimming and playing in the water. Then, we were sitting on a towel, whispering incredibly inappropriate things in my ear. His fingers had touched my sensitive spot and I felt everything tighten. I had woken up just as I had orgasmed. It was embarrassing.

I had literally gotten up and showered at two in the morning, then drank a red bull and cleaned my room. I wasn't able to fall back asleep.

"I say, just try it. Don't let your parents find out, but if you two are really hitting on each other-"

"There's more, Mish." I add.

Mish sets the cashbox down, the front door chime goes off and Phoebe rises, "I'll get it. Just fill me in later."

I nod and lean close to Mish, "When we went to the bookstore, Teddy and I had really been flirting with each other and we almost kissed."

Her eyes widen, "Oh my god. Allison Marie Hennings, you better go home and jump his bones."

"I'm not jumping his bones, Mish. He's dealing with something personal right now. I don't want to further complicate it for him."

"Well then at least start flirting back. And not the shitty flirting you used to do at the beach parties." She replies as she quickly fills her water bottle.

I nod, "Maybe I will."

CHAPTER 10
TEDDY NOVAK

"Maybe I will." I reply as Allie stands in my doorway in a tight yellow crop top and denim shorts. She wears her beat up, white converse and a bow holds her hair back.

"Dude, you never say no to a party. You practically used to beg Ana and me to go with you. What changed?" She pleads.

"Well for starters, I only know you." I reply as I take out an earbud. I close my laptop, "Second, I'm not really in the mood."

"Novak."

"Hennings." I reply mockingly. Allie rolls her eyes.

"Get off your ass and come with me. Please. You don't even have to drink." She jumps onto my bed, bouncing on the mattress. God, she really is beautiful right now.

I sigh, "We saw how well that went last time. You got drunk and I had to carry you home drooling,"

"I was not drooling."

She absolutely was. Though, it's not like she would remember, she was sleeping, knocked out by the alcohol consumption and the bickering and puking.

"You definitely were, Allison. All down my shoulder as I carried you home." I reply and she sticks her tongue out at me, mockingly.

I roll my eyes, going over to the dresser and pulling it open. I take out a red shirt with the sleeves cut off, the sides completely exposed. It's yet again, another Allister shirt, albeit, faded from time and numerous wash cycles. I don't care that she's sitting there on my bed as I lift my t-shirt up over my head and discard it. Her eyes flit between my eyes, my shirtless torso, and the floor.

"You don't have to be bashful, Als, you've saw me in just a towel before." I flash her a smile and she rolls her eyes, but her gaze doesn't leave my body.

She shakes her head, clearing her thoughts, "Well, that was before we almost kissed at a bookstore and you told me I looked hot in my work uniform."

Oh, she looked incredibly sexy in the small, powder blue polo shirt, top button undone and that short, white skirt that showcased her long legs. Allie was tall, don't let her fool you.

She'll act like she's not tall, but compared to Ana, Allie has some height to her. Her frame is full, built well from years of dance practices and conditioning, she's not skinny, she's not overweight, though, there would be nothing wrong if she was.

In any form or way, Allison Hennings would still be incredibly sexy to me.

I grab my leather flip flops from the corner that I've discarded my shoes in, between the blue wall and the white dresser.

"So you're going with me?" She asks excitedly, bouncing on the bed.

I nod, "Yes, Allison, I am going with you."

She giddily jumps up and down. Didn't know that me going with her would have such a big impact on her mood.

I grab my phone, sliding it into my pocket and I follow her upstairs.

"Mom! Dad! Teddy and I are going to Mish's party. Don't wait up for us." She shouts up into the main level of the home. From the kitchen, her Dad shouts back.

"Be safe! Don't do anything stupid."

She takes my hand, pulling me out the front door as quickly as she can. Fuck, she really does want to go to this party. Why, though?

As we approach Mish's house, I realize how incredibly stupid this is of us.

Mish lives right down the road from the Hennings and her house is busier than any frat party I've gone to in my college career.

Lights are flashing from inside, the music pumping. People are spilling out onto the porch, mostly the losers who would rather sit outside and smoke a joint the entire time.

We head up the steps and to the front door, which is held open by a large rock.

Allie's eyes widen at the first sight of the crowd and quickly, her hand jolts out and takes mine. The warmth of her palm against mine brings me back down to earth, reminding me that we're really here, together, in this moment.

"Do you want me to go first?" I ask and she nods, moving behind me, but never letting go of my hand. I make my way through the door, pushing past the people congregating in the entryway and I lead us into the living room.

An old *Fall Out Boy* song is playing loudly, the room shaking. I fuck with this song, but no time to enjoy it right now, first, I need to help Allie find Mish.

The LED lights taped to the ceiling begin flashing with the beat of the music, shades of blue and purple soak the crowd. How are there even this many teenagers and college students in Eldridge Bay?

On the far side of the living room, Mish sits in a large

beanbag chair with the blonde haired girl I've saw her with a couple of times. The girls legs are draped across Mish's lap and they both hold cans of *White Claw* as they laugh quietly about something. As the party grows rowdier at the chorus, Allie's hand moves out of mine and her arms wrap around my waist.

Don't get hard.

Her hands are locked tightly around my abdomen as she uses me like a shield to get her through the crowd of people. Her face is pressed into my back, body against mine as I maneuver us through the crowd. We finally reach Mish and I tap Allie's hands to alert her to that fact. She releases and comes around me. Mish jumps up when she sees Allie, hugging her.

"I wondered when you and your hunk would get here!" Mish slurs over her words, long gone to the alcohol.

Hunk? What?

Allie rolls her eyes, "He's not my hunk."

"Not yet." Mish looks to me and winks.

What the hell is Mish talking about? A second later, another girl and guy join us in the corner. I haven't met these two before.

"You made it!" Allie and Mish say at the same time and Allie quickly hugs the rose-gold haired girl.

Allie releases and turns to me, "This is Phoebe. She is mine and Mish's boss at the country club."

Phoebe fakes a gasp, "Don't say it like that. It makes me seem old."

"Well, you are, so," Mish says with a laugh.

Mish's date rises, "Introductions are in order!"

Allie nods and turns to me, "This is Teddy. He's one of my Dad's players who is staying with us for the summer."

I give them a small nod as a hello and Phoebe and Mish exchange a knowing gaze. What the fuck is happening right now? My eyes wildly dart from Allie to her two friends.

"This is Stella, she and I have been kind of seeing each other. She's staying with her Grandma for the summer," Mish yells as the song changes to another frat party classic.

"It's nice to finally put a name to the face." I reply, shaking her hand. I've saw her around a couple of times with Mish.

Phoebe giddily jumps up and down, "Okay! I'm Phoebe, I'm Allie and Mish's coworker, and this is my fiancé Lucas!"

The tall, blonde haired guy looks like he belongs on a California beach with a surfboard. He's got a deep tan and wavy blonde hair. He's attractive enough. They're both hot together.

I give them a small smile, attempting to be friendly to these two strangers at a party that I really don't want to be at, "Mish, we need drinks. Are they in the kitchen?"

Mish nods, "Kitchen for canned or bottled drinks. Back porch for the keg, though, Cameron is already incredibly drunk, so I would avoid the keg. I hid your mini bottles in far corner of the kiddie pool cooler."

Allie nods and grabs my hand as the crowd settles some. She leads me to the kitchen where an inflatable kiddie pool is set up on the floor, it's filled with canned and bottled drinks and ice chunks.

She reaches down and takes out two small shot bottles. *UV Blue*. Nasty.

"Mish got these for me, but you're taking a shot with me, first."

I nod. I didn't exactly want to drink tonight, but I guess it couldn't hurt to have a single shot of shitty vodka. She hands me one and we both twist off the lids. She hands it to me and I pocket both. We clink the small bottles and tip them back.

It taste like fucking cough syrup as it goes down, the cool sensation tickles the back of my throat and leaves me coughing afterwards. She finishes the shot before me, setting the bottle on the counter.

I've saw Allie tip back shots before, so I'm not exactly

surprised at her speed, but she barely even flinched, let along coughed like I did. I reach past her, setting the small bottle down and my hand brushes the side of her arm. The heated sensation pulses through my veins and goes straight to my cock.

"I think I need another shot." Allie mumbles.

I nod in agreement. Fuck, if I'm going to survive tonight, I'm going to need at least three more shots.

———

Three shots in and Allie and me are in the middle of the room. She's discarded her crop top, and hair bow, dancing in front of me in just the short denim shorts and a white lace bra with a small bow between her breast.

Our bodies are close, the temperature between us growing. My chest feels heavy as she begins to rub her body against mine. Part of me wants to puke as the anxiety bubbles in my stomach, not cooperating with the liquor, but another part of me just wants to lean in and kiss her. I reach over my head and pull off my old t-shirt and her hands move to my exposed skin quickly. Her sweaty palm and fingers press against my sweaty chest. Her fingers brush the sensitive skin of my nipples, they go rock solid, then I watch as she traces her fingers down my chest.

Her fingers graze over my abdomen and my breath hitches. She laughs loudly, throwing her head back and moving her arms to the back of my neck, pulling us closer together. Her breast are fully pressed against me and I feel as though I'm going to spontaneously combust.

The restraint for me to not kiss her, right here, right now, is getting harder and harder to control by the second. The anxiety has subsided as I realize, there is nothing more that I want to do right now. I just want to press my lips to hers, while our tongues explore each other's mouths, and I hitch her up, holding her up by her thighs.

She pulls back for a second, jumping up and down, her hair frizzy as it bounces. The song begins to fade into the next one and she leans towards me.

"I have to pee. I'll be right back." She wanders off through the crowd, leaving me standing in the middle of the party. What the fuck is she doing to me?

I stand there and watch as she quickly runs upstairs, leaving me alone with my wild thoughts.

ALLIE HENNINGS

Within minutes, I find myself in Mish's bedroom with Mish, Phoebe and Stella.

"I think I'm just going to do it, I'm just going to kiss him." I tell them as Stella passes around water bottles.

Phoebe nods, "You should. If he were living with me, I'd be jumping his bones immediately."

"Again, aren't you engaged?" Mish asks and Phoebe waves her hand dismissively.

"Lucas left like half an hour ago. He said it was childish. I told him I would probably just stay the night with you, Mish."

"Ouch." I respond and she nods. Mish frowns, as though Phoebe has thrown a wrench into her plans.

Stella takes a drink from her water bottle, "So what if you kiss your Dad's star player? It can be nothing more than a one time thing."

Mish and Phoebe nod in agreement, "Could just be a summer fling."

"The problem is, he lives across the hall from me again next school year and I sure as well don't want to deal with the awkwardness of running into him randomly. Besides, what if he doesn't even want me like that and he's just playing around?"

Phoebe bursts out laughing, "A guy who's 'just playing' wouldn't almost kiss you, then make a comment about how hot you look in a skirt. Baby, this isn't just playful bickering and jabbing. It's straight up, unadulterated sexual tension."

I nod, processing this. Am I ready to make that kind of move on Teddy? What if he truly just wants to make jabs at me and doesn't actually want to be with me? Do I even want a relationship. Mish takes out a mini bottle of vodka and hands it me.

"Liquid courage, girlfriend. Go jump his bones." She pats my back, and I quickly down the shot, then head back downstairs to find him. I'm gonna do it. I'm going to just get it over with. I'm going to kiss him.

When I arrive back to the party, Teddy is leaning against the bannister, waiting. He smiles softly when he sees me, "Everything okay?"

I nod, "I just wanted to fix my makeup while I was up there."

He nods and reaches a hand out, helping me downstairs and back into the party. A remixed version of a *Tate McRae* song begins to play and we begin to sway against each other. My heart is racing, my body is shaking as I work up to my next move.

I lean in, "Can I ask you something?"

He nods, our body's are sticky against each other as the crowd moves around us. My heart is thumping out of my chest as I push myself closer and closer to him, pressing my body against his.

His green eyes are sparkling under the pulsing red and orange lights. Everything begins to slow down as I press myself against him. His muscular arms wrap around me, holding me tightly, but he puts a small gap between us.

"Can I kiss you, Novak?"

He thinks silently for a moment and as my hand moves up his stomach and to his muscular pec, I can feel his own heart racing. The beat drops to the song and in the same moment, everything slows down even more.

Instead of responding, Teddy leans in toward me with extreme caution, his lips find mine and my hand quickly moves up his chest and my arms wrap around his neck, drawing him closer to me. Every inch of skin feels like it's heating up as he pushes deeper into the kiss, our lips doing a dirty dance with each other as his tongue finds its way into my mouth.

I'm fully making out with Teddy. I'm making out with Teddy Novak. This is insane. I feel him pulse in his shorts and at the same time, my own body begins to react to him and his kissing. I've saw him kiss so many girls at Allister. I've watched them stumble out of his room at two in the morning. And I never wanted to admit it, but a small part of me was jealous of those girls.

Because deep down, since the day I met Teddy, I've wanted to kiss him.

If someone told me on move-out day, that before the Fourth of July, I would be kissing Teddy Novak, I would've told them to go fuck themselves.

But here I am, drowning in his lips, his taste, his touch.

I finally pull myself back to take a breath and both of us are panting as our eyes lock under the lights. There is no one else in the room, just us.

Metaphorically speaking.

Because right now, I feel as though there is no one else in this moment but Teddy and me.

"Fuck, Allie." His hand moves to his lips, shocked, but not upset about it.

I nod. *Oh Teddy, I definitely want to fuck you.*

His eyes widen. *Fuck.* Did I say that out loud? There's

another still moment of the two of us looking into each other's eyes, holding the space for each other to say something, but neither of us are able to. I press up on my toes and kiss him again.

"Are you sure?" His voice is low, his lips near my ear. I nod and he takes my hand, leading me to the kitchen. We reach for our tops out of the cupboard and I quickly pull mine on. He does the same. Now my heart is really racing. As we exit the party, I take out my phone and text Mish and Phoebe:

We're going home ;)

Mish immediately responds, before I can even pocket my phone,

SHUT UP! SHUT UP! SHUT UP!

I pocket my phone and take his hand, leading the way off of Mish's front lawn.

We make a quick escape from the party and rush down Mayberry Street, heading back to the house. We have to do this in his room. My room is right next door to my parent's room and I am too drunk to be quiet right now.

My mind is racing as I imagine what sex will be like with Teddy. My cheeks and my ears are heating up as my imagination races. We barely make it through the front door before his lips find mine and we are hungrily kissing each other all over again. He presses me against the wall, his hands holding my ass, pulling me towards him. He lifts me and continues kissing me as he slowly makes his way down the carpeted stairs. Teddy fully carries me down the stairs. I knew he was strong, but fuck. It makes my heart race and my body heat up as he does it.

He presses me against his bedroom door and I continue kissing him quickly, my hands moving up into his tousled hair. He sets me down, but doesn't pull away from the kissing and he twists the doorknob, opening the door.

I pull out of the kiss at the last second, just in time to see into his room.

Though, I immediately recognize that something is wrong. No light peers in through the small window. There isn't the soft smell of cologne lingering in the air. The room smells stale, the cold air prickling against my skin. I realize where we are.

The forbidden bedroom. Part of me doesn't even want to know what's in here. What if it's like a creepy sex dungeon left behind by my grandparents? What could be in this room that is usually locked?

I swallow back the alcohol as it rises with the bile in my throat.

I flip the switch on the wall and any pent up arousal I felt fades away when I'm met with pale blue walls, clouds painted on them. A small, toddler sized bed is in the center of the room. The bed is still made, toys lie in the corner, untouched.

What the fuck is this place?

I look to Teddy and he looks at me, confused. There's a picture on the small nightstand by the bed. I walk wobbly across the room, my legs feel like jello as I do, and I collapse to my knees on the carpet, my fingernails dig into the threads as the room begins to spin crazily around me. I reach for the frame, taking it in my shaky hands. I feel Teddy come up behind me, kneeling down and rubbing a hand up and down my back.

My stomach knots as I stare at the picture. It's a young boy, about four or five, holding a baby, sitting behind them, are two parents.

My parents, and I recognize that baby.

It's me.

So who is he? I look quickly to Teddy, who, in his slightly-less buzzed state has put together the pieces before I even had the chance to think about it.

I throw the picture to the side and throw up everything in my stomach onto the light blue carpet.

Tears burn in the corners of my eyes as I fully begin to process this situation. What the fuck is happening right now?

There's a commotion upstairs and a second later, standing in the open doorway with shocked looks on their faces are my parents. They don't know what to say. My mom looks as though I've unearthed something that was never supposed to be unearthed. My dad is in such a state of shock, that he looks like he could faint. I've never saw either expression on their faces before.

"What the fuck is going on here!"

CHAPTER 11
ALLIE HENNINGS

The four of us sit at the dining room table. It has to be three or four in the morning. Teddy and me have both showered, and I've snacked on crackers and sports drinks, trying to calm my upset stomach.

"So what was that?" I ask quietly. Not angry or upset, but processing, my eyes are locked on the bowl of fruit in the middle of the table. I can hardly look them in the eyes without an answer.

"Just know, we love you a lot and we did this because of how much we love you." Mom starts and I shake my head, ignoring that response.

"Be straight up with me." I don't beat around the bush and I don't want them to either.

Dad nods, "It's a lot, Allie. We just need you to understand why we didn't tell you about it."

Teddy looks between my parents, then back to me, as though he's asking if he should leave. I shake my head slowly and he brings his hands together, resting them on the table. Under the table, his leg is bouncing nervously.

A silence looms. I set the picture frame on the table, sliding it towards my parents, "Who is this?"

"That's Adam. Your brother."

Everything begins to spin. A brother? I don't even remember having a brother?

What?

My brother. I don't even remember having a brother.

I have a brother. I feel as though my entire world has been thrown off axis and everything shifted in that moment.

The thought rings through my head line a broken alarm. I have a brother. *Had.* I *had* a brother. Everything begins to hurt and bile rises up the back of my throat as it sinks in. Tremors rumble up my legs and through my back and a chill comes over my arms. I rub my hands up and down my arms, attempting to control the goosebumps as they take over.

Tears prick at the corners of my Mom's eyes, "He was three when you were born, and he passed when you were three."

He was six years old? I lost my brother.

What?

Everything I thought I had known has come crashing down around me and I feel absolutely sick. I bite my tongue to hold back the puke. I can hardly breathe.

"He-"

"Why didn't you tell me?" I cut my Dad off, "Why didn't you two tell me that I had a brother?"

My dad takes a deep breath, "You watched him die, Allison. You watched him die, then within a month, you continued on with life as if nothing happened."

I can't even remember it. I watched my own brother die and I can't even remember it. I don't have a single memory of him. There's nothing in my mind, no matter how quickly it's racing, that remembers any trace of Adam. I dig as far back in my memory, but it's all hazy. Everything is clouded, like I'm driving through a heavy blanket of fog.

I can hardly breathe.

"The psychologist called is dissociative amnesia. You

witnessed something incredibly traumatic as a toddler, then blocked it out. It's common, for young children, especially. While it hurt us, it was easier for us to raise you, without reminding you of it." Dad explains and everything really sinks in. Tears prick at my eyes.

Amnesia? I just completely erased my own brother's death from my mind to make coping easier. Wow, I'm an incredibly fucked up person. The hurt, the pain, begins to churn in my stomach into something stronger. Something worse. Anger. I'm angry they never told me. They had to live with this grief, watching their daughter continue living her life as though nothing had ever happened to her brother. For seventeen years, they've carried the burden of losing their six year old son, while also pretending that he didn't exist for my sake and my well-being. The thought alone drives me insane. I feel like a shitty person.

Mom nods, wiping her eyes with her sleeve, "We knew, eventually, we were going to tell you when you were eighteen, but what happened senior year, made us feel like you weren't in a good enough place to handle it."

Senior year.

I never told anyone about that. Not Teddy or Ana or Logan or even Mish.

Back in high school, a freshman girl on the dance team that I had been training had died. She had taken her own life. *Eden Watts.*

I feel Teddy's eyes on me, waiting for me to say something. To reveal something, but I can't. Not right now.

"Tell me what happened."

"I don't think-"

"I don't care." My voice tensing as my mind races, "Tell. Me. What. Happened."

Dad leans in to say something quietly to Mom as she starts to cry. She silently gets up and goes to her room, leaving me with my Dad and Teddy. Our eyes all linger on the closed bedroom door. Dad takes my hand from across the table.

"You were three. Grandma Maeve was watching you and your brother while me and your Mom went to see a concert in the city. She had you both playing in the kiddie pool on the back porch and had quickly gone inside to grab an extra towel. She thought that, with your brother being six, she felt comfortable leaving you with him for a moment," He pauses, taking a deep breath.

I reach across the table and take his hand in mine, he squeezes it tightly, "One minute, he was fine, the next he was having a seizure. He fell over, blacked out. He was shaking and drowning. You started crying loudly and Grandma rushed outside. By the time the paramedics arrived, he had drowned."

Teddy lets out a pent up sigh and I look over, seeing tears brimming in his own eyes. He covers his face with his hands as he processes the information. He's only been seriously in my life for two months and the story has even brought him to tears. I feel sick to my stomach.

"Your mom and I rushed home. God, Allie, I don't think I've ever driven faster in my life. I went nearly one-hundred all the way back. Your mom was screaming, sobbing into the phone to your Grandpa. I was nearly pulled over twice, but I stopped and told them and they just let me go. It was hard. We got home and he was in the hospital. He was cold, lifeless and in the morgue. The last time your Mom and me saw him, he was lying on a metal table-"

He stops himself, not wanting to share the details. I don't want those details, "We buried him here, in Eldridge Bay. He was born here and we wanted him to also lay here. That fall, I was offered a full-time coaching position at Allister College and we decided it would be for the best."

I don't even remember that. I had thought, that all this time, he had been coaching before I was born. There's never been a clear, definitive date on how long he's been coaching at Allister. I knew it was a while, but by a while, I had always thought he meant before I was born.

Not when I was three. Was I even born in Allister? Or was I born here, in Eldridge Bay? So many more questions fill my mind as I sit in silence, processing all of what my parents have shared.

I can't believe that I witnessed that. I witnessed my own brother's death and I can't even remember it. I shake my head, attempting to make my thoughts stop for one damn second, though, I know that method won't do me any good.

My stomach knots as my brain attempts to imagine the small boy in the picture between us lying in the cold, sterile morgue. The image begins to occupy and overwhelm my brain as it swirls about. It twists and turns and stabs at the deepest parts of my heart.

"Can we see him?" My voice comes out quietly.

"Like now?"

I nod, "Right now."

———

I had been to the Eldridge Bay Cemetery a few times in my life, but it was always for people I knew and loved and remembered. I don't even remember Adam.

It's just Dad and me, Teddy headed to bed and Mom hadn't come out of their room. Dad had peeked his head in to tell her where we were going, but all I had heard was the quiet cries of her from within the dark.

How do you even process something like this? How do you go on with life now knowing you watched a sibling die? A sibling that you can't even remember?

We park the SUV and the walk from the road is only a couple steps. I recognize this spot. Only a few graves over were Grandma and Grandpa.

The tight feeling in my chest grows. We had been here so many times since he died and I had never noticed. I had never, ever noticed the small headstone with the name Adam Scott. He's been here the entire time. When we buried grandma and grandpa, Adam was only a few feet away. I had probably walked right past his grave every single time I came with my Mom to pay respect to her parents.

All this time, all these years, Adam has been here.

I kneel down in front of the small headstone, my Dad kneels next to me and rests his hand on my shoulder as we both stare intently at the engraving. It's in clean condition, meaning someone has been coming to clean it. Who else knows? Who else was in on this secret that apparently I was the only person to not know about?

I trace a finger across the lines that make the A in his name and everything hurts. My head is spinning from this revelation and the alcohol I consumed hours ago, my stomach aches from the puking, my lungs hurt from being out of breath from kissing Teddy.

I kissed Teddy.

However, after the information I've learned, it seems so inconsequential. So what? I kissed a hot guy at a party and almost hooked up with him.

Compared to what is going on now, I think there are much bigger things to worry about that don't involve Teddy Novak. Salty tears brim in the corners of my eyes and they burn as they drag down my cheeks.

Oh my god. Kissing-

Adam Crushem. My first boyfriend. The pieces click in my mind. My parents had to watch me date a guy with the same name as their dead son for a handful of months.

They were always on edge whenever he came around, and I finally understand why.

I turn around and face my Dad, throwing my arms around him and holding him tightly against me. I cry into his grey pajama shirt, my tears soaking the shoulder as he wraps his arms tightly around me and holds me. I melt into my father's embrace, feeling so many things at once and craving only one thing. *Comfort.*

I want comfort from my parents right now. I want my mom and my dad. Fuck, I feel so bad. They had to hide this.

Something so life-altering was hidden for seventeen years.

My dad releases an arm and takes out his phone. He opens a photo app and nudges me to look at it. I pull back from the hug and settle next to him, legs sprawled out on the top of my brother's grave as I see an entire photo library before me. It's four thousand pictures and videos.

"This is how we remember him, Allie, and it should be the way you do too." He slides his phone into my hands and I click the first image at the top. It's Adam, probably one or so, standing up against a couch. He wears only a diaper and has a large smile on his face. His cheeks are rosy and plump with baby fat. His one hand is bracing him against the couch, the other holds a plastic block.

I scroll to the next one. He's in a small *Mickey Mouse* life-jacket, sitting on my Dad's lap as they sit in the boat. Sunscreen coats his little face as he smiles with missing teeth. It has to be from the same year as the last picture.

That boat sat unused in our backyard until I was thirteen. Then finally, Dad sold it.

The next one, from the same day, is Adam wearing a small straw hat and sunglasses. He's sitting with Mom and it attempting to take her sunglasses off her face.

The next picture really breaks me, though.

He's sitting between Grandma and Grandpa. Grandma is in the middle of booping his nose and Grandpa's head is thrown back in a fit of laughter from something. These three people are my family, but they are no longer a part of my life. My grandparents died when I was a kid, Adam died and I erased it from my memory.

That's the part that really hurts. My grandparents died pretending that Adam had never existed. They closed their eyes and never woke up without getting to properly acknowledge their dead grandson.

My Dad slides the phone from my hands and scrolls ahead a few hundred pictures. He stops on one. It appears to be the Fourth of July based on the decorations and America-themed attire. Adam is a little older now. His blonde hair has grown into a mess of curls on top of his head, his eyes wider and his teeth are almost all there as he smiles.

Except, it's a video. He hits play and holds it out between the two of us.

From the voice behind the camera, I assume that Grandma is filming. Dad comes around from behind the camera and looks at the wrapped box. Adam starts to pick at the white paper.

Even my parents look significantly younger. My mom's blonde hair is longer, my dad's hair has no grays, and he's clean shaven.

"Can we open it?" He asks. His voice. That's my brother. I feel as though a knife has stabbed me in the chest. A pain forming and sprouting, sending tremors down my spine.

"Not yet, bubby. We gotta wait for Grandpa to get down here."

I recognize the kitchen counter they stand in front of. Although it's been renovated, it's the same layout at the kitchen at the summer house.

I hear Grandpa approach in the background, Adam excitedly jumping up and down on his barstool. Mom wraps two arms round his waist, in case the stool tips.

"Okay, now you can open it!" She says cheerfully.

Adam quickly tears away at the white paper, tossing it on the floor excitedly. He removes the lid of the decorative box underneath and a series 0f pink balloons fly out. At the bottom is a small baby doll, wrapped in a pink blanket. He looks up at our parents, confused.

Grandma and Grandpa gasps.

"Martie! No way!"

Mom nods happily as tears form in her eyes, "It's a girl!"

Adam still looks confused, "Adam, bub, you're going to have a baby sister!"

It registers in his brain and his eyes widen, but then fall again, "I don't want a sister. I want a brother."

Everyone laughs, including Dad and me now, in the silent cemetery. I wrap an arm around my dad as he uses a free hand to wipe the tears out of his eyes.

The video ends and Dad goes silently to the next one. Adam is sitting on his bed, playing with plastic animals, "Hey Adam, what should your sister's name be?"

He holds up a plastic crocodile, waving it around. Only, it's not a crocodile and suddenly, I feel sick all over again, "Ali, like Alligator!"

"Dad…" I turn to him, pausing the video. He attempts to smile through the pain.

"Your brother named you, Allison. He wanted your name to be Allie." He says, and I completely lose it. I feel a choked back sob rise out of my throat. Tears run down my face like rivers, and my body bobs as I let all the emotions pour out of me in an exhausted rush. Dad presses the back of my head to his shoulder, allowing me to once again cry into his shirt.

None of this feels real. Not a single second of it feels like reality to me.

I attempt to calm my breathing, controlling my emotions. I look from my Dad to the grave in front of us.

I press a hand to the stone, to his name, "Adam. I'm sorry I forgot you, but I promise you, I'll never forget you again."

TEDDY NOVAK

The revelations from tonight alone make me feel sick. One minute, I was kissing Allie. I finally had gotten what I wanted. The girl that has been the object of my desire since day one at Allister. However, I lost her as quickly as I got her. It's not her fault though, I don't even know how I would react if I learned I had a brother I watched die when I was a toddler.

I've only been fully integrated into their dynamics for a couple of weeks now, and even I feel grief for them. I feel sick that Jesse and Martie had to live silently with their grief. I'm even more upset about the fact that Allie had no idea. Her entire world just came crashing down around her.

Suddenly, my problems seem so inconsequential.

I stare up at the ceiling fan, watching it slowly spin above my bed. My body is sticky with sweat, the sheet is tangled with my legs and my stomach burns from the alcohol. From upstairs, I hear the front door open and then close. There's silence for a moment, then footsteps head downstairs.

Coach?

There's a soft knock at my door, then it cracks open. It's not Jesse Hennings.

It's his daughter.

She stands in the doorway, even with the minimal amount of light coming from the plug in by the door, I can see her eyes. They're puffy and red.

"Hey." I say quietly as I sit up.

"Hey." She mutters back. We both linger in a burning, antagonizing silence as we process everything that's happened in the last twelve hours.

"Can I sit in here with you? I don't want to be alone right now." She says quietly, her voice is nearly a whisper.

I can't even tell her no. I just give her a soft nod. There's the quiet sound of her kicking off her shoes, then, her sliding out of her hoodie. She wears an Allister Dance Team tank top underneath.

Allie says nothing as she climbs into the queen sized bed at my side. I don't bother saying anything back. I can't even imagine the way that she is feeling right now. I don't want to imagine it. She lifts the sheet up and stays strictly on her side of the bed. I roll over, not facing her as we both lie in silence.

I can tell she's crying. The soft sound of her breath hitching, the movements of her body. What should I even do in this moment? My coach is just upstairs, her *Dad* is right there. He would kill me if he knew she was lying in my bed like this.

Fuck it. She was there for me that day I had a panic attack. I have to be there for her. Right now, we both may be beaten down, but we both need someone, and that someone is each other.

I roll over, her back to my chest and I scoot closer to her. I wrap one arm around her waist, the other under my pillow. She stops crying for a second, rolling over to face me, and she leans into my chest, resting her head in the space between my pec and my bicep. My arm is still wrapped around her and I pull her closer to me, as she closes her eyes.

I don't fall asleep immediately. She doesn't either. We just linger in the silence of the house. We linger in this moment with each other.

I wait until she falls asleep on my chest. This beautiful girl who has just learned earth-shattering information. The beautiful girl that I've wanted to do this with since the day I met her. I've wanted to lie at her side and hold her as though she's mine since day one. I didn't think it would be under these circumstances.

I reach over to the nightstand with a free arm and grab my phone. I tap into my messages app and start a new message thread with Logan and Ana.

> I know it's 5 AM, but how soon can you get to Eldridge Bay?

> Something just happened and I really think Allie needs her friends here with her.

I quickly send the two messages. They probably won't see it for a few more hours, but that's fine. I need sleep. I set my phone down at my side and Allie rolls in her sleep, facing the other direction, but I don't remove my arm. I won't, until she asks me to.

Because truthfully, there is nothing more I want to do right now besides give her comfort.

She gave it to me when I had the moment on the beach, and I will keep giving it to her for as long as she needs because she deserves it. If you asked me two months ago who my best friend was, I would've said Logan, but in this moment, I've come to realize that my real best friend is now Allie.

CHAPTER 12
ALLIE HENNINGS

I wake up to the feeling of hard, but warm muscle underneath my neck. I sit up, sun peering into the bedroom and I remember where I am. Lying next to me, wearing only athletic shorts, the sheet kicked back, is Teddy. One arm rests on his stomach, the other is sprawled out under where I was just laying.

Everything hurts. My stomach, my head, my neck. Every bone in my body aches in some way. I grab my phone out of my pocket, the battery is low, but there's a text on screen.

It's from Ana.

> Teddy texted last night saying something
> was going on and he was worried about you.
> Logan and I are coming a day early. Call me
> if you need to. I love you <3

He texted Ana and Logan? I don't know whether to be pissed he talked to them, or thankful he notified my close friends before I had to myself.

I slide out of his bed, and grab my sweatshirt and head back upstairs. The house is eerily quiet as I make my way into the kitchen and turn on the coffee pot. There's a sticky note on the counter.

'*Your Mom and I are going to see Adam. Breakfast is in the fridge.*'

I open the fridge door and take out cold waffles. I throw two onto a plate and put it in the microwave. I need to eat something, then I need to shower and get myself cleaned up. As the waffles warm up, I notice something sitting on the dining room table. A book? A sticky note on top has my name on it. I grab the leather bound book and open it. It's filled with pictures and journal entries in my Mom's handwriting. There's a page marked with the silk ribbon and I flip to it. It's a picture of Mom, Dad and me from last years Homecoming Tailgate. I rush into my bedroom and fall onto my bed, eyes scanning the journal

The journal entry accompanying it is dated from today.

Allison Marie Hennings,
There are plenty of reasons as to why we never told you about Adam Scott, but it wasn't because we were hiding him from you.

I feel my chest tighten. Oh my god.

Your father and I have a lot of things we haven't told you yet. Many of these things are heartbreaking things, things we've struggled to deal with ourselves, and within that first year of Adam passing, it was easier for all of us to slowly erase him the same way that you had. Though, we didn't get the dissociative amnesia that you did. We had to live with that pain. We had to wallow in that pain and learn to move forward in a world without our first born son while raising a daughter who had quickly forgotten about his existence. We do not resent you for that, we never have and we never will. We know very well now that it was your toddler brain coping with a traumatic event.

There are exactly 216 entries in this journal. 216 pages of one page, written letters to Adam.

He had passed away in July, I began writing one letter every month following his passing, give or take a few. My therapist said it was a healthy outlet and it has been for the last seventeen years, but now, I believe that you deserve to know everything. My beautiful daughter, you deserve the truth. The complete, bare naked truth. It's an ugly truth, but it's also beautiful. The truth I've been writing within these pages for the last eighteen years is messy; your Dad and me have made plenty of mistakes as parents, as husband and wife, and I wrote these issues to Adam.

At first, the entries were solely about him and my grief, but Adam became more than my eldest born son, gone too soon. He became an outlet for me to write every single one of my *thoughts. Every thought and memory, every muse, every burn.*

So this truth may be hard to swallow at some points, but trust me, that everything that has happened, happened because we loved you.

Love, Mom

I stare down at the page, skimming my finger over the handwritten words. I flip to the previous entry and it's a picture of Adam holding a flower. It's dated May 8th:

Happy birthday Adam.
Today, you would've been twenty-four-

My heart skips a beat as I imagine what life would be like had Adam lived.

Would we have ever moved back to Allister? If we did, would he have gone there too? What would he have studied? Would he have played hockey? Would he have been incredibly overly protective over me? Or would we have bickered? I would've been a freshman at Allister if he was a senior. Would he have joined a fraternity? Would he have played an instrument?

I realize, the answer to these what if questions are probably buried within this journal.

What would he have looked like as an adult? Would he have had Mom's naturally blonde hair like I do, or would it have darkened over time and become a more brown shade like Dad's?

There's a knock on my doorframe and Teddy stands there,

arms crossed, but not sternly. He's watching me as though I am a bomb that could go off at any moment.

"Get in here." I tell him and he enters, sitting down on the edge of my bed. I adjust to sit criss-cross and I hold the journal between us. He stares at the page.

"What am I looking at?" His eyes scan the pages.

"My mom has been writing monthly journal entries for the last seventeen years. They're all letters to him." I reply as I flip through it. My eyes stop on one.

It's dated August 10th. From the same year he died. I realize it's the first entry.

Dear Adam,

I don't think I can read this right now. The truest form of grief. The snippets I saw from the recent letters are less in the grief, as time had passed, but these letters are fresh from when it had happened. From the gravestone, I know that August 10th was exactly one month after he passed.

I don't know if I'm ready to open that door yet. I don't know if I'll ever be ready to open that door. What good could come from me reading the deepest parts of my mother's grief. I flip forward and an image catches my eye. It answers one of my questions. It's Dad, he's teaching Adam how to skate.

Last November, just before Allie's Birthday, you had told me that when you grew up, you wanted to play hockey. Just like your Daddy. I had a feeling you would want to start learning how to play soon. The four of us headed to an ice skating rink and your father taught you how to skate. You were too small to join an Elementary

Team, but they said maybe next year. That's now, and you aren't here to join, but the team you were going to join had a night dedicated to you. It was beautiful. Your father also began coaching hockey at his former college. If only you could've been there when he signed the contract. He was crying. He said he did it for not only himself, but for you.

Teddy's eyes are following mine across the page and he lets out a quiet gasp. I close the journal and turn to him.

"Last November, right before thanksgiving break. Do you remember the charity game?" His eyes tiredly look at me. Where's he going with this?

I vaguely remember it, "It was the night with the highest ticket sales right? And the auction?"

He nods, "Do you remember the organization we were raising money for?"

I don't. Though I wish I had. It was the Thursday night before my birthday.

Teddy types quickly on his phone, then turns the screen to face me. It's a website homepage. It's an organization dedicated to giving money to families who have lost a child or who have a child who has an illness.

Teddy quickly pulls up the schedule and shows me. It's the same date as when we went to the ice skating rink when Adam was little.

Everything is just getting more and more complicated. More and more difficult to process and deal with. I cover my eyes and start to cry into my hands. Teddy wraps his arms around me quickly, holding me tightly like he had last night.

His chin rests on top of my head as my curled up form collapses into him.

"It's okay, Allie. I'm here. I'm here." He whispers to me. We linger in this silence. Me in his arms. It's comforting. It's the comfort I need right now.

I slowly pull out of the hug and face him. Our eyes meet. I know I shouldn't do this. Not after how the past twenty four hours have gone. But something in my head is screaming at me to just lean in. Just to close the gap. Slowly, I lean my head forward. His nose nudges mine teasingly.

Through all the emotions I've felt in the twenty four hours, there is only one that I am absolutely positive with.

And it's this.

Our mouths are so close, nearly touching, I can taste his warm, breath against mine. Our lips are touching, but aren't locked.

Then, the moment ends. Teddy backs up quickly, his hand moving to the back of his neck to rub it anxiously.

"Allie," He shakes his head, standing, "I can't kiss you. You're grieving, you're feeling a lot of things right now and I would feel like I'm taking advantage of that."

I shake my head, rushing to my feet as he heads to leave my room, "Teddy, wait."

I follow him into the kitchen. The microwave has been done with my waffles for a while now. At this point, I mind as well just start it again.

"Teddy, I'm sorry, I-"

He shakes his head, "Allie. It's okay."

"It's not okay though. I'm sorry. I'm just not thinking clearly."

He turns to face me, his eyes staring at me as he shrugs, "That's why I can't kiss you, Allie. You aren't in a good head-space right now."

"Is that why you texted Ana and Logan?" I ask, not accusingly, or angry, just wanting to know.

Teddy nods as he pours a cup of coffee, "You need to be surrounded by your friends. I didn't tell them what happened, just that you're going through something."

"Why?"

"Because even through all of our bickering and all of our flirtatious banter, I do care about you. More than I should. I always have."

His words make my heart jump a beat, but not in the same way it did last night when I was learning so many things about the past.

"You may have despised me. Hell, you may still despise me, but the way I feel towards you is stronger than I feel toward anyone. I haven't felt this protective over someone since-" His words trail off. He is silent as he stares at me. His tongue swipes across his bottom lip as he bites it, thinking carefully to himself. God, he's so wrong. I'm still fully processing my feelings, but I don't think I ever truly despised him.

"The last time I cared this much about someone, they broke my heart, Allie." He doesn't look away from the cup of coffee as he mixes in cream and sugar.

"Your high school ex?" I rub my arms and grow closer to him.

He nods, "She cheated on me. With someone older."

"What? Like a coach?"

He nods, but doesn't elaborate on it.

There is so much trauma in his life that he has locked away with a key. The same way my parents locked away Adam and his death. He definitely has bodies in his attic, ones that he doesn't want to look back at, and I can't push.

I want him to be able to tell me. I want him to let me in and see what bothers him. He just witnessed, probably the darkest moment in my life, behind the death of Eden during senior year. He knows almost every trauma in my life. He knows about Eden, he knows about Adam, I've told him and

Logan and Ana and Luke about my past of getting bullied in Middle School.

"If you care about me, Teddy. Please don't shut me out." I tell him, crossing my arms and he sighs, then takes a sip of coffee and sits down at the island. I lean against the counter next to him.

"Remember how I told you about my grandfather?"

I nod.

"I know why he went to prison," he starts, "I'm the one who testified and sent him to prison."

Oh.

Fuck.

"He was sexually abusing my nanny. I found him doing it, and testified against him in court. She was only fourteen." His hand tightens around the mug and I reach across the island, taking his hand.

"Teddy…" I frown and he shakes his head.

"Allie, It was when I was six. It was fifteen years ago. I hardly remember it in vivid detail. I just remember sitting on the stand and staring at the man I called Grandpa sitting there in an orange jumpsuit. His eyes shooting darts at me. From that point forward, I couldn't sleep. I was worried he was going to break out and kill me for doing that to him." Teddy explains quietly and I nod, listening intently. The emotional exhaustion from the last twenty-four hours setting in. I can see it in his eyes. I can feel it in myself.

"That's where your anxiety comes from?" I ask and he nods, bowing his head.

I squeeze his hand, holding it tightly in mine. In this moment of silence, I know that we both need a distraction. I know that we both need a reprieve.

"How about we get out of here? Go do something fun?"

He looks at me, unsure at first, "What are you thinking?"

"How do you feel about amusement park rides?"

———

Within two hours, we're dressed, fed and arriving to a local amusement park. It's a small park with a couple of roller coasters and flat rides.

We park the car and head in. The crowd is pretty quiet, quieter than the previous times I've come here with my parents and Mish. Usually, we just come for the waterpark though because Mish, as well as my parents, hate rides for some reason.

"So, do you come here every summer?"

I shrug, "We used to a lot when I was younger. A little less now, but I did come here last summer with Phoebe and Mish. Phoebe rode some rides with me, Mish hates amusement park rides, so we spent more time in the waterpark."

He nods as he looks around, "Is that fucking *Snoopy*?"

I laugh and nod, "It is. He's all over the place here."

"He was the mascot of my home amusement park. I didn't get the chance to go a lot, but I always enjoyed going when I did."

I assume it's another park owned by the same company that owns this one, but I don't know enough about their other locations.

Besides the big one in Ohio that I went to with Phoebe for her birthday two summers ago.

We stop in front of a large map, "So. What are we riding first?"

We start on the Scrambler. The spinning ride that is at every local county fair. Teddy immediately sat on the inside, arm behind me. And every whip and spin, I'm sent sliding into his side. We get off the ride and head towards a small food stand. It's a hot day in Michigan. My phone's weather app says it feels like one-hundred.

"Fuck, it's disgustingly hot out." Teddy says, then tips back his bottle of water. I nod.

"Maybe it wasn't the best day to go to an amusement park?" I laugh quietly.

He shakes his head, capping the bottle, "No. After yesterday and this morning, it's just what you needed."

"What *we* needed."

He nods in agreement and takes out the paper park map we found on the ground during our walk to the Scrambler.

"We could ride this roller coaster. It's only a little further up the path." He points to it, showing me. It's an older roller coaster, but I've ridden it and I love it. I nod, taking another drink.

We finish the drinks, then head toward the roller coaster and move quickly through the line. We get into the forrest green train and buckle up, then bring the bar down to our laps.

"When was the last time you rode a roller coaster?"

"Uh? I think I was seventeen, senior ditch day?" He replies as the train bounces out of the station and towards the lift hill. The further up we go, the more and more of a pit forms in my stomach. I love roller coasters, but even with riding ones much bigger than this one, my stomach always feels like this as they creep to the top of the hill. I feel my hand slide over and grab tightly onto Teddy's. He looks at me, but doesn't say anything and just squeezes my hand tightly in his.

If the lines weren't so blurry, if life wasn't so messy, I might've considered this a first date-

And the train meets the top of the hill and goes down. As it goes, I let out a loud shriek, Teddy looks over to me, laughing, but he keeps holding my hand as he throws our hands up into the air. With every quick turn and abrupt dip, my grip tightens. His fingers interlock with mine and our palms are pressed together.

The ride goes by quickly and we get off the rollercoaster. We stop in a shaded spot underneath an old oak tree. He takes both of my hands into his and he looks to me in silence.

"Thank you, Allie. This is a good distraction."

I nod with a small smile, "It's no problem. This place makes me feel like a little kid again."

He smiles at this and slowly leans towards me, "Would it ruin the moment if I just kissed you right now?"

I look back to this morning, when he pulled away from the kiss and said he couldn't. So I throw it back at him.

"I thought you said you couldn't do it this morning."

"You mean after we just cried with each other about your brother? That moment was not the right time to, but right now. I want nothing more than to kiss you." He tells me and I just nod.

"Then kiss me, Teddy."

He quickly leans in and presses his lips to mine.

Today has been an absolute shit show of a day, but if there is one positive thing that has happened out of all the emotional heartache and mess, it's being with him. Crying with him, lying in bed with him, listening to him as he laid his trauma out in front of me, being here with him and riding roller coasters and fair rides and just pretending to be a kid again. Kissing him.

It's all worth it.

———

We arrive home around ten. Mom and Dad are sitting at the living room couch and Mom is watching reruns of *Grey's Anatomy* on some streaming service. It's her comfort show. I don't understand how. Almost all of the main cast has a near death experience every season.

We come up the stairs and to the living room.

"Hey, there's our girl." Mom says with a small, comforting

smile and I sit next to her on the couch. Teddy sits on the loveseat next to the couch and sprawls out.

"Hey Momma." I tell her and rest my head on her shoulder.

"Where'd you two go?" She wraps an arm around me.

I recount the day to my parents as Teddy lies in silence, staring at the ceiling and unwinding from our insane day. There's only one part I leave out, and it's how many times Teddy and I kissed. They don't need to know that. Not right now.

"That sounds exciting. I'm glad you finally found someone to ride those stupid roller coasters with you." Dad laughs and this gets a smile out of Teddy.

He sits up and Dad turns to face him, "How do you ride those things?"

Teddy shrugs, "Life is already a roller coaster. The ride itself is just a physical manifestation of it all."

Both of my parents heads turn to face him. They're almost surprised at his philosophical approach.

Both of us burst out laughing, realizing the joke before they did, "I'm kidding. I just like the thrill of it all."

I snuggle into the couch next to my Mom and in this moment, I feel as though the piece I've felt like I was missing has been put into place.

Even with all of my grief, I feel safe. *Secure.*

At peace.

CHAPTER 13
ALLIE HENNINGS
ONE WEEK LATER

Dear Adam,

It's the Fourth of July. The first Fourth of July without you. I still miss you. I miss seeing your face in the glow of the fireworks. I miss your bright, beaming smile and the way you would cover your sister's ears when they exploded in the sky, and

close the journal as a knock sounds at the door. It's not technically the Fourth of July, not for another seven hours, but the knock at the door signifies one thing.

My best friends are here. I jump out of my bed and rush to the living room, looking over the stairwell as my Dad answers the door.

Since learning about Adam, my parents and I have been spending a lot of time in what was his bedroom. My mom and I usually find the time once everyday to go and sit in there and go through old photo albums that had been stuffed away into his closet.

My Dad must've been down there, in Adam's room, because Teddy is not here at the moment. He's working at Carla's until 8. He seems to enjoy it, and he gives me free ice cream, so I guess he can keep working at my comfort spot in town.

Either way, I am too excited to even think about anything else as Logan and Ana enter. I rush down the four steps, practically skipping all of them as I throw my arms around my best friend.

I can't contain my excitement. I can't even contain the smile on my face. After the drama and issues that this summer has brought so far, I am glad to see the faces of the people I spend the most time with standing in my doorway.

Ana's dark, curly hair is shorter, cut to her shoulders. The last time I saw my roommate, it had cascaded down her back. She's wearing an oversized blue t-shirt. One I assume belongs to her boyfriend, and her classic white converse high tops.

Logan looks no different than he did a month ago. His dirty blonde hair is still parted in the middle, green eyes that can come off as yellow or blue in different light, and a jawline even stronger than Teddy's.

"I missed you!" I say loudly as I lift Ana. I remove an arm and pull Logan into the hug, "I missed both of you!"

Ana pushes her boyfriend out of the hug and keeps hugging me, "I missed my Allie."

It's in this moment that I'm reminded of why I love Ana so much. She's my best friend. She's the twin flame I had always hoped for. Having her in my life for the last year has been the best thing I had once never had.

Ana and I have been through so much together in the nearly a year we've known each other. When I met her, she was really struggling. She was struggling being around Logan again, she had been grappling with a loss that I can't even imagine facing, and she had come into college a year later than others her age. I got to watch her slowly connect with

Logan again, then fall in love with him all over again. I was there to console her through her grief, playing games and just spending any free minute we had together.

From tears after practice, to skipping parties to eat ice cream and watch shitty book to movie adaptions, Ana has quickly become my platonic soulmate. Mish is the same, here at least. I have two platonic soulmates for the two places I live and I have never been more grateful.

I lead them downstairs, to Teddy's room, which he has so graciously cleaned up for them to stay in for the few days that they're visiting. Teddy is sleeping on an air mattress in the basement living room, but after how the last week has gone, I doubt that will last.

It's something we agreed to not tell anybody, but Teddy and I have been sleeping together. Every night. In the seven nights since I had found out about Adam.

And I don't mean sleeping together as in having sex, I mean, we truly are just sharing a bed and holding each other. Granted, I'm usually in a baggy t-shirt and shorts and he usually only wears boxers, but we aren't having sex.

Yet.

It's not like I was clawing to jump his bones, but I feel like we've made a lot of progress with each other over the last month. We've been incredibly civil, *too* civil, even.

If kissing can be considered civil, nowadays. Logan throws their bags down and Ana plops onto the bed, but flinches when she realizes, quickly sitting up. Logan laughs, dropping their things on the floor.

"You washed the sheets, right?"

"These aren't his sheets anyway, his are on the air mattress. These are just extras." I lean against the doorway and Ana nods, falling back and sprawling out on the bed.

"We just drove sixteen hours straight, Allison. *Sixteen*. Do you know how good it feels to fall into bed right now?" Ana asks as she basks in the fresh sheets on Teddy's bed. I roll my eyes.

"Why yes, Analise, I know how it feels to drive sixteen hours. It is my house."

Logan laughs quietly at his girlfriend and comes over to me, he leans toward me, "She took an edible like four hours ago."

Of course she did. Ana may be an incredibly dedicated student, but even the most dedicated students let loose sometimes.

She's not an addict by any means, but anything to take the edge off.

And those are her exact words.

"Ana," I say to her, however, she's too busy cherishing the bed to realize. I snap my fingers like she's a dog and say her name again. She sits up, alert.

"How about we go bother Teddy and get ice cream?" I attempt to bribe her and she shoots up, as though her entire spiel about the bed and the long drive meant nothing.

"Where is Teddy?" Logan asks as he grabs the car keys from the water bottle pocket of his backpack.

"At work. He's one of two employees so he only gets a day or two off a week." I reply and the two of them follow me upstairs so I can get my things. Ana's eyes wander around the house, looking at everything she can. They dart around like flies buzzing spot to spot. *Oh, my Ana.*

"Where does he work?" Logan stands outside my bedroom door as I grab my purse and a hair tie.

"The ice cream place." I quickly tie my hair back, out of my face.

Logan bursts out laughing, "You're kidding, right?"

I shake my head, entertaining his reaction with a smile, "Dude, I wish I was. I'm surprised he didn't tell you."

"He didn't even tell me he had a job. Whenever I asked

what he's been doing, he'd just say hanging out or watching TV or going on a run."

"Well, he does do all those things, just before or after he goes to serve ice cream to the folks of Eldridge Bay."

"I never imagined Teddy working at an ice cream shop. Shit, I didn't even imagine he would do any working over the summer, unless it was working out." He jokingly flexes his biceps and kisses at them playfully.

"In Teddy's defense, he did have a summer job back in Philly." I reply. Logan looks at me, confused for a moment.

"Did you just defend Theodore Steven Novak? I'm shocked, Allison." He feigns a dramatic sigh. I wince at the use of Theodore, knowing the background behind it and how much it bothers Teddy. *They don't know.* It's not my place to share, so I bite my tongue and keep quiet.

I walk past him to the kitchen counter to set my stuff down. My eyes drift to the couch, where Ana is clutching a blue decorative like it's a life preserver, and she quietly snores.

I approach her, "Ana?"

She's out like a light.

Of course she is.

Another quirk of Ana. She loves her sleep.

Don't get me wrong, so do I, but Ana really likes her sleep. She has to have six alarms set to ensure she wakes up in time for class.

Logan sighs, but has a smile on his face. He lifts her up with ease, "I'm going to put her in bed. We can still go bully Theodore without her."

Knowing the truth, I feel protective over the information he shared with me about that name. Hearing Logan continuously say it, just sounds wrong.

Logan heads downstairs, walking slowly as he fully carries Ana, bridal style, and he returns a second later, "I think the excitement wore off and she crashed."

"Like a kid after a candy store."

"Just like a kid after a candy store."

———

We enter Carla's and it's quiet. Only a mother and her two children sit in the booth in the corner, closest to the bathroom. The natural sunlight pours through the wide windows and brightens up the exposed brick.

Teddy doesn't notice Logan and me at first. He's too busy scrubbing away at dishes to notice.

"Novak!" Logan shouts in the same way he does at practice or games. Teddy's head shoots up like a dog who is startled by their owner. He turns quickly and his face lifts quickly when he realizes it's his roommate.

He fully vaults the counter and first pulls him into a bro-hug, then, they do some weird handshake thing that I just stare at, processing. There's no verbal cues I can use to give me a hint of what the handshake means. It's entirely silent.

Seeing Teddy with Logan, reminds me of how much of a kid he truly is at heart. I cross my arms.

"And nothing for me? Jerk..." I tell him and he turns.

"Oh, you want a hug, Allie-cat? I'll admit, I'm pretty sticky and sweaty, so it probably won't be the best hug in the world."

I lower my voice, "Maybe you wouldn't be so sticky if you stopped jacking off in the bathroom every half hour."

"Oh and you know all about my self-pleasure habits."

"It's hard not to when you live right underneath me." I bite back.

He feigns a dramatic gasp, "Oh shush, don't pretend you aren't listening for your own pleasure."

"I would rather stick forks in my eyeballs."

"That could be arranged."

Logan coughs as though we forgot his existence. We both turn to him.

"So, are you two fucking or what? Because that banter felt incredibly sexually charged."

From the corner of the room, I see the mother look at us with a concerned face. She quickly gathers her things and her children and they rush out. We all watch and when the door closes behind them, I turn to Teddy, "Awww, you're scaring away dear Carla's customers."

"Psh, she was totally coming onto me when she got here."

"Oh, I bet she was. A mother with a child, who's wearing a wedding band bigger than my watch." I push back. Even though I have an incredibly intimate and personal relationship with Teddy, there is still something exhilarating that comes with bantering with him.

"Guys, question." Logan bounces in again, both of us turn to him and in unison say no. His eyes flit between the two of us.

"You both are fucking weirdos." He shakes his head and Teddy rounds the counter, this time like a normal, functional human being and approaches the register.

We order and Teddy just gives us the ice cream for free, even after both of us say that we'll pay. He's going to put Carla out of business at this rate. We pull two chairs behind the counter and he sits on the wooden stool as we eat and Teddy recaps everything that has happened so far.

Well, sort of.

An altered truth, if you will. There are plenty of details that Logan doesn't need to know.

Logan informs us of how summer has been back in his hometown with Ana. She returned to the waitressing job she's worked at since high school. Logan has been working at a roller rink, just to pass the time. He says he does it just so he can skate more, but I don't fully believe it. Teddy and I have a theory that Logan is going to propose to Ana for Christmas.

It's not like when they got together in May, it was for the first time. Engagement rings are a lot of money, so it makes sense that he's working as much as he can to pay for it.

The two of them had grown up together. They were practically raised from diapers together. Their Mom's were roommates at Allister back in the day, similar to Ana and me. They were freshman when my Dad was a senior. Apparently Logan's Mom had a big crush on my Dad.

And now we're here.

Life is funny like that sometimes. It's just crazy, that our family legacies are so interwoven. Our parents were there at the same time. My dad was an R.A, like Luke, and Logan and Ana's mom's were like Ana and me.

We continue sitting with Teddy for another nearly two hours until Ana finally texts Logan, having woken up, wondering where we all went.

Should I tell her about Teddy? I know we agreed that we wouldn't tell, but Ana is my best friend. She's my roommate. I feel like I should tell her.

But I also want to tell her about Adam.

Maybe leaving the Teddy of it all out of the picture is better for now? I make a mental note that we'll save the Teddy drama for a later time and date.

Or maybe I just won't talk about it at all. Who knows when this thing between us will eventually end. Not to say there is anything going on besides kissing and lying next to each other. But even that could end the minute we go back to school.

We return back to the summer house and Ana is sitting at the kitchen counter with my Mom. She's eating an apple with peanut butter, drinking from a glass of water.

"Oh there you are!" Ana says excitedly as Logan and I approach. I sit down next to her and Logan leans against the counter at her other side.

"Where'd you kids go?" Mom asks as she works on dinner

for tonight. The speaker in the corner quietly playing *Fleet-wood Mac*. Her hair is tied up into a messy bun and the sleeves of her sweater are rolled up to her elbows.

"We just went to bully Teddy at Carla's," I reply and Mom laughs quietly.

"Of course. Always bickering. You two are like an old married couple." Mom says. I know she doesn't know. She can't know, right? But it's enough to draw suspicion from Logan.

His eyes immediately flit to me, telling me that he knows something. He doesn't know anything. Unless Teddy mentioned something when I went to the bathroom. He wouldn't, right?

I take out my phone quickly and shoot a text to Teddy. He gets off work in an hour, but I have to know if someone is in on our little secret.

When I look up, Logan has turned his head to face my Mom. She's talking to them about the apartment situation next year. The thought of it makes me sick.

Next school year, Ana and me, as well as my freshman year roommate Jenny, and a randomly assigned person are living in an apartment style suite on campus. It's an upcharge, but Ana and I made the executive decision after she and Logan were back on, that we want our own rooms. We'll each have our own rooms, as well as a full kitchen, living room and two bathrooms. Ana, Jenny and me are all working to pay our share of the increased room and board charge.

Shit, my parents offered to pay the lump-sum of three-thousand dollars.

I immediately said no. I don't want to flaunt my parent's wealth and success. It's not mine to do so. It's theirs. Even if I am their daughter. I want to work to pay the difference

It just so happens that Logan, Teddy, Patrick and Nik are

living across the hall from us because of course they are. I can't escape Allister Sharks, no matter how hard I try.

Patrick and Nik are the same year as the rest of us, juniors. They're on the hockey team too, with Nik as goalie. They're okay enough, not annoying like Teddy, but they aren't saints. Nik is the cliche, tattooed bad boy with enough angst to fill up a shitty romance novel and Patrick is the sweet, golden retriever guy who's an education major.

I would've preferred Luke moving into the apartment with them, but he's an idiot and chose to be an R.A again for the free room and board.

Okay, maybe he had the right idea, but whatever.

"Allie?"

I snap up from looking at my phone. Mom holds a spatula and stares at me, Ana and Logan's eyes are also glued on me, "Sorry, what?"

"I asked if you girls know anything about your fourth roommate?"

I shake my head quickly. I wish we did. The three of us are a roommate group, so we knew from the day of selection that we would be together. We don't find out who our fourth is for another week or two.

"I wish." I reply quickly and my phone vibrates.

No, I didn't tell him. U think he knows anything?

If anyone figured it out, it would be Logan bc ofc it would… bro is like a walking romance detector.

I tuck my phone under my thigh and face Ana, "I hope to every god in the universe it isn't Bella."

"Bella from down the hall? God that would be a tragedy." Logan asks. Ana and I both nod.

Bella the Bitch, as Ana not-so-cleverly came up with last fall, is a girl from down the hall. She was always getting in other people's business and trying to start shit. One time, she told Ana that she saw me flirting with Logan in the Math building.

Funny, Bella, neither of us took math last year. In fact, we didn't even take the same math credit.

Sure, there is a lot of class overlap between Logan and me. We're both psychology majors. While I'm studying criminal psychology, Logan is studying plain-old psychology to become a therapist. We had two classes together in the spring and one in the fall.

Ana didn't believe Bella's bullshit for a second.

"Anyway, as long it's not Bella, and she's not a stuck-up bitch, I could care less who it is." I reply and Ana nods in agreement, biting on the apple.

"What time is your friend going to be here, Allie?" Logan asks.

I lean over the counter to look at the oven clock, "Soon, why?"

"Because I think she's here." Logan says and I go to the front window and Mish is getting out of her Volkswagen Bug, purse on her shoulder, makeup done, and hair perfectly curled. She's wearing a tight, white crop top and denim shorts.

I rush down to open the door, Ana and Logan following behind me and standing at the top of the stairs. Mish bursts in, throwing her arms around me.

"My god, work was incredibly tragic today Allie! Mr. Kavanaugh tried to slide a fifty into my bra in front of Phoebe and god, she about-"

She stops and smiles when she sees Ana and Logan, then turns to me again, eyes wide and filled with intrigue, "Why are all your friends so hot, Allie?"

"Down girl." I tell her and she comes up stairs behind me.

I stand between them and introductions are shared with each other.

Out of everything that could happen this week, this is what I feared. Mish can sometimes be very… forward with her thoughts.

What I mean by that, is that she doesn't exactly know when to keep an inside thought, an inside thought.

"You are GORGEOUS." Mish says loudly as she takes Ana's hands. Ana chuckles quietly, a small blush coming over her face.

Her bisexuality is showing, as she would say.

Ana had come out to me almost immediately after moving in with me, to which I replied, that I will support her in anyway possible and it changes nothing.

Because it doesn't.

"Thank you." Ana giggles and Mish releases her hands, turning to Logan. She tilts his head to the side, then the other. He laughs anxiously, eyes looking to me for help.

"You have an incredible jaw line-" I grab Mish's hand, pulling her away.

"Alright, enough of that, *Fondle-Me-Elmo.*" I take her hand and lead her, and the others to the back porch. We take a seat on the patio table and spend the next half-hour talking. Mish tells Ana and Logan all about her life back in Chicago, Ana recounts her's and Logan's incredibly dramatic relationship to Mish, who listens intently.

They seem to be getting along well, thank god. I had a feeling they would. I tend to attract the same type of person

Then Teddy gets home from work and joins us on the patio, still wearing the light blue polo shirt and the khaki shorts. His hair is a sweaty mess and he pulls up a chair between Logan and me.

Mish's eyes move to Teddy and me, then Logan and Ana, as if she's asking if they know. I shake my head.

"What was that?" Ana pipes in, then takes a sip of her soda.

"What?"

"That look she gave you, then the head shake."

I look at her, acting confused. Now I feel all eyes burning on me. Fuck. I knew I should've briefed Mish before they showed up.

"Allison Marie, I live with you nine months out of the year. I know that the look Mish just gave you meant something. What aren't you telling us?" Ana leans towards me. My eyes do everything they can to avoid looking to Teddy or Mish for help. I cannot give them any hint of what is going on.

The sliding glass door opens. Saved by the bell. Mom steps out with salad, followed by Dad carrying the Alfredo dish. Ana looks at me, eyes stern.

"We aren't done with this conversation."

Well fuck.

CHAPTER 14
TEDDY NOVAK

Well fuck.

That dinner was incredibly awkward. Jesse spent most of it talking hockey with Logan and me. Mish and Ana would talk occasionally about work or school, but Allie sat in silence, poking around at her food.

This could be a big fucking mess.

Though, it's not that Allie and me are together. We're just kissing sometimes and sharing a bed.

Though, I think I want more. Insane statement coming from me, *I know*, but the last month that I've spent with Allie has been insane and the insanity has only drawn me closer and closer to her.

I wanted her to be my everyday. I wanted her to be there when I woke up in the morning, and when I went to bed at night. We could be king and queen of our own kingdom, our own world.

After the sun set, Mish agreed to take us all to Cameron Kavanaugh's party. The last Cameron Kavanaugh party I went to, Allie was wasted and he was making a move on her, then she threw up in the sand at his feet, and I had to carry her home as she drooled.

We cannot have a repeat of that night. It's a short walk to the beach where the party is taking place. The same place as the last party. Allie does everything she can to avoid me, which admittedly feels pretty shitty, but I understand why.

We don't want anyone to know about what's going on between us. Besides the fact that Mish already knows, but Allie said she trusts her with the secret.

The five of us approach the large fire that lights up the beach with an orange glow and a sweltering warmth. I work in the morning. So no drinking for me, though, that's probably for the better.

Ana grabs Allie's hand as Allie goes to walk and the five of us stand in a circle, "We're circling back to that conversation, Allison."

"Not now, Analise. We're at a party together for the first time in nearly two months." Allie attempts to argue, but Ana grabs her shoulders. Mish watches from a foot or two away, in case this goes sideways.

"Yes now. What did that mean? I'm not stupid." She shakes Allie aggressively.

Logan looks to me, almost as though he knows. Allie was right. Out of everyone, somehow, Logan would pick up on it first. Maybe it's the psychology degree? I see the gears turning in his brain, then it finally clicks.

"Oh my god," he looks between us, then to Ana, "They're totally fucking."

"Absolutely not." I say

"No sir." Allie says at the same time. Mish looks nervously between us, then takes off towards the party.

Ana approaches Allie, growing close, "Are you and Teddy together?"

Allie is speechless, unsure of how to respond. Well, that was fun for the few days it lasted. Now word will spread, Jesse will inevitably find out, and boom, I'm back to being homeless. The thought alone makes me sick.

"We're not, *not* together." Allie starts. She looks to me as if she's asking for my approval. If she really wants to do this, then we'll do it. Though, the consequences scare the absolute shit out of me.

"We've just kissed a couple of times and we shared a bed, once."

Lies, but I won't say that, not right now. I refuse to be the one to add fuel to the fire.

Ana's eyes widen and Logan looks shocked, they turn to each other, then Ana opens her clutch and takes out a fifty, handing it to her boyfriend.

"What the fuck was that?" Allie asks. The two of them burst out laughing. Now that it's out in the open. I slide my hand into hers, gripping it tightly. She's my girl. Not technically, but if we've gotten to a point where our friends made a bet, and with everything we've done-yeah, she's my girl.

"We made a bet at the beginning of summer, that by the time we visited, you two would be getting together. Logan said not a chance, though, his opinion changed a bit when he saw you two interacting, but I've been on the Tallie train since the first day of the bet." Ana explains.

I don't know whether I should be angry or if I should laugh along with them. Also, Tallie? Now I know she didn't just give us a fandom ship-name like we're a popular movie couple. I've spent enough time on the internet to know what a ship name is.

"Guys, we're not dating. We're just-" she stops for a second, "It's complicated."

"How complicated?"

Allie shakes her head, "We just have both been dealing with a lot and just turned to each other for a bit of comfort in our complications."

Just looking at Allie speak and try to make sense of whatever we are makes me want to kiss her. I want to grab the back of her neck and lean her towards me, slowly pressing my lips into her's.

She looks to me, Ana and Logan's gazes are still planted on us. I nod.

We're doing this.

We're really doing this.

Ana and Logan give us a small smile. Ana comes over to Allie, wrapping her tightly in a hug, "Just embrace it. I pushed that feeling away for so long, and it just makes it worse."

Allie nods, releasing my hand and hugging her roommate back, "I love you, Anabear."

"You too, Allie-cat."

Ana slings an arm over Allie's shoulder and they rush to the beach to catch up to Mish. Logan stops me, "Good for you, Teddy, but if you hurt her, I'll kill you."

"If I even considered hurting her in anyway, which I don't, I would be axed from the team immediately and lose my scholarship, so…" I trail off and Logan laughs quietly.

"Oh, you are in quite a predicament, Novak."

"Just promise you and Ana won't tell,"

Logan motions zipping his lips and tossing the key, "Alright, where's the keg Mish mentioned."

———

A song called "Dirty Little Secret" plays as Allie and me dance together in the crowd of people, and frankly, it feels incredibly appropriate for the moment.

Allie and I have gotten ourselves into an incredibly complicated situation. I don't know how she really feels about me, but I know how I feel about her, and it's serious. I've felt that feeling since the day I got here and laid my eyes on her.

But the situation is so fucking complicated. My coach, the

man in charge of my entire future, is her dad. If I even want the chance to go pro after college, I need him on my side. Hell, if I even want to finish college and get a degree, I need to stay on good terms with him. I highly doubt me dating his daughter would be on "good-terms".

Her body grinds into mine, pulling me back to this present moment where I feel incredibly tense, but also freed at the same time. I feel free because there's no one here who could, or would want to, ruin my future and I can freely dance with the girl I like.

I also feel tense though, because at any moment, something could swing in and it could all come crashing down.

It's not even an if, it's a when.

I'm Teddy Novak. My life sucks, sometimes. From my shitty parent situation, to my grandpa going to jail, then hanging himself for being a creepy loser, to this new, crippling anxiety disorder.

At this point, I just know the ball will drop and I could lose everything I've worked my ass off for.

The thought makes me feel incredibly sick. My entire chest feels heavy and my entire body goes cold as goosebumps appear on my arms and everything begins to feel sweaty. Dizziness takes over and the only thing that brings me back down to earth is Allie's hand moving to the back of my neck and pressing my forehead down to her's.

I close my eyes and gulp back my anxiety, pushing it as far down as I can until I feel the release of stress roll of my back.

"You okay?" Allie leans in and asks.

I nod, but she shakes her head, "You're not. I'm not a dumbass, Novak."

She takes my hand and leads me away from the party, down the beach some way, to a small lifeguard post. We sit down on the small, wooden base and her hand moves up and down my bicep.

"What's going on in that pretty head of yours, Teddy?"

"Nothing, I promise." I can't tell her that it's the situation we're in that's making me anxious, because knowing her, she would end it immediately and I don't want that.

It's a struggle. Part of me truly wants to be with her, loud and proud with her, but part of me knows that there will be consequences, even if Allie is happier than ever with me. I won't get out of this scot-free. This murky situation, one, where we aren't even in a relationship and we've kissed a couple of times and share a bed, is a double edged sword. I have never felt the kind of relief that I feel when I'm with her, where everything feels so light and free, but I haven't felt anxiety like this in an incredibly long time. It's inescapable, really, because no matter what happens, I'm fucked.

"Teddy Steven Novak, I can see that you're lying right through your teeth." She leans into me, wrapping both arms around me as her head rests on my

I let out a deep, pent up sigh as I attempt to control my breathing, "It's just that, I feel- stuck. The anxiety I'm feeling right now is about me and you."

This causes her to lift her head, looking into my eyes with deep concern. A moment of silence passes, "How so?"

"It's hard, Allie. I want to be with you, like actually be with you. This last week alone, going to that amusement park, and kissing you and sharing a bed with you- it has meant so damn much to me. It has made me feel like a big weight has been lifted off my shoulders, but I can't be with you because if your Dad finds out, then my college career is over. He'll kick me off the team and without hockey, I lose my scholarship and I'll get kicked out. My dream of going pro or even having a career is over because I'll get kicked out of Allister."

She nods, listening intently, "You want to be with me?"

I give her a hard nod in response, "Allison, I've wanted to be your boyfriend since Welcome Weekend freshman year."

"Really?"

"Yes. I have wanted you to be my girl, for an incredibly long time. That's why I've bickered with you and banter with you. I realized quickly that, the bicker and banter was the only way I could keep you in my orbit, because the feelings I have for you are as immense as the stars in the sky." I tell her and I notice her eyes immediately glass over with those words. I've struck her in a way I don't think she even considered.

She turns her body to completely face me, "Why did you never say anything?"

"Your Dad, Allie. Being at school, it was easy enough to distract my mind with partying and kissing other girls and studying and practice, but being here? All of the things that distracted me are gone, and you, Hennings, are the only thing I can see. You're the only thing in my headlights as I drive through my complicated feelings." It sounded better when I was thinking of what to say, but the cheesy line makes her raise a hand to my cheek, thumb caressing it delicately.

She melts at these words and I feel my heartbeat increase.

"Teddy," she takes my hand and squeezes it, "First off, this isn't a shitty romance novel. My Dad won't be pissed at us dating. The dynamic will change, sure, but he's not going to punish you for it. He's not a prick. He is probably the most forgiving person I know."

I want to believe her, I truly do with every ounce of my heart, but it's so fucking impossible to believe these words when I've saw how the world works when dealing the deck to me and my family.

"And second, you could've just told me how you felt. Shit, I wish you did!" She starts laughing as she rubs her eyes with the back of her free hand. I laugh as the mascara smudges across her cheek.

"Teddy. You have always frustrated me. Everyday, for two years, you annoyed me, you got on my nerves and I never knew why. But I think I know why now. I liked you. It's like the concept, that when you're a kid, if there's someone you like on the playground, you're mean to them. While archaic, I think it's the only way I can describe how I feel about you." She rambles and I feel my own eyes begin to water as I process everything that is going on in our lives.

Everything. My anxiety and my trauma, the situation with her brother, now this? Life is getting more and more complicated by the second and while it makes me feel sick, I feel as though this is exactly what is supposed to happen.

The things that make you the most anxious, are usually the most worth it.

This is one of those moments.

"So what do you want to do about it?" Her voice comes out quietly and I let out a soft sigh as I close my eyes and press my forehead against hers.

"I want you to be mine, for me to be yours." The words slip out. I didn't even take a second to think about what I wanted to say. It just came out so naturally. Like it's a muscle I've been training for the last two years now.

The pent up, anxious feeling reappears, but I ignore it as I lean forward and kiss her once, then twice. It's in this moment, that I realize the one thing that's been missing from my life, all this time, has been her. It's always been Allie.

She doesn't know it yet, but there's one thing I've never told her. None of it was accidental. I rigged the roommate assignments last year. I asked a girl I went on a date with, who worked in housing, where Allie was living as she was in group one for selection and she told me as if it wasn't confidential information.

So when it was my turn to select my room the next day? I selected the one across the hall from her. Hell, half the team picked the rooms lining the hallway just because we always live in a pod with each other. Just because I placed us in a pod where Allie was conveniently also living, doesn't mean that they wouldn't follow.

She has been the thing keeping me afloat. Seeing her everyday, bantering and bickering with her everyday.

She stops, pulling away and biting her top lip, "So, we're together? Like, together, together?"

I don't respond. I look into her deep blue eyes, swimming in them like they're moon-lit pools for me to get lost in.

"If you want us to be? Then yeah, you're my girl." I mutter and she nods quickly, wiping her eyes.

"Then I guess that makes you my boyfriend, Teddy." She throws her arms around my neck and I pull her onto my lap. In a moment of silence, so far from the party, all that matters is her.

I smirk, then lean forward and press my lips against hers, slowly turning us around, and lying her down on the deck of the lifeguard stand. The quiet, cool summer breeze blows in from the lake. The soft sounds of the waves lapping at the shore, the music and cheering from the party in the distance, it all goes silent as I allow myself to drown in the moment with her. I made her mine. I finally got the girl I've wanted for nearly two years.

This is better than winning any trophies for games, better than getting a good grade on a test, better than sex, even.

Because in this moment, I finally feel as though I am allowed to feel and absorb the love that I've deserved for an incredibly long time.

Her chest presses against mine. I can feel her heartbeat faintly. It's racing. So is mine. It is in this raw, intimate moment, that I feel like I'm drowning in her, becoming completely consumed by this love by the second.

I lean deeper into the kiss, then, I pull back. Our eyes locked in a pregnant silence. She breaks it by bursting out laughing, "What?"

"I just like looking into your eyes knowing that I finally got the girl." Her eyes. *Fuck.* Her eyes are like a siren's curse, pulling me further and further into her.

"You finally got the girl, eh? I would've never known." She smiles up at me, hands cupping my face.

"I thought that the kissing made it pretty clear, no?"

We sit up and she punches my shoulder, "It was loud and clear, but just because we're a thing now, doesn't mean I'm not going to take up every chance possible to bicker with you."

"Oh, really? Every chance you get, you're going to bicker with me?" I tease.

"Well, when we aren't kissing." Allie shrugs, leaning in to quickly kiss me again.

"Then shit, we mind as well already break up." I shrug. Allie shakes her head quickly. Then, she takes my hand in hers.

"You're not ending this. Not a chance in hell." She rest against me, both my arms around her.

"Never planned on it, baby." I stare out at Lake Michigan, the moon reflecting on it. Her head moves to resting on my shoulder. It's in a quiet moment like this, that I realize everything I ever wanted, has been right in front of me all this time.

I've just been to scared to reach for it.

CHAPTER 15
ALLIE HENNINGS

...and how you would point out what each and every firework looked like. Some would look like animals to you, others, cars or emojis. Whenever someone asked what your favorite holiday was, second behind Christmas, was always the Fourth of July.

Last Fourth of July, I remember spending all afternoon wiping popsicle juice off your face and out of your shirt. We decided to not come back to Eldridge Bay this summer. It was a hard decision, but it's one we needed to make. I wish we had come back. I wish we had come to see you, but it's hard. Dad and me have really been struggling, baby. So has Allie. We don't understand why, but she doesn't remember you. At all. Not a single moment or memory. She's *still little, but it's all a mystery to her. But I haven't forgotten you. I haven't let you go. I don't think I ever will.*

Love,

Mom

lie on the air mattress next to Teddy. He's snoring quietly besides me, arm tucked under the pillow with his bare back on full display. I'm wearing his t-shirt from last night it smells like beach and bonfire, but it also smells like him. My fingers trace over the words my Mom wrote so many years ago. I close the journal, bookmarking it with the ribbon at the Fourth of July memory from sixteen years ago.

Today is the Fourth of July. I'm twenty. I'm not three. I'm not four. I'm a full-grown adult, and only now, am I learning about my older brother.

I slide the journal under the air mattress and change back into my oversized hoodie, tossing Teddy's shirt to the side. We told Logan and Ana that we finally made it official last night, Mish too, but she was too far gone to the liquor to probably remember it today. I head upstairs and my parents are sitting on the couch, talking in quiet voices to each other.

They stop when they see me.

"Morning, kiddo." Dad says as he stands up, grabbing his coffee mug and walking to the kitchen to get more. I look from him to my mom.

"What are you two talking about?"

"Nothing."

"It's not nothing. I can tell. Who died?"

Alright, poor judgement on my part, saying that, just a week after learning about my dead brother. It's a small wince, but it's one that tells me it doesn't bother them as much as I initially thought it would.

They look between each other and Dad approaches, "No one died, Allie. Just- there's a problem in Allister."

"What kind of problem?" *Shit.* I pray that it's not something tragic like our house burned down or Dad lost his job. That would just make this summer even more complicated.

Dad returns to the couch and sits down next to my Mom. I sit on the coffee table in front of them.

"There was a water-line break at your mother's bakery and it completely flooded the place. We have to meet the insurance people, then start working on repairing and rebuilding what we can."

My mom looks upset. I understand why. First, her business, that she spent years building up, has been destroyed. Second, she has to leave her hometown earlier than expected.

"Mom? Do you know the condition of the place?"

Her bakery and cafe was a hotspot in downtown Allister. It looked like a comfy, cozy autumnal cafe with dark brown counters, a dedicated bakery case, and booths with dark blue cushions. Think Central Perk from *Friends* meets Karen's Cafe from *One Tree Hill*. Granted, that's probably where her inspiration came from. If there's anything to know about my Mom, it's that she's obsessed with TV shows, especially trashy dramas. I too enjoy a fun, soapy CW drama, but she has an obsessions with these types of shows. She did grow up on shows like *90210* or *Dawson's Creek*, which factors into her love for the genre. She practically raised me watching these shows. While they aren't my favorites, they're a good palette cleanser from all the dark and brooding drama shows we have on TV nowadays.

She grabs her phone from the table, turning it on and opening a message thread with the manager of the location. The place is destroyed. It's dark, making me guess that the power no longer works, water damage peels away at the paint and the floor boards.

It breaks my heart for her. She's been building that business up ever since I was in the second grade. It's been a big part of her life.

Just like *Adam*.

That cafe was another child she conceptualized and birthed from her mind, and it's gone. She's lost her actual child and her metaphorical child.

"So, when are we going back?"

"Friday."

That was the day Ana and Logan were supposed to leave. Now we're all leaving. The reality sinks in. We're leaving Eldridge Bay so soon. We're going back to Allister. What about Teddy?

More specifically, what about Teddy and me? Living in my childhood home together for the next month until we can move into the on-campus apartments.

We have to give up everything here already. Everything happened so quickly. The summer *just* started. I've only worked a couple of weeks at the country club. Mish and me have only hung out a couple of times. Teddy hasn't worked much. We just started dating.

And now we have to say goodbye to all of it.

"What if Teddy and me stay, the rest of the summer? We can keep working, close down the house in August and come home." I spurt out and they look at me, confused.

"Do you think that's a good idea? With how you two bicker and argue?" Dad asks, his eyebrow cocked.

I shrug, "I'm only about half-way to my goal of paying the extra fee for the apartment. I'm sure Teddy's in the same boat."

They look between each other, "I don't think it's a good idea, Allie."

"Come on. I'm twenty. He's twenty-one. You were living on your own by then. You guys know me," and I turn to Dad, "And you know Teddy."

They sigh. Dad takes a sip from his cup, "Let us think about it today."

He heads to their bedroom to assumably start packing, leaving me with my Mom.

She leans forward, looking over my shoulder to her now closed bedroom door, then back to me. Her voice is low, "How long have you and Teddy been together?"

The question knocks me off my feet and a stinging feeling forms in my chest. I do everything I can to not look shocked that she discovered this. And so soon-

We just officially started dating last night.

"What? We're not-" I shake my head quickly, attempting to deny it, but I know it's far too late for that.

"Allie. I went downstairs last night to get insurance files from my lockbox in the storage room and I saw you two in bed together, and it wasn't like two people on opposite sides with pillows between them. He was holding you and you were using his chest as a pillow." She keeps her voice low and she has a caring, sympathetic look in her eyes

Busted. Not even twenty-four hours after we started dating.

Dating. I'm officially dating Teddy. A giddy feeling forms in my chest until I realize that my Mom knows, and it instantly dies.

"We started dating last night." I say quietly. Did she already tell my Dad? Is that why he wants to "think about" Teddy and me staying here the rest of the summer?

She nods, squeezing my hand. She sees the concern in my eyes, "I didn't tell your dad. You're going to tell him."

"Do I have to today?"

"No, but I would before the end of summer, if this is serious. If this is nothing more than a summer fling, keep it on the low. I don't know how he would react if he found out and there's already so much on his plate right now…"

I nod, "I just-"

I move to the couch and rest my head against her, "Teddy and me just found comfort in each other through all the shit we've been dealing with. His anxiety, me finding out about Adam. It's just been a lot. I haven't even slept with him, we've kissed maybe twice, but it's just complicated." The kissing part is a lie, of course. We've kissed way more than twice. In fact, we stayed up for three hours after returning from the party, just kissing and talking.

She nods understandingly.

"He's so worried that if Dad finds out, then he'll kick him off the team, and everything Teddy has worked for will just end. He'll get kicked out of school. He'll lose his chance to go pro." I explain, tucking a strand of hair back. Mom grabs the coffee pot and refills her mug.

"Do you think it's just a summer thing?"

I shake my head, "Truly? No. He told me yesterday that he's had feelings for me since we met at the Meet the Team event at the house Freshman Year."

Her eyes soften at these words, "I feel like, subconsciously, you always knew. Didn't you?"

I nod, "All the bickering and fighting. Everyone has always said we sound like an old-married couple, maybe because we are meant to be a couple?"

Mom stands, rising to her feet, and pushing the stool in, "We're going to have a girls day. Get away from your Dad and Teddy. We can take Ana and Mish and we can talk more about this."

I stand too.

"Do they know?" She asks.

I nod, "Mish probably won't remember. I told her we were official, but she had like six beers from Kavanaugh's keg."

My mom cringes with a smile, "I dunno how she drinks that garbage. The Kavanaugh's liquor has always tasted like dog crap."

I laugh quietly and nod, "It's easily accessible for her.

Can't buy anything because she's not twenty-one yet, can't steal from her Dad because you know how he is."

Mom nods and I follow her to the kitchen as she rinses out her mug, "Yeah. He's super protective over her."

I stand next to her in silence, then hug her, "I'm sorry about the cafe. And that you found me with Teddy, and Adam and everything. I'm sorry, Mom."

She turns off the sink and tightly embraces me, "Don't be sorry for things that are out of your control, Allison. You couldn't have prevented Adam's death, you couldn't have prevented the cafe, and you sure as hell could not have prevented falling for Teddy."

I nod, "I've been reading the journal. It breaks my heart. Seeing how hard it was. I wish I could remember that time of my life."

I wish I had my own memories of Adam. Not just my parent's memories of him.

She shakes her head, "No, no, no. We all agree that it's better that you don't remember the specific details. That's why we gave your the journal. So you could learn the filtered details. The ones that are worth remembering."

"Even if I had my own memories with him and they're just gone?"

She nods again, smoothing my hair back, "All the good ones were saved, Allison. Just keep reading. You'll find them all there. I kept a journal for seventeen years.

I nod, then hug her again, "I'm going to go downstairs and see if Ana is up yet, then we can get this girls day on the road."

She smiles, nodding, then I head downstairs quietly.

Teddy is now rolled over to his back, his phone perched up on his chest as he types quickly at the screen. He sees me at the entry way and sits up. Good god, he's gorgeous. He's like a greek god, carved from marble.

Even with the bed head and the light sunburn on his arms.

He smiles and I bounce over to the air mattress, jumping on and sitting at his side, "Good morning, beautiful."

His voice is hoarse from all the talking and singing last night. I lean in and kiss him quickly.

"Good morning to you too, boyfriend."

"Boyfriend? Really?"

I swat at him, "Oh hush. As if your monologue on the beach meant nothing."

"It meant more than nothing," he pauses for a dramatic moment, "It meant everything."

Cheesy. So incredibly *cheesy*.

I mount his lap, straddling his legs between my thighs. He looks at me with fresh, morning eyes.

"I can hardly believe it."

"What?"

He pushes the rogue strand of hair behind my ear, the one that's been escaping all morning, and looks deeply into my eyes.

"I can hardly believe that I am finally your boyfriend."

"Insane, right?"

He nods with his golden smile, "Pretty insane."

I kiss him once, then again and he rolls me over onto my back with his body over mine, palm pressing into the pillow to hold him up. His hand moves underneath my shirt and to my side, his long fingers snake around to my back and he presses me against him.

I feel him harden over me as he presses himself into me. We've never had sex. I've only saw him naked once and it was at a frat party where we were both drunk. I always made fun of him and said he was small, but judging by the way it feels as he presses it against me tells me otherwise.

I'm wearing shorts and he's wearing boxers, but it strains at the material. We can't have sex here. Not now.

I might've finally gotten the boy, but we're not going to fuck immediately. At least not when my parents are both awake upstairs and Ana and Logan are on the other side of the door. I'm not an asshole.

I cup his face in my hands, then pull out of the kiss and run a hand against his jaw line. A soft, stubble of facial hair is growing in. So light, it's almost blonde.

"Was that okay?" He asks, unsure as I stare into his eyes.

I nod slowly, softly, "It's perfect. You're my boyfriend."

He smiles proudly and rolls onto his back, "I want to know everything about you, Allison."

I sit up against the pillows, turning to face him. I thread my fingers through his messy curls as he lies back and stares up at the ceiling, "Oh yeah? Like what?"

"What are you scared of?"

"Snakes and vampires."

He laughs out loud, "Like Twilight vampires or Dracula vampires?"

"Both. It's just so creepy! They sink their teeth into skin and just drink from a vein like it's a straw. That just-" I tremble dramatically to emphasize how much it bugs me.

"Like this-" he turns his head inwards towards my neck and I wither as he kisses at the delicate skin. He drags his top row of teeth against it. I squirm, pushing him back.

"What about you?"

"Going to the dentist. Don't get me wrong, I'll go, but I'll be freaking the fuck out the entire time."

"Dude, seriously?" I sit up, laughing.

He nods with a small smirk, "They have all those lights and drills in your mouth? The small needles that numb it? Absolutely not. That shit is scary as fuck."

I think of another question, something random, "Favorite color?"

"A deep red, maroon. You?"

"Cliche, but a light, hot pink. Like *Mean Girls*." I reply. His eyes study me for a second as he thinks.

"You kind of look like the main girl from that movie," he

says with a quiet laugh, turning my jaw as he looks at my face inquisitively.

"Which one?"

"The one played by Rachel McAdams. Not the Lindsay Lohan character." He clarifies. I dunno if I should be flattered or offended. She's pretty as hell, but her character is a massive bitch.

"And you look like Shrek." I shoot and he rolls his eyes.

"Ouch, Als."

He gets up and grabs his shorts from last night off the couch, where he had tossed them, then his t-shirt that I had slept in all night, "What is your shoe size?"

He looks at me, "What?"

"What is your shoe size?"

He bursts out laughing, "Allison, if this is a tricky way of asking how much I'm packing, you could just ask me to show you. It's not like I'm shy."

"I'm not! Like what if I want to buy you shoes for something? Or we go bowling or skating and I go to get shoes or skates?" I defend myself and he makes a face that says '*Mhm, sure.*'

"I'm a size twelve and a half, sometimes thirteen. What about you?"

"Ten in women's."

I rise off the mattress and move the topic away from these goofy questions we're asking each other, "What time do you have to be to work?"

"Uh, eleven? I might get there a few minutes early."

"Okay. Take Logan with you. Mom wants me and Ana and Mish to go out and have a girl's day with her."

He nods, "Okay. Or he can help your Dad with whatever the hell he's doing today."

I intentionally haven't brought up the summer ending so soon. I know it will alter his mood and make today worse for him and his anxiety. I'll wait until there's a definitive answer.

"I'm gonna wake them up and then I'll meet you upstairs," I tell him, kissing him one last time before banging my fist against the door.

———

Two hours and two pots of coffee later, the three of us girls are in the car. Mish isn't joining us today as she's been puking all morning. *Go figure.* Even I had a feeling that was going to happen.

My mom parks the car in the parking lot of a zoo. She said the place we were going was a surprise.

I didn't expect it to be a zoo, especially one they used to take me to when I was little. The three of us get out, Ana pulls on Logan's baseball cap, yet again another piece of Allister College merchandise.

"Mom, when you said girl's day, I didn't expect this."

"Well, we haven't been in forever! They have a new butterfly exhibit that's supposed to be so pretty and I really wanted to see it with you girls." She exclaims.

Ana shrugs, "I like zoos. I didn't get to go often when I was a kid."

Ana's father had died when she was eight. She was raised mostly by her older sister and grandma. Her mother had started working three jobs to just keep a roof above their heads.

Then, right before she graduated high school, grandma passed.

We head into the zoo and begin exploring the different exhibits. Something pinches in the back of my mind when my eyes land on a lion statue. It's a memory. I stop and close my eyes, doing everything I can to scoop it up as it slips through my fingers.

It's a brief moment. Only a second or two. I'm in a stroller with him.

With Adam.

My heart sinks and when I open my eyes, they're glassy. Mom and Ana turn around when they realize I'm not following them. The memory, as it comes back, makes me feel dizzy, as though the world is spinning and I am struggling to keep my balance.

"Allie? What's going on?" Mom asks with concern as she walks over quickly

Ana rushes over, grabbing my shoulder, "Allie. Babe, is everything okay?"

"I saw him."

In any other context, the way I said it would make it sound like I was talking about some extraterrestrial being or demon, but for Mom, it registers immediately.

"Adam?"

Ana looks confused, "Who's Adam?"

Fuck, I forgot that I only explained Adam to Logan, and he must not have had the chance to talk to Ana about it. I ignore her for now, I'll fill her in at home.

"Mom. I saw a memory with him. We were here. I was in a stroller with him. He handed me a popsicle, I think."

A small smile comes over my Mom's face, she nods, "And you dropped it. He was so upset with you that day, but by bedtime, he felt so bad that he wanted you guys to have a sleepover in his room."

The expansion of the memory from my Mom makes my heart hurt even more than it did from the initial memory. Did she write about this moment? Is this what life is going to be like? The more that I read, the more that pieces of the past will come back to me.

Ana silently stands between us, confused, "Who's Adam?"

I take a deep breath and grab her shoulders, "I had an older brother, when I was three. He died and until a few days ago, I never remembered him. I completely erased him from my mind and this summer, I found out about his existence."

Ana's eyes widen in shock, as though I'm reciting a soap opera plot to her, "Like, actually?"

I nod, "Actually."

She just looks stunned, "And you just found out about him? How?"

"Teddy and I had gone to a party with Mish. Teddy was drunk so I was leading him downstairs to his room, we opened the wrong door and found what was Adam's bedroom." I tell her and Mom realizes, that was not the true story. Her eyes shoot daggers at me.

"Okay fine, Teddy and I were making out at a party and it was getting hot and heavy, then we went to go to his room and went into the wrong room." I explain and Mom's eyes are also filled with shock at the true story. Ana looks about the same right now.

It would be kind of funny if the story didn't have such a tragic ending.

Ana goes to speak but stops, covering her mouth, "My mom knows. She found me on the air mattress with Teddy last night. My Dad doesn't know though."

"But I thought you started dating yesterday?"

"We did, but we had kissed a couple times before that. There's been a weird tension between the two of us for an incredibly long time now. It was just up to the circumstances." I explain and Mom nods understandingly. Based on the stories I've heard about her and Dad, I have a feeling she knows exactly what the feeling is. She may be the only person who really does understand.

My words sink in. It truly was just based on the situation. We had been drowning ourselves in our hobbies and sports and academics at school, at each other's throats any time we were together because we hadn't spent enough time with each other to realize what the feeling truly was. It was a feeling so strong, so unexplainable, that it's overwhelming.

"All we needed was a push toward each other. That push, was him coming to stay with us for the summer. If it wasn't for that push, we would've just kept bickering. I think the way I feel about him, is the realest thing I have felt with a guy in an incredibly long time."

They both nod understandingly. Mom takes my hand, giving it a gentle squeeze.

Mom smiles, "You know, you and Teddy remind me of your Dad and I? The playful bickering, the emotional pining, and I fell for your Dad when we lived seven hundred miles apart."

Ana and I both nod, "You girls are lucky now, with smartphones and FaceTime and cheap airfare. But you're also lucky that the people you fell for have been right in front of you, or in your case, Allie, across the hall from you for the last two years."

"Ana, I don't know much about your relationship with Logan, just that you used to be together in high school then got back together recently, but now that you have him back, don't ever let him go." She tells Ana with a small smile and Ana nods, "That goes for both of you. Allie, your relationship is so new, and Ana, you's has been through so much, but don't let go of that feeling. Even when it gets hard."

"Thank you, Martie." Ana says appreciatively, hugging my Mom tightly. I join in on the hug. Her arms wrap around both of us.

Mom winks at her, "No problem. I'm always on your sides."

She releases both of us and we begin walking up the path, I turn to her with a small, loving smile, "Now let's go see the butterflies you've been hyping up."

———

TEDDY NOVAK

It's eight p.m when I finally switch off the open sign and lock the door. I still have so much shit I have to do to close for the night. I start off by sweeping.

As I mop, there's a knock at the door. Standing against the glass is Allie. She's smiling, wearing my hoodie. I rest my mop against the counter, and quickly unlock the door, letting her in.

"What are you doing here?" I ask, locking it behind her.

"I wanted to see you." She says with a small smile, climbing up to the edge of the payment counter and sitting down on the ledge. I approach her, pressing my hands on the counter at her sides. She spreads her legs apart and I step between them, my body fitting perfectly between her outstretched thighs.

"Are you sure that's it?"

She nods, "Yep."

I look deep into her eyes, trying to get her to break.

She does within two seconds, "Okay fine, I wanted ice cream and my parents are out on a friend's boat, and Logan and Ana are going to watch fireworks and I really didn't want to third wheel."

I completely forgot that it was the Fourth of July until she mentioned fireworks. I shake the thought from my mind and focus on her.

We're really together.

It's kind of insane if I think about it.

Two months ago, Allie and me would've laughed if someone came from the future and told us that we'd be together.

But I've wanted her to be mine for so long. So *fucking* long.

I step away from her and round the counter, opening the freezer.

"Alright, Princess Allie, what can I get for you?" I spin the scoop in my hand, a trick I've been practicing the past few shifts.

"Superman?"

Superman Ice Cream has to be a Michigan thing because before having this job, I had never heard of it… ever.

It's a mix of pink, blue and yellow and its flavor is interesting because I can't exactly pinpoint what it tastes like.

I pull the big carton out of the freeze and grab a plastic cup, scooping it out and handing it to her. She grabs a plastic spoon. Then tries it.

"Teddy, this taste off. Can you try it?"

It shouldn't, I just put it the big freezer a minute ago. I approach her and she scoops some more, holding it out to me.

She takes the spoon and goes to feed it to me like I'm a baby, but at the last second, her hand jerks downward and she presses the cold scoop to my neck.

"Oops." She says with a flirtatious smile, "Let me get that."

She leans in and begins to lick the small clump off my neck as it drips under my shirt. *Fuck.*

Her lips suck softly at my skin. I feel my heart begin to beat faster, pumping blood downward.

"Finish up and meet me in the car," she grabs the keys off my belt loop, then her cup of ice cream in the other hand and she heads to the door.

"Allie! Wait-"

She walks out without turning back around, her silhouette framed by the glow of the streetlights. I don't know what tricks she has up her sleeve, but I want to find out. Now.

I scramble to clean the shop, my heart racing as I throw the last of the supplies into their places. I open tomorrow, but who gives a fuck about the condition I leave it in as long as no product is ruined? It's just ice cream.

I lock the door with the master key, nearly fumbling it in my haste, and dash toward the black SUV parked a few spots away from Carla's. The windows are tinted, but I can see Allie's silhouette inside, a teasing smirk on her lips that makes my pulse quicken.

I slide into the passenger seat, the interior air conditioned, the sultry beat of the radio filling the space. Allie's hand plays with the buttons of my polo, her fingers dancing over my chest.

"Allie, what are we doing?" I ask, my voice barely above a whisper, thick with anticipation.

"Just playing around, Novak," she replies, her voice sultry and playful. She leans over, her breath hot against my ear. "Now take off your shirt."

I don't hesitate. God, how could I? My erection is growing in my shorts, and every fiber of my being screams to give in to her. I pull my shirt off, tossing it to the back, exposing my skin to the cool air of the SUV.

She grins, eyes sparkling with mischief as she takes the soupy ice cream and slowly wipes the spoon against my collarbone. The chill of the ice cream shocks my skin, and I shiver, feeling the cold spread like fire through my veins. She drops the spoon into the cup in the cup holder between us, her focus entirely on the trail of ice cream dribbling down my pec, then my nipple.

The sensation is insane. The cold drips down, drawing a jagged line toward the waistband of my shorts. Just as it passes my navel, she leans in, pressing her warm tongue against my skin, and I nearly lose my mind.

"Fuck me," I groan, arching my back as her tongue glides along my body, following the path of the dripping ice cream. I watch, entranced, as she drags her tongue up my chest, following the trail up my abs, then my pec, her tongue flicking against my nipple, sending jolts of pleasure shooting through me.

"God, Allie," I breathe, eyes wide with desire. I could break apart at the seams if she keeps doing this.

She leans in closer, her breath mingling with the cool air inside the SUV, and I can smell the sweet, creamy scent of the ice cream mixed with her tantalizing perfume. It's intoxicating.

Allie continues moving up my body until she reaches the finish line at my collarbone, her lips brushing against my skin, and my heart races. Her hand tilts my face toward her, and she presses our lips together forcefully, fully throwing me into the moment.

It's electric. Her lips are soft yet demanding, and I can feel the heat radiating from her body, drawing me in deeper. I kiss her back with equal fervor, our mouths moving in sync, the taste of ice cream and something sweeter lingering between us.

Suddenly, she tosses off her sweatshirt, and underneath, she's wearing nothing but a lacy, yellow bra. My breath hitches at the sight, the delicate fabric accentuating her curves and leaving little to the imagination.

Before I can even speak, she leans back in, her lips trailing down my neck, sending waves of heat coursing through my body. I can't help but reach for her, my hands finding her waist, fingers lightly brushing her skin. The sensation is electric, and I want more. I want all of her.

Allie tilts her head back, exposing her throat, and I can't resist. I lean in, kissing a trail down her neck, tasting her skin while my hands explore the curves of her body, fingers grazing the lace of her bra.

The feeling is intoxicating, and I can't help but tease her, my fingers dancing along the edges of the fabric. "What if someone sees us?" I murmur against her skin, the thrill of being caught mixing with the desire coursing through my veins.

"Let them," she replies boldly, her voice a sultry challenge. "It's the Fourth of July, and you're my boyfriend."

With that, she pulls back, her fingers deftly unclasping her bra and letting it fall away. My breath hitches at the sight of her bare skin, the way the soft light catches the curves of her breasts. I'm captivated, my desire for her igniting like a flame.

"Allie…" I breathe, my voice thick with need. I just stare for a moment. She's the most beautiful girl on the planet.

"You gonna just stare, or are you going to do something, Novak?" she urges, her eyes dark with longing, and I can't hold back any longer.

I reach for her, fingers exploring her softness, marveling at the sensation of her skin beneath my palms. She gasps as I caress her, her back arching slightly, urging me on. I lean in, capturing her lips again, pouring every ounce of desire into the kiss.

The SUV feels small and hot all of a sudden, the air thick with tension as we lose ourselves in each other. Her hands find their way to my shorts, teasing the waistband as she pulls me closer.

This girl is a wildfire, and I'm ready to get burned.

"Allie, what's gotten into you? That was hot as fuck. " I murmur, my voice low and thick with desire, and she simply smirks back at me, that wicked look in her eyes promising an adventure I can't resist.

"I watched a movie with Ana a little while ago and it gave me the idea, but that's not the end of my little surprise." She sits back down in her seat and buckles up, backing up and taking off.

It's only a short drive north until we arrive at a small private beach. Allie parks the car, quickly pulling her bra back on and clasping it, then, she opens her door. I don't say anything, I just follow her out.

"We allowed to be here, Hennings?" I ask as I slam my door closed. The summer air is brisk, but sticky.

"Well, it's my parent's property. It's where my Mom's siblings used to park their campers when they came to visit." She turns around, walking backwards and facing me for a moment. She turns back around and rushes down towards a small, sandy patch of land just at the edge of the lake. I watch as she quickly kicks off her sandals, then undoes the button to her denim shorts and drops them.

"Take them off." She nods at my shorts. I nod, undoing my belt. I fully toss it to the side, then undo the button and slide out of my own khaki shorts. I kick off my tennis shoes and pull of my socks, throwing it all to the side.

She takes my hand, "Follow my lead."

"For?"

She cocks her eyebrow and smiles, "You scared, Novak?"

"No, but what are we doing?"

"We're going for a night swim. You ready?" She replies with a daredevil smile. I nod and follow after her. She runs down the small wooden dock and jumps in and I jump in right after her, splashing into the lake. It's cold, but with our interaction in the car, it's probably for the better. My body temperature was quickly rising and I need the cool down.

Or do I?

She comes to the surface just before I do, both of us are treading water, bobbing up and down. She smiles and swims towards me. She wraps her legs around my waist, her arms move around my neck and she begins to kiss me again, except this time, the lake it lit up by fireworks going off in the horizon.

It feels like a movie moment. The one where the main guy has fought through all the bad guys and finally gets the girl. The fireworks going off, the sticky summer heat combined with the cold water of Lake Michigan.

I've never felt this way about anyone before.

Through all the drama, I feel as if I am right where I am meant to be.

CHAPTER 16
ALLIE HENNINGS

Everything is changing.

And I can't decide if it's for the better or not.

This morning, Dad and Mom had announced that they are returning to Allister, and that Teddy and me can finish out our summer here.

Upon receiving this news, Mom winked at me, making me nervous that she was going to tell dad about Teddy and me at some point before she and my father arrived home.

I had quickly excused myself from breakfast and my feet carried me quickly into my bedroom, closing the door behind me. Now, I'm three journal entries deep, as I flip to an August entry, from the first year we spent here without Grandpa and Grandma.

Dear Adam,

As summer comes to a close, I am reminded of how blessed I am to have the family that I do have.

Back in March, Grandpa passed away. He

went to heaven to be with you and Grandma. Allie has been taking it really hard, being back in Eldridge Bay with both Grandma and Grandpa gone. I can't even imagine how it would effect her if she remembered losing you too. It's harder for me to process that Allie is now older than you were, when you passed. She's turning nine this year. It's been six summers since we lost you, Adam—

I close the journal as tears brim in the corners of my eyes and I roll onto my back to stare at the ceiling, the plastic stars have been stuck to my ceiling since I was little. Probably when I moved into this room that summer. This used to be my parents' room before Grandma and Grandpa passed. After they did, my mom and dad moved into their old room, and made me a full "big girl" bedroom. I was eight. The room had felt incredibly mature for an eight year old, so to lighten the mood, my Dad hung plastic stars on the ceiling. Then, I littered the walls with posters of *One Direction* and *Harry Styles* and *Niall Horan* at nine. They were my first husband's.

One of the posters still hangs from the wall. It's the album cover for their second or third album. Whatever one had come out right before I moved into this room.

There's a knock at the door and I sit up. Teddy cracks the door open, balancing the plate I left at the table on top of a glass of water.

"You okay, Als?" I uses his foot to kick the door closed behind him.

I look to him with exhausted eyes, "Do I seem okay?"

He sets the food and water on my dresser, then, he pads

across the room and sits down at my side, his hand resting on my thigh, and his thumb moving in soothing circles.

"No, that's why I'm asking, baby." He apologizes. I shake my head, Teddy has nothing to apologize for. Nothing at all. It's not like it's his fault. Yesterday was a nearly perfect day, and so was the day before that, but this morning, after they told me their decision, everything felt like it was losing color and going into a mute, greyscale. It shouldn't feel that way. I got the boy. I get to stay here for another month with him-

Any other girl my age would jump around at the idea of getting a beach house alone with her boyfriend for a month.

"I just- it'll be the first time I'll be here without them, and it's only been a few days since I found out about Adam, and it just feels like a lot right now." I attempt to explain to him, but he just nods and listens intently to me, even if what I'm saying isn't coming out clearly.

"Is there anything I can do to make you feel better?" He tilts my head up to face him, looking into my weary eyes. God, his eyes. They distract me from what's really happening. The real world goes dark and all I see is him.

I just nod and bow my head out of his grip.

"Just be here, with me." I try to add but he leans forward, pressing his lips to mine as he lies me gently on my bed, he hikes my thigh up around his waist and his lips move away from mine and to my neck. The distraction works. My entire body heats up as I drown myself in his embrace, his touch. Every part of my body, every inch warms up to him.

He releases and sits up, looking down towards me. My arms are out at my sides and I know I look like a hot mess. No doubt about it.

"I still get giddy thinking about how you're now my girlfriend." He says with a boyish grin and I nod, wiping away my tears.

"Me too." I attempt to smile. He gives me his classic smirk, a Teddy Novak trademark at this point.

"I'm your girlfriend?"

I let out a laugh and not, "Yeah Novak, you're my girlfriend."

Everything between Teddy and me is so complicated, but now that we're together, it feels so much easier.

It really felt like I had met my match. I'm no longer carrying this all on my own. I don't know how I would be able to carry the weight of my grief without him being there with me. *For* me.

I bring my thigh down and sit up, grabbing his sharp jaw line and kissing him again.

Then, the door opens. *Oh fuck, oh fuck, oh fuck.*

I pray to god that it isn't my dad.

Teddy quickly falls to my side. to my side and luckily, it's not.

Ana stands in my doorway, shocked, but also like she has something to say and doesn't want to say it.

"Sorry you had to see that, what's going on Analise?" Teddy asks, fixing his hair as he gets up. She looks frazzled, but giddy as though she now has a million questions.

"I just wanted to talk to Allie, but I can go-" She quickly shakes her head and goes to close the door. Teddy stops her.

"No need. I'm gonna go shower, then head to work. She's all yours." He looks back at me and winks. He fucking winks. *Be still, my heart.* Then he heads out to the living room. Ana closes the door behind her and sits on my bed. I'm trying to be happy about the fact that I get a month alone with Teddy, just the two of us, but it's hard.

"So, did you guys hook up yet?" She's bouncing up and down excitedly.

I swing a pillow at her, "Seriously Ana?"

She laughs, "I'm kidding…"

A pregnant silence passes, eyes darting back to me quickly. "Or am I?"

All I can do is roll my eyes at her. Ana is always so extra. It's why we all love her.

"For your information only, no, we haven't hooked up yet. We've laid together and cuddled, we've kissed, we did some foreplay last night," I know that she's gonna get hung up on the last part.

"Foreplay?"

"Think Ice Cream on a totally ripped, halfway naked hockey-player body."

Ana's jaw practically hangs to the floor in shock, "No!"

I nod, "I put ice cream on him, let it drip down and I licked it up, then he may or may not have played a bit with my boobs. It was probably the kinkiest shit I've ever done."

"Speaking of crazy, I need to talk to you about something. Something big." She takes one of my hands quickly, squeezing it so tightly, I feel like she's cutting off my circulation.

Oh.

She reaches into her shorts pocket and takes out a small, black velvet box. *No.* It *can't* be.

She flips it open and sitting inside is a small, thin, gold band with a small diamond on the top. It's tiny, but it's very Ana. She's never been overly flashy in the jewelry department. My eyes widen at the image of the diamond ring sitting inside the box.

"Is this what I think this is?" I grab the small box right out of her hand and scan the ring, looking at it carefully. *Holy shit.*

She nods, "Yeah. It happened last night!"

It's a fucking engagement ring? Logan proposed to Ana. This summer has truly been crazy. The news about Adam, Teddy coming to stay here and me very quickly caving to his charm, and now this? My best friends are getting married! I close the box and toss it to the side.

"Analise Flores, you saw me last night and didn't even tell

me!" I shout, taking her hands excitedly. She smiles, bowing her head somewhat bashfully, then softly nods.

"You didn't tell me about the foreplay, so I guess we're even." Those two things are not even on the same level?! My best friends are getting married! I may have been in a somewhat shitty mood earlier, but this definitely boosts it.

"We absolutely are NOT even, girl." I jump off my bed, the feelings that washed over me moments ago are now flushed away as I jump up and down excitedly, filled with giddy.

"I wanted to tell you today, so I could ask you an incredibly important question," She starts, setting the ring aside and taking my hands in hers, gripping them tightly, "As you know, my sister is in Europe right now doing god-knows what. She said she'd try to make it back for the wedding, but didn't want to make any promises. So, I was wondering if you would possibly be my maid of honor."

I nod excitedly, then release her hands and throw my arms around her, wrapping her into a tight embrace and squealing. My best friend is getting married! Analise Flores, who I met a year ago when she was reeling from her's and Logan's breakup, is now marrying him. The thought is mind-boggling. It's just crazy how fast the world changes when you're an adult.

When you're a kid, the days pass by slowly, feeling like the days and the weeks and the months drag on. At a certain point, you grow up, and everything is happening and changing so quickly that if you blink, you'll miss it.

"Of course I'll be your maid-of-honor, Ana! I can't believe it!" I look deeply into her eyes as they begin to glass over with tears, "You're getting married!"

She throws the ring box down on my bed, taking my hands as we jump up and down excitedly. Oh my god, does this mean I have to plan the wedding with her? I don't know what a usual maid of honor does?

———

"You're getting married?!" Teddy nearly chokes on the toothpaste as I sit on the edge of the bathtub and Ana and Logan stand in the doorway. He puts down his toothbrush and spits out the paste.

"Next summer!" Logan tells him, slapping Teddy's back, hard. Teddy chokes, spitting out the toothpaste and rising his mouth with water.

"And you want me to be your best man?" Confusion fills his face.

Logan nods, "Exactly."

"When did this happen?"

Ana laughs, "Last night!"

Teddy looks at me, flabbergasted, then back to them. It is kind of crazy that they already have their wedding party planned out, but don't even have a set date or invitations or anything. But leave it to Logan and Ana, the couple who have defied the odds for an incredibly long time. They've probably been planning their wedding since Kindergarten. .

I can't think of a more perfect ending for the two of them.

"What about the guys?"

"I have groomsman, Teddy. Have you never been to a wedding?" Logan asks jokingly, but Teddy's face falls.

"Dude, are you serious?"

Teddy nods, "Never have."

"Oh my god," Ana feigns a fake a dramatic expression. It's kind of sad, honestly. It reminds me of how shitty his upbringing was.

He has barely scratched the surface with the things he has told me, but it makes me reminds me that not everyone had a semi-good upbringing like me. He never went to family weddings, probably never had a big family Thanksgiving or Christmas. Our lives are so, insanely, infinitely different.

Or at least I had thought. That thought is kind of altered with the whole dead brother thing.

"So, my groomsmen are going to be Nik, Luke, Patrick. Ana has to find some more bridesmaids, but right now she's got Allie and Jenny, and then her cousin."

I sit up, "Do Jenny and your cousin know that they're gonna be your bridesmaids yet?"

Ana stops and thinks, then bursts out laughing, "No, they don't. We wanted to tell you two first."

Teddy exchanges a look with me and both of us look at Ana and Logan.

"Well, congratulations to both of you. Really." Teddy says with a small smile, throwing an arm around Logan in a bro-hug, then he hugs Ana.

"We're both so happy for you!" I shoot up and hug Ana again. I move to her boy-

Fiancé. I move to Logan and hug him tightly next.

These two are absolutely made for each other. Soulmates.

Whatever their souls are made of or whatever that Brontë quote is.

Teddy's phone buzzes with a call and he grabs it off the counter, flipping it over and reading the screen. His face falls. His entire body tenses and his eyes furrow. I catch a peak of the initial and only one person comes to mind. Only one person could get to him like that. I pray it's not her, though.

His *mother.*

"I'll be right back." He heads to his room and the three of us linger for a moment, watching intently as he marches quickly to his bedroom door and slams it shut.

"That was weird..." Ana says and I nod. He got all weird when he saw the screen. Who else could it be for him to get all cagey? It makes me fear that my initial guess of who it is, is correct.

TEDDY NOVAK

"Mom?"

"Teddy, baby, hi." Her voice sounds so happy. This is the first time I've heard her voice since May. All I've gotten are pictures and messages here and there. She was so busy with Pierre or whatever the fuck his name is to even remember that she has a son.

She couldn't even return my call when I had my anxiety episode a few weeks ago.

"Why are you calling?"

I'm sure that people would probably raise hell for the tone I just took with her, but how can I not be angry with her after everything she's put me through?

She lets out a soft sigh, "I wanted to check in on you. See how your summer is going?"

"Well, besides having to go back into therapy again, it's been fine."

"Why'd you go back to therapy? I thought your anxiety died out?" Leave it to my Mom to be completely oblivious to the fact that part of my anxiety stems from her being absentee.

"Take a guess."

"Theodore Steven. What happened? Is Coach treating you badly?" I wince. She knows. She signed for me to not use the name Theodore anymore. She knows the background and how fucking traumatized I was. Yet she's so wrapped up in Pierre, that she can't even bother to remember that.

The words come out before I can stop myself, "No, not at all. If anything the Hennings are treating me better than you ever did."

There's a silence. One where I can just hear her breathing on the other end of the line.

"Teddy, I'm-"

She goes to make an excuse and I quickly cut her off, "No

Mom. I don't want another excuse. You haven't even bothered to return my calls for the last two months and then you call out of the blue like nothing happened. Well, shit happened and you weren't even there for me."

"What happened, Teddy?" Her voice comes out sharper, snippier.

"I had a panic attack because I started to fall for a girl I shouldn't have, and I couldn't even talk to my Mom about it. I couldn't go to the one parent that was still, somewhat present in my life because she's too busy getting dick in Paris or London or wherever the fuck you went!" I feel my own temper rising, bubbling. My heart starts to race, my palms feel sweaty, my body tense.

"Theodore Steven Novak. Do not talk to me like that." She says sternly through the phone, "If you're not going to talk to me like an adult, then I'm not going to call you."

"Age wise, I may be an adult, but internally, I am still a kid. I am still growing up and learning how to adult and you aren't even here for me." I fight back, "And you can't even remember my real name? The name you legally helped me change, Mom.

"I want to be there for you, Teddy. That's why I called!" I can almost hear the tears in her voice. Truthfully, I don't want her crocodile tears. They mean nothing to me. Just like I mean nothing to her.

"Teddy, I'm moving back. With Pierre. He wants to move to the states, and meet you, especially with the news we have."

"What could be so important Mom, that you're going to move back to Philly with your French guy?" I shoot, just exhausted at this point of whatever the hell she has to say. Whatever she says won't impact me in anyway. As far as I'm concerned, this is the final time that I'll speak to her in my life.

"We're having a baby."

Nevermind. That definitely changes things.

The feeling that surges through my body is one that I can't explain. I'm frustrated. I'm upset. I just want to burst out into tears or laughter and break shit. The world just keeps changing. The list of blows and hits from this summer alone are enough to knock me flat on my ass.

I don't say anything. I just remove the phone from my ear and press the big red button, then I fucking chuck it at the wall as red fills my vision. My hands grab the edge of the dresser and I throw it to the floor, sending everything on it to the floor. It's not even my stuff. It's Ana and Logan's, but right now, all I can see is red. The door opens quickly and Allie, Logan and Ana are all standing there in shock.

My chest is heaving, my face red with so many different fucking emotions.

Before I can do anything else, Allie comes over and throws her arms tightly around me, squeezing as tightly as she can.

And I break down. The minute her arms tighten around me, tears form in my eyes I just allow myself to let go in her arms.

CHAPTER 17
ALLIE HENNINGS

t's been twelve hours since my parents left to go back to Allister and it feels wrong to be here without them.

At least I'm not all by myself. Teddy is softly snoring at my side, his back rising slowly as he breaths, with half his face smushed into the pillow. He is absolutely sprawled out and taking up more of the bed than he should be.

I flip through the pages of the journal, reading entries, skimming my fingers over the printed pictures that are glued in.

Mom's emotions are so raw. They're so real and deep and emotional. It hurts to read them, but something is nagging at me to read every single entry. To find out as much as I can about Adam Scott.

Dear Adam,

Allie got her drivers license today and your father is freaking out about it. He's so scared that something will happen to her behind the wheel, though I know her. She's an incredibly careful driver. She picked up my driving skills, obviously. Your father has a bit of a lead foot, if you remember.

I keep telling him that he's just as likely to get in an accident as she is, but he begs to differ.

I trust her so much, I just wish you could've been the one to teach her. That just feels like something a big brother would do for his little sister. You would've driven around our neighborhood with her, staying calm as she abruptly hits the breaks or presses down on the gas too quickly. You would've given her the calm that she absolutely did not get from your father.

To celebrate getting her license, we finally got her a car. It's an old Honda CRV that an old friend of your father's was selling privately. Your dad got it for cheap- in exchange for season passes to Allister's games, if you'd believe it.

It's looking like it's going to be a good season, your dad is confident about it. The team does look really good. Allie also qualified for states in dance. She'll be performing in Washington D.C in December.

She's also planning on auditioning for her school's hip hop spin on The Nutcracker. I wish you could see her. She's brilliant.

This entry feels extra personal. It feels like it reaches into my chest and yanked out my heart, then threw it on the ground and crushed it into a million little pieces.

I close the journal and hang my head back, eyes drifting to the ceiling. Out of all the entries, the ones where she is directly telling Adam about things that had happened in my life hurt the most. It makes me realize how different our lives would've been if he hadn't died.

Next to me, Teddy stirs in his sleep. He looks so peaceful. His eyes flutter under his lids, his lips slightly parted and his brown hair a mess. I carefully run a hand through it, fingers catching in the curls. He stirs, but doesn't wake. Truthfully, I wish he got to always be this peaceful. But his life is just as, if not more, fucked up as mine.

There's a soft sound of laughter emitting from the kitchen and I slowly slide out from underneath his arm and slink out into the kitchen where Logan and Ana are standing above a pan, attempting to make breakfast.

"Well, good morning, sunshine!" Logan says loudly. Ana's eyes dart up and she smiles.

"Don't mind us. We're just trying to make breakfast." Ana says as she attempts to flip the pancake on the pan.

"I don't mind, as long as you don't burn my house down," I tell them and reach for the glass coffee pot, starting a brew cycle, "And clean up your mess when you're done."

Logan shoots a finger gun and click his tongue at me, and at the same time, Ana flips the pancake off the pan and straight onto the hardwood floor.

"Whoops." She says loudly, throwing her hands up in defeat and looking down at the mess she made.

I can't help but laugh, stepping in as she backs up. I pour batter onto the pan and take over pancake making duties.

"The mop and mop pads are in the closet by the stairs," I tell her as she rushes to get cleaning supplies.

I turn to Logan, "Looks like you'll be doing all the cooking, buddy."

He laughs, "That, I already knew. Bless Ana's soul, but she can't cook for shit."

"I heard that!" Ana shouts from the cleaning closet.

At the same time, Teddy saunters out of the bedroom with tired eyes. He's only wearing athletic shorts.

Logan wolf whistles at him, "Welcome to the party, you sexy bastard."

Teddy flips him off, "It's too early."

"It's ten in the morning, my hunk of a roommate. You wake up earlier than that during the school year," Logan corrects and moves the bacon off the skillet and onto a plate.

"Yeah, for hockey, or class. It's summer break." He groans and buries his head in his arms, face down against the counter. I take the pancake off the pan and round the island, running a hand up and down his back.

"Oh, my poor baby." I tell him in a playful voice and he sits up, looking at me with a gobsmacked look in his eyes.

"So I'm the baby?" He stands up, body angled towards me and my eye glaze over his taught chest. I can tell he's tensing his muscles, making them more pronounced. I put a hand on his stomach.

"What are you gonna do about it?" I start, moving a hand up and down, "Baby?"

A wicked smirk comes over his lips and he lifts me up, throwing me over his shoulder. I yelp in response and he opens the sliding glass door into the backyard.

"Teddy Novak, put me down!" I shout as he rushes to the lake. He runs down the metal dock, then tosses me straight into the icy cold water of Lake Michigan. That *ass*. Part of me is mad at the fact that he just threw me into the lake, but the other part of me wants to climb up there and yank him down with me.

But before I can, he's cannonballing into the lake. I breach the surface, kicking to stay afloat as he swims towards me, wrapping his arms around me.

"Who's the baby now?" He mutters, water dripping off his face and from the loose strands of curls. Our bodies are so close together. I can feel his chest pressing against mine as my legs hike up and wrap around his waist.

"You're trouble." I splash him. Despite this, he swims towards me, wrapping his arms around me. My legs hook around his waist tightly.

"And you're incredibly sexy." He leans in and presses his lips to mine, drowning in the kiss, savoring it. No one has ever made me feel this way before. It's such a strong feeling. One that gnaws at me and my soul, absorbing every inch of me until he has fully consumed me. He pulls back, pressing his forehead to mine in a soft, tender moment.

"I don't think I can ever get you out of my head." His voice is low, a whisper. A soft, delicate whisper.

"You couldn't even if you tried." I tell him and he moves back in for the kissing. I press a hand to the back of his head, knotting my fingers into his wet curls.

"Hey! Stop fucking in the lake!" Logan shouts from the back porch, startling both of us and we quickly pull apart. I burst out laughing at the fact that Logan and Ana probably saw all of that.

"Race you, pretty girl." He whispers, letting me go. He pushes me further into the lake, cheating. I splash him quickly.

"Cheater!" He laughs and takes off, but not before I launch forward and grab onto his back, arms around his neck, legs around his waist.

Like a koala bear clinging to a tree. He doesn't bother kicking me off, even after he walks up the shore and back into the backyard. His hands grab the bottoms of my thighs as he lifts me up.

And at the door, Ana now waits with towels, like my Mom would've done if she had saw what just happened.

———

After drying off and having breakfast, the four of us are packed into the SUV and heading towards another one of my favorite Michigan locations.

The Sleeping Bear Sand Dunes are only an hour drive from Eldridge Bay and they are gorgeous. The sand is warm, the lake is a bright shade of blue. I feel almost like a giddy little kid on Christmas. Mom and me usually go every summer, but getting the chance to show my friends and my boyfriend one of the prettiest spots in Michigan, makes me feel with so much happiness.

We reach a state park toll booth and I quickly pay the lady. Ana sits in the passenger seat, the boys in the back. Her legs are up on the dashboard.

"I thought we were going to sand dunes?" Logan asks, leaning forward from the backseat.

We weave down the winding road, green trees and pushes all around us. The *Pierce Stocking Scenic Drive* is a nearly eight-mile drive through the woods of Empire, leading up to the highlight of the drive, the *Sleeping Bear Sand Dunes* Overlook. It's stop ten of the tour and is always the busiest, especially on nice days like today.

"We are. It's the second to last main stop of the drive." I reply giddily and roll down the windows, inhaling the fresh, summer air. Ana turns up the radio, not to a point where it's obnoxious, but enough where we can still hear the music over the rolled down windows.

I don't stop at any of the lookouts, not until we get to the best one. The parking lot is full, families and groups of people coming and going from the trail into the woods.

"We're here!" I shout as I pull into a parking spot and stop the SUV.

"Where's the dune part of it all? I just see woods." Logan comments and Ana turns around, swatting her boyfriend. Mine leans forward and kisses my cheek quickly.

"Better be worth it, Hennings." He whispers and I turn around to face him.

"It will be."

We climb out of the car and the sweltering heat no longer feels good as the sun burns down onto us. Teddy lifts his t-shirt, sliding it into his back pocket. *Fuck*, my boyfriend is sexy. Logan pulls on sunglasses and Ana lowers her Allister hat down over her head, covering her eyes from the light.

Teddy takes my hand and the four of us follow the crowd to the mouth of the trail. Another couple walks by, the girl mounted on the girls back and I stop them.

"Teddy, bend down." I tell him quickly. I want what that girl had. He eyes me.

"Excuse me? Here?"

"Trust me."

He does it and I jump onto his back, like I did earlier. Instinctively, his hands grab my thighs, holding me up and my arms lace around his neck. The sweat of his back sticks to my clothes, and I rest my chin on my arm. He doesn't even struggle to carry me. We're so close in height and it's like I weigh no more than a sack of potatoes to him.

Which is nice, because I kind of enjoy him carrying me around like this. It's fun.

The sand begins to take over the dirt of the trail. He sets me down as we all kick off shoes and sandals, the warm sand under my feet reminds me how close I am to the most beautiful spot in this state.

Then, a couple more steps, and we've made it to the best part. The lookout point over Lake Michigan, where the golden sand meets the vibrant blue waters. Where families are racing down the dune and people are taking pictures.

I literally hear Ana audibly gasp when we make it to our destination. Teddy sets me down, marveling at it.

"This is really fucking nice." He mutters and I take his hand, resting my head on his bicep.

"It is. It's my favorite spot in Michigan." I reply and he looks at me with a small smile.

"I understand why."

Ana and Logan are already busy taking pictures, but Teddy just focuses on me.

"The view is incredibly pretty from here." He says as he spins me to face him, taking both of my hands, "But you're prettier."

Sure, it's a cheesy line, but it's the way that he says it with such certainty that makes my heart skip.

I squeeze his hands in mine, "That was really cheesy."

He laughs, nodding, "It sounded better in my head."

"But I appreciate it."

He does the thing that he did from this morning in the lake. He presses his forehead to mine. It feels so passionate. So right.

"It is true though. Allie, you're fucking gorgeous." He says and I smirk as I lean in for a kiss.

"No, that's all you, baby." I tell him between kisses and he stops, pulling back with a wide grin.

"Oh, so we're back to this?"

"You bet your ass we are."

He shakes his head, "I'm not baby, you're baby."

"No, no, no Teddy. You're my pretty baby."

Ana gags, "Guys, we're in public."

"You've been dating for what, two days? This is insane behavior from both of you." Logan mutters and Teddy flips him off.

"Not all of us spent thirteen years pining after our girlfriends, Finlay." Teddy replies as the four of us regroup. *Touché*. It makes me wonder, how long did Logan really have feelings for Ana before they finally got together? Did he ever have feelings for someone else, or were they put on this earth destined to be with each other?

"Well, for your information, Ana and me kissed when we were five, got together at fourteen and now we're here." Logan gestures at him and his girlfriend.

I want that. I want mine and Teddy's relationship to be something that is written in the stars like our roommate's relationship. The two of them, despite the one year break-up, have been in each other's orbit since birth. They've been destined to be together like their love story was written before they were even thought of. I want that. I want to believe that.

Mine and Teddy's relationship is one that was destined to happen, but truly, it's hard for me to convince myself of.

Because the world doesn't always work that way. I'm reminded of Adam. If mine and Teddy's relationship was destined to happen, does that mean that Adam was destined to die? Because if so, that's incredibly cruel. It's evil and heartbreaking if that's the way the universe works. If that's the universe we live in, that I don't want anything to be destined.

"Als, is everything okay?" Ana grabs my shoulder and I quickly turn to her.

"Hmm?"

"You dazed out for a second? I just wanted to make sure everything was okay?" She asks. Teddy and Logan are now staring down the edge of the dune, talking about god knows what.

"Yeah, I-" I stammer, "I was just thinking about Adam."

She frowns, nodding and taking my hand in hers, "How has all of that been going?"

I shrug as we walk away from our boyfriends, to a shaded spot under a tree, "It's hard, for sure. But I think being able to read my Mom's journal entries has made it a bit easier. I read one and I learn something new about him, I see pictures of him, and I form an image of him in my mind."

We sit down on an exposed root. She sits behind me and takes my hair out of a ponytail and begins to braid it.

This is something that we used to do in the dorms after a long day or a stressful class or practice or meeting. We would sit on the floor and braid each other's hair like young girls at a sleepover. She's way better at doing a braid than I am, so it's mostly her braiding my hair as one of us vents about our problems.

"Tell me something about him." She says as she tightens the strands, but not too tightly.

"He named me." I mutter as my face heats, emotions taking over. I didn't even hesitate to share that fact. It's easily the best thing that I have learned about my brother.

"Really?"

I softly nod, careful to not disturb my roommates delicate process.

"He wanted to name me Alligator, but Mom and Dad compromised with him and settled on Allie." I laugh at the idea of being named after a reptile and she chuckles quietly.

"He liked animals?"

"Yeah, apparently a lot. Dad showed me a picture before they left of Adam setting up a zoo in his bedroom with legos and plastic animals. He had his lego figures touring it." I explain to her and she nods. Tying back part of the braid with a hair tie.

"But he named me, and ever since I found out about him, I can't stop imagining what my life would be like if he was still here." I turn to face her, braid unfinished and she drops her hands to her lap, nodding, "Dad thinks he would've played hockey at Allister."

"Well of course he does, he's Jesse Hennings."

She's not wrong. Had Adam grown up, he would've

wanted to play hockey, and my Dad sure as shit wouldn't let him play for any other team but Allister.

Does that mean Adam would've played with Teddy and Logan and the others? He was three years older. He would've been a junior or senior when we were freshman. The thought makes me sad again.

Ana glances past me, "Uh, where'd the boys go?"

I turn around and sure enough they're gone from where they were standing. Well, I can be sad later. Because fuck, I know exactly what they've done. We get up quickly and rush to the spot they were, looking down the steep slope of the dune. Of course, they're on the fucking move, racing down the dune.

"They did read the sign, right?"

Ana turns to look at me as she crosses her arms with annoyance, "What sign?"

I lead her to the sign and she reads it, "It could take two hours to climb back up or cost three-thousand to be rescued."

"Yep. They're gonna bitch about this all the way home."

"I doubt they read that sign." She replies as her lips straighten into a thin, annoyed line. I nod in agreement. I also highly doubt they read that sign.

Hell, Logan probably didn't even get the chance before Teddy took off. If you asked Logan if he would jump off a cliff if all his friends were, he would do it with no hesitation.

Especially for someone like Teddy.

CHAPTER 18
TEDDY NOVAK

We absolutely did not read that sign before we decided to race each other down the sand dune, and we should've. Now, I'm sprawled out on Allie's bed, utterly wrecked, while she sits on my back, kneading her hands into my sore muscles.

"I can't believe you didn't read that sign, you baboon," she teases, pressing her cold hands into my warm skin. Not only do I have a sunburn from hell, but my body aches like I was body-checked after a brutal game.

"In my defense, Logan was the one who suggested it, and I just followed after him," I attempt to argue, but by the sound of her groan, I can almost hear her rolling her pretty blue eyes.

"So if Logan jumped off a cliff, you would too?" She lifts her hands and stands on the mattress, a playful glint in her eyes. I roll over, and she crosses her arms, staring down at me. I reach up and grab her thighs, bringing her back down onto my lap.

"Probably. He'd do it for me without hesitation. But you're going with me."

"Ah, so murder-suicide? Got it." She nods, her lips curving into that devilish smile I can't resist.

"If I'm going, you're going with me, babe. I don't make the rules." I smirk, but the moment is quickly overtaken by her hands rubbing deeply into my biceps, pushing at the knots in my muscles.

"Fuck, babe. That feels good," I grumble, closing my eyes as she continues. This is what I get for spending half the climb on all fours like a fucking dog.

Her hands move up my arms and onto my chest, pressing into my pecs, and the minute her fingers knead over my nipple, I feel myself tense—with pleasure. My body reacts instinctively, and her eyes dart to me, a mix of surprise and excitement.

"Oh!" She's startled but keeps going as I tuck an arm behind my head, watching her, mesmerized by her every move.

She stops at the waistband of my boxers, her fingers hovering. "Can I—"

"Fuck, Allie. Yes," I hiss, my breathing growing heavy, my body warming up under her touch. Her hand rests over my cock, the fabric between us driving me wild as she moves it up and down slowly, creating a warm friction. My chest tightens, my legs tense, and my toes curl—literally.

She looks up at me, her lips slightly parted, excitement radiating from her. "Keep going?"

"Yes. God, yes," I mutter, and she continues, her movement steady and deliberate. As she rubs, her lips find their way down to my abs, planting sweet, delicate kisses on each one. It's all way too fucking much, especially this early in the morning.

If she keeps this up, I'm going to fucking explode.

I stop her, pulling her up, and she pushes back her messy hair, staring at me with wide eyes. "What? Did I do something wrong?"

I shake my head, my voice low and smoky. "No. I just want you. Is that okay?"

She sits up, nodding eagerly, and I flip her onto her back, pressing my body down over hers. I lift her baggy t-shirt, exposing her yellow panties, and my breath hitches at the sight. I slide my fingers up both of her thighs, and in one quick motion, I tear her panties in two.

She gasps, her hips buckling in surprise. "You're a panty-ripper?" She watches me, her eyes wide with a mix of shock and arousal, my face just inches from her sweet pussy.

I shrug, a cheeky grin spreading across my face. "Not always."

"Teddy Novak, have you been reading more romance novels?" She asks, and I can't help but smirk back at her.

"Maybe?"

Before she can react, I push my tongue down onto her warm, tender skin. She yelps, her fingers digging into my curls, but she doesn't pull me away. Instead, she pushes me forward with urgency.

Fuck me.

I keep going, hiking her thighs up and over my shoulders. She crosses her ankles, and I dive in deeper. Who gives a fuck that Ana and Logan are downstairs? We heard them going at it last night; this is our moment.

I've known her for over two years, seen her drunk off her ass, crying about a test, and throwing up in the grass. We've only been together for three days, but I feel like I've known her forever. I replace my tongue with my fingers, rubbing three of them against her, and she moans, her breath hitching.

"Are you wearing a bra?" I ask, my voice thick with desire.

She shakes her head quickly, and I lift her shirt, sliding my head up into the darkness. I cup one of her breasts with my free hand, the other stroking her quickly. Her entire body trembles beneath me.

"Fuck, Teddy," she breathes, and I nod as I suck on her skin. She tastes fruity, with a strong hint of coconut, intoxicating and addictive.

"Shhh, baby. Don't make a sound," I pull my head out of her shirt, and her eyes meet mine, dark with lust.

"Can I put my fingers in you, babe?" I ask, my voice low and raspy.

She nods quickly, her urgency palpable. "Yes, fuck. Just do it already, Teddy."

With no other warning, I slide two fingers slowly into her. She goes to let out another loud moan, and my hand moves from her breast to cover her mouth.

"Be quiet, loud girl. We don't want our friends to hear us," I tease her, and she shakes her head in defiance.

"Fuck them."

I shake my head. "No. I'd rather fuck you, pretty girl."

I pump my fingers back and forth, watching her face as I work her up. Each thrust sends her closer to the edge, and she moans again, the sound driving me wild. Her body reacts instinctively to my touch, and it's fucking sexy.

I grow harder as she moves a hand up, feeling the erection straining against my boxers. She grabs it, and I clench my teeth, a hiss escaping my lips as she moves her hand up and down while I continue to stroke her.

I keep going until she comes, her release washing over me, and I don't stop until I'm spilling into my boxers, gasping as pleasure overtakes me.

I fall onto the mattress beside her, both of us panting to catch our breath, the air thick with heat and desire.

"Was that worth it, Allison?" I ask, still trying to process what just happened.

She turns onto her side, facing me, then shrugs a shoulder, a playful glint in her eye. "Solid six out of ten."

I shoot her a look, incredulous. "What do I have to do to get a one hundred out of ten?"

"Next time, you have to go all the way," she mutters, and I freeze, her words hitting me like a punch to the gut.

"Oh, really?"

She nods, her eyes sparkling with mischief. "Yeah. Then maybe you'll get a ten out of ten at least."

"Am I that bad?" I frown. She's gotta be fucking joking. Right?

She shakes her head, leaning in to kiss my lips, a hand resting on my face. "No. I'm just busting your balls."

She kisses me again, and then she gets up to gather her things for a shower, leaving me lying in her bed, staring at the ceiling, still reeling from what just happened.

Fuck. What is she doing to me?

———

For Logan and Ana's last day here, Allie has tasked us with cleaning out the attic. She was supposed to do it with her Mom, but instead, she has stranded Logan and me up here.

The girls are down in the living room, sorting through the totes and boxes and suitcases, sorting them into separate piles. Logan opens a tote.

"Dude, it's Coach's old stuff. This is weird, isn't it?" He asks as he slides it across the wood over to me, inside are old jerseys and new paper clippings from when Jesse was young. One on the top is laminated, it's a picture of him and two other boys, probably eleven or so.

"It's kind of weird. I don't know I would've believed someone if they told me that we would be cleaning up the attic of Coach's house." I reply and he continues digging through the tote.

Logan pulls out a blue jersey.

"Shit, man! It's an old Allister jersey."

He holds it up to me and sure enough, it is an old Allister College jersey.

It's dark blue with white font and the old logo in the middle. He flips it and on the back, in big, bold font is his last name and his number. 26.

Logan reaches back into the tote as I look at the jersey that is now in my hands.

It's weird. We've always known that Jesse was once an Allister Hockey legend, but seeing a piece of his career right here, in my hands, puts it into a whole new perspective. One that I didn't anticipate whatsoever.

It makes me feel even more connected to my coach.

As though he's a father figure for me.

Logan holds up two pairs of rollerblades, bringing me back to the present moment, "Dude, are you thinking what I'm thinking?"

I cock an eye at him, "Trash?"

"No, Teddy. Let's play a pick-up game of street hockey." He shakes his head and takes off his own tennis shoe, checking the size.

He compares it to the size of the rollerblade, "Shit, I wear the same size. You're a size bigger, right?"

"Compared to you? Yeah."

He shoves his hand into the old rollerblade, the holds it out to me. I pull it off his hand and turn it over in my hand. Would this even fit? It's not even my size. I kick off my shoe and slide my foot into it. It's a tight and crammed, but my foot fits into it.

"Okay, even if we wanted to play a pick-up game. We don't even have sticks or pucks or a net to play." I reply and he looks at me as if I'm speaking gibberish.

"You realize who's attic we're in, right? There's no way he doesn't have equipment up here. Fuck, he had two sets of rollerblades." He shakes his head, rising and padding across the attic, taking down a large cardboard box and lifting the lid.

"Found sticks."

He drops it to the floor with a thud and continues his search. Admittedly, the idea of getting to play a game with my roommate makes my heart thump harder in my chest. I haven't gotten to play since the beginning of May. That was two, almost three months ago. Hockey, on the ice, honestly seems so inconsequential to everything else in life. I finally have Allie, I've cut off my parents.

He takes out another box, one with a small folding net. It's definitely not a new made for hockey, but it could work. Underneath the net, were knee pads.

I should've known better.

Of course Jesse has everything for a pick-up game in his attic. Why wouldn't he?

The more the thought lingers in my mind, I realize, maybe hockey isn't the be-all, end-all for me? I'm gonna have a college degree in business and marketing in two years time.

"What's taking you two so long? Bring down another tote!" Allie shouts from downstairs and I grab another tote, one we haven't even opened, and I walk it down stairs, dropping it on the floor in front of them.

Her blonde hair is still damp from her shower and she's wearing my t-shirt again, tied with a hair tie, paired with her usual denim shorts. Ana is still wearing sweatpants and a tank top, not bothering to get dressed after Allie shared the group's agenda today. I lean in and quickly kiss Allie, cupping her soft face in my hands, then without saying another word, I head upstairs to continue working through bins with Logan.

As I pass the threshold of the attic, Logan has an empty cardboard box filled with the small net, the rollerblades, the pads and the practice balls. He has two sticks tucked under his arm.

"You know we have to finish the attic, right?"

He shrugs, "It's only eleven in the morning. We have all day."

Oh, Allie will have a heyday with that response.

———

She absolutely had a heyday with that response, but she gave my persistent roommate the ultimatum of one hour of play time, then we have to get back to work.

We drove up to the basketball course and Logan sets up a net on one end, and a cardboard box on the other. The girls sit in the metal bleaches on the side of the court and I tighten the skates.

"You're going down, Novak." Logan says with a cocky smile as he tightens his knee pads.

"You wish, Lo." I slide out onto the pavement, attempting to catch my balance for a second. It's been three months since I've last skated. Of course I'm going to be shaky.

Logan skates past with no problem. As if he never stopped skating.

Though, knowing Logan's proximity to campus, he probably never did stop. He can drive an hour and be right back on the ice we play on day in and day out.

Allie throws the first ball in and I swing outward for it with my stick, attempting to catch it, but Logan quickly skates in and steals it, carrying down the court.

I skate fast, sweat already prickling on my skin. We've been here ten minutes, what the fuck?

It doesn't help that it is once again an hundred degree day, with the sun full in the sky and beaming down on us. I'm going to be as red as a tomato after this. I steal the ball from Logan, sweeping it between my legs and to behind me, quickly pivoting to run it up my side of the court.

"Fucker!" Logan shouts, skating to me and bumping me in the hip. I bump back, harder.

"Oh, game on, Finlay."

And suddenly, all of the shitty things that have happened this year float away. I have the girl. I have my friends.

Nothing else matters.

Not even the game itself.

———

ALLIE HENNINGS

So the boys had gone well over the hour break I had originally given them, but whatever. They showered and we finished cleaning out the attic.

Life with them here, in Eldridge Bay, has been nice. Peaceful, even.

I roll over and check the time on my phone. It's seven a.m. My alarm is set to go off in a half and hour and I absolutely do not want to get out of my bed. Teddy is asleep next to me, curled into the fetal position as if he's going to get attacked at any second. I kiss his temple, then throw back my covers and get out of my bed, heading into the living room where Ana has already started getting things ready for their departure.

Today is the day. After a full week of visiting, Ana and Logan are leaving us. Leaving me and Teddy.

Alone in this house. *Yikes.*

Part of me is incredibly nervous about the fact that Teddy and me will be spending two more weeks in Eldridge Bay, alone without Mom or Dad or Ana or Logan there as a safety net. We'll be living domestically, like an actual couple. It's odd, it's scary, but it's also thrilling?

"Good morning," Ana says quietly with a smile as she attempts to zip up a suitcase.

I head over to the coffee pot and start it, "Do you really have to leave?"

Ana gives me a sad smile, standing up quickly and rushing towards me. She throws her arms around me and lifts me off my feet, then quickly sets me back down, "I do. Logan's parents are going to celebrate their anniversary next week and they need Logan home to watch Davey and Tyler."

Davey and Tyler are Logan's younger, twin brothers. They're thirteen. Davey is super into hockey, has even gone to a practice or two with his brother just to watch. I've never met Tyler, but from what Ana says, he's an incredibly gifted musician.

"But they just need Logan home, not you!" I plead with puppy dog eyes, knowing the exact answer. She's going to say no. I understand. Her and Logan are like a package deal. The only time that they're apart is on campus, when they're doing their separate activities and classes.

Is that going to be Teddy and me once we get back to Allister?

"Allie, we move in three weeks from tomorrow," her hands hold my arms, "You'll have your two weeks of silence and peace with Teddy, so many miles from home, then you two will come back to Allister and we get to move into the apartment, and start junior year."

I nod, "I know. I'm just nervous, about being here alone with Teddy. And I know it's making him anxious too."

Ana nods, "Logan told me that Teddy opened up about his anxiety struggles a bit when they were climbing the dune."

He told someone else about his struggles? Is he even the same guy that sauntered into this house with a cocky smirk on his face, or has he changed?

The thought makes me wonder… if he has really changed that much in a month, what *else* will change about him?

"Yeah, I never knew about it until he showed up at my bedroom door in the middle of the night. Ana, he was super pale and trembling like a leaf. I've never saw anyone like that before." I explain and she frowns, nodding.

"I understand. The same thing happened with my brother

after Dad died." She bows her head for a moment, processing. Ana doesn't really talk about her Dad very often. He passed when she was fifteen. I don't know how, or why, but I refuse to pry. She's my friend and I won't do that to her.

I lean against counter, the cold countertop pressing into my back, "It's just... everything I've learned about psychology in that moment, every textbook, every lesson or lecture, just vanished. I didn't know what to say or what to do."

"What *did* you do?"

"I hugged him, held him tightly, ran my hand up and down his back the same way my parents used to do to me when I was sick."

She nods, processing this for a second, then hopping up on the counter to sit across from me, "And ever since the stuff with his Mom, he's really been on edge?"

"Exactly. I'm thinking that maybe we should just go home too at this point?"

"Do you think that's the best choice? I mean, you practically begged your parents to stay here?"

I just shrug. I don't know what the right choice is anymore, to be honest. Like that one song says, should I stay or should I go?

Maybe I really do need to talk to Teddy about it?

"I-" A voice interrupts us and we both turn around. Teddy stands there tiredly, his hair a mess. He's wearing only athletic shorts.

Ana looks at me, unsure, then back to Teddy, "I'm going to go wake Logan up. Maybe you two should talk?"

She rushes out of the kitchen and back down to the lower level as Teddy tiredly saunters towards me, "I think we should go home, Allie."

I meet his gaze, "Are you sure? I'm conflicted."

"Why?"

"Because I want to stay and show my parents that I am

independent and can do this, but at the same time, it feels…
wrong, and I know it's not helping your anxiety any. Yesterday, after you and Logan played hockey, you seemed so on
edge. Like something was bothering you." I try to unpack it
all and his hands rest on my shoulders as he meets my
gaze.

"You don't have to worry about my anxiety, babe. I promise. If you want to stay, then we'll stay. But from what you're
saying, it sounds like it would be better if we go home." His
hands rub up and down my shoulders and I wrap my arms
around him, hugging him tightly.

"You won't be mad?"

He shakes his head, then rests his chin on my head, "No,
Allison. Nothing could ever make me mad at you."

I lean further into the embrace, pressing my cheek to his
chest. I listen to the soft beating of his heart.

"I love you, Allie. I really do."

Hearing him say it makes me feel dizzy, but not in a bad
way. It makes me feel off-balance, as the euphoria of the
words pulse through my veins.

"I love you too, Teddy." The words just come out with
little effort, as though they've been on the tip of my tongue
for a while now.

He lifts me off my feet and swings me back and forth as he
holds me. I burst out laughing and he sets me down, releasing
me and our eyes meet.

"I think we should go home, really. It just feels wrong
being here without mom and dad." I tell him and he nods
understandingly.

"Call your mom. I'll start getting stuff packed up."

My parents had taken the rental SUV back to the airport,
leaving us with my mom's SUV to drive back to Allister.
Between Teddy and me, we could probably make it back
without stopping.

It feels weird, to just up and leave randomly. Usually,

Mom has a big barbecue with all our friends from here and we have a send-off party.

But we're leaving quietly, barely making a peep.

I go to my room, quickly pulling on shorts and shoes.

"Guys, I'll be back. I have something I need to do!" I shout, grabbing the keys and rushing out the door.

The Country club opens in a half-hour. Both Phoebe and Mish are working. If I'm truly leaving, I need to say goodbye to them. It just would be wrong not to. Right?

I wish we had time to party and hangout one last time, but from the way Teddy made it sound, we're leaving with Logan and Ana later today. Now is the only chance I'll have to do this.

I arrive and park in my usual spot next to Phoebe's Volkswagen Bug, then slam the door closed and rush inside, to the backroom where they will for sure be sitting and gossiping about god knows what together.

I turn the corner and see something I didn't expect.

Mish's lips pressed against Phoebe's, holding her face tightly, fingers threaded through her hair. Phoebe presses into the kiss, accepting it.

"Oh!" I yelp in shock and they both turn to face me.

"Oh my god!" Phoebe yelps and covers her lips, embarrassed. Mish looks between Phoebe, then me.

She walks over quickly, "Allie, what are you doing here?"

"I had something to tell you both, but-"

"It's not what it looks like. I swear." Mish says quickly. I look past her to Phoebe, who's reapplying her lipstick.

"Are you sure? It looked like you two were kissing."

Mish's eyes quickly dart to Phoebe, then back to me, then back to Phoebe again.

Phoebe sighs, "Okay, yes, we were kissing."

"What about-"

"We ended our engagement last night."

Oh.

Well *fuck*.

"I didn't know you were-?" I add and Phoebe shrugs.

"I dunno if I am, Als. Mish and me ran into each other at the bar after I ended things and we ended up kissing and now we're here." Phoebe explains.

Mish quickly tucks her shirt back in.

"I'm sorry about your engagement." I tell her, approaching slowly.

Phoebe quickly shakes her head, grabbing my hands in her's, "Don't be. He was an ass."

I quickly hug her, wrapping my arms tightly around my friend. I'm about to make today even worse for her, aren't I?

She releases from the hug, "Anyway, what were you coming to tell us?"

I quickly take both of their hands in mine, my eyes darting between the two of them, "We decided this morning that we're going home, so I'm leaving Eldridge Bay earlier than expected."

Instantly, their faces fall.

I just ruined their days. Shit, I probably ruined the rest of their respective summers. Mish looks at me silently for a second, as though she's asking if I'm absolutely positive. I nod a quick, short nod.

Mish's eyes glass over first, "I'll miss you, Allie."

I pull my summer sister into a tight embrace. We hardly spent time outside of work together this summer. I was so busy with Teddy and finding out about Adam and she was so busy with her summer fling. We didn't get nearly enough time together.

I hug her even tighter.

"You better still come visit me in Allister, you bitch." I mutter and we both laugh quietly. She nods.

"Of course. As long as you come see my performance in January."

"Deal." I respond quickly. She's doing a dance showcase

in Chicago, and the grand prize is ten thousand dollars. It means a lot to her, and she was there when I did the dance thing in Washington D.C. back in High school. There's no question of me being there.

I turn to Phoebe and pull her into a tight embrace next, "Wherever your life takes you, Phoebe, just know that I will always love you and support you. No matter what."

She nods, crying into my shoulder. I don't know the next time I'll really see Phoebe. We don't text often, like Mish and I do once the year begins.

It's only then that I, too, begin crying.

———

Five hours later, Teddy and me have officially resigned from our jobs. Carla was sad, but understood that we needed to go back. She said that if Teddy comes back next summer, he's got a job. For my sake, I didn't need to resign. Phoebe just kind of picked up on it from the fact that I had gone to say goodbye to her and Mish.

I promised that I would never tell anyone about the kiss. Not even Teddy.

We almost have the car entirely packed up by noon. Teddy and Logan are attempting to put everything in like *Jenga* pieces. I re-enter the house. The only thing left, food wise, is the frozen and refrigerated stuff, which Mish and Phoebe said they'll come and take after their shift. The dry food is packed away into a box in the backseat.

I re-enter the house and go downstairs with one empty box. There's only a few things I want to take home.

I enter Adam's bedroom and turn on the light, setting the empty box on his bed. I start by packing away the picture frame that I had found. The one that lead to me learning of his existence. There are more pictures on the walls and I take down every single one, packing them in. Then, I grab a photo album that sits on the dresser and add it in. No more leaving him in Eldridge Bay. Adam finally gets to come home with me.

There's one more thing. I haven't touched it until this very moment, as I wanted to leave his room the way that it had been left. But I want it. I want a part of him.

The alligator plushie that sits on his bed, next to his pillow. It's a pale green and has a white smile, its eyes closed. I squeeze it tightly, hugging it and inhaling the dusty scent. I imagine that somewhere in that scent, is a remnant of my brother.

Tears drip down my cheeks and are absorbed by the plushie. There is still so much that I don't know about my brother. So many unanswered questions. Like missing pieces of a fucked up puzzle.

There's a knock on the doorframe. I quickly turn, the alligator still tucked under my arm. Teddy is wearing khaki shorts and a blue Allister College shirt.

"You okay, pretty girl?"

I look around the room, then back to Teddy and nod, "Yeah. I'll be okay."

He approaches me and wraps his arms around me, "Do you want to go see him before we head out?"

I nod into my boyfriend's chest, the alligator trapped between us, "If we could."

He hugs me a little tighter, then releases and grabs the box, leaving me in Adam's room for an additional second.

I take it all in one last time. The walls, the furniture, the toys. Everything that was once his.

I turn off the light, but I don't close his door.

I'll never close that door again.

———

"I want to read something. Something that Mom wrote about Adam on what would've been his tenth birthday." I say as my friends surround me.

All of them. Including Phoebe and Mish, who only know a little bit of what happened regarding Adam. In the week after the discovery, I did tell them about it. They made the journey over here on their lunch break to say goodbye. The six of us stand over Adam's headstone and I open the leather-bound journal to the bookmarked page.

Dear Adam,

Today would have been your tenth birthday! It's bittersweet. Allie is now older than you were when you passed and it's hard for me and your dad to comprehend. She's growing up so much. I wish you could have grown up with her.

Not a day goes by that I don't miss you or think about you. Your sweetness. Your beauty. You were my baby boy, my first born, and you were taken away from me so quickly. Your father and I traveled back to Eldridge Bay this past week to visit your grave. Allie had been begging to go to a summer dance camp, so we let her go and we came back here to see you. It still doesn't feel real. Even four years later, I still look for you at the park when we take her. I still wait to hear your voice. I see the things that you loved at the store and think about buying them for you, though, you would never be able to use them, because you're not here.

It's hard, Adam. It really is. The more time the passes, the more and more that I forget about you. Your laugh, your voice, your scent. These things that made you, you, are fading from my mind slowly. Like sand in an hourglass. I can still see your face. I see it as clear as day. You're right there. But the rest of you is fading away slowly. Though, I still can hear your laugh in your Dad and your sister, although it's not yours exactly, it's similar. Allie also scrunches her nose sometimes when she laughs, like you used to when you were little. The memory of you grows further and further away from my reach. You fade as the time passes and it breaks my heart.

Your sister has no idea still; I don't know if we'll be able to tell her anytime in the near future. The therapist keeps telling us that it's for the best she doesn't remember you, that we should just you stay buried. But it's hard. I'm combing through our photo albums and hard drives and all I see are the memories of you. I so badly want to remember you in the way that you deserve to be remembered, but we can't. One day, we will tell Allie. We will take her to your room and show her your things. We will tell her the truth about you, Adam. One day.

But that day is not today.

It's not going to be tomorrow.

Hell, it probably won't be for a few more years, but eventually, your sister will learn about you. We will finally be able to look at the memories of you and remember you in the way that you deserve to be remembered.

But until that day, my sweet boy, just know that I love you. Your dad loves you. Grandma loved you until her dying day. Grandpa continues to love you. He goes to the cemetery in Eldridge Bay everyday to see you. Deep down, somewhere inside her mind, locked away like the princess in that storybook you used to love, Allie loves you. Even if she doesn't remember.

Love,

Mom

Tears line down my cheeks and I look up from the journal. There's not a dry eye among any of the six of us as we stand together over my brother's grave. I lean into Teddy, and he wraps his arms tightly around me as I close the journal and break out sobbing into his t-shirt. A hand makes it way to my back, moving up and down slowly. From the nails, I can tell it's Phoebe. Then, I hear Logan and Ana and Mish pile in.

This is my family, too.

My parents and Adam are my family, but so are these

people. My roommate and our boyfriends, and my summer sister Mish, and my boss, Phoebe. We're all a family.

That family also goes beyond the people standing here today. It's also Patrick and Nik and Luke. It's my teammates from the dance team. It's the players my Dad has helped over the years.

Family is so much more than what I thought it was, once.

We break from the hug and I wipe my eyes with the back of my hand. I turn and face Mish and Phoebe.

"You two behave. Don't trash the house later." I tell them, hugging Phoebe first.

Phoebe nods, "We won't. We'll just take the food and lock-up."

I release, then hug Mish next.

"I'll miss you, Allie-cat."

"You too, Mish-Mish."

We hold each other for a prolonged second, then we release each other and I look between my two friends one last time. I hand Mish the house key, then take Teddy's hand and follow him back to the SUV.

It's time to go home.

CHAPTER 19
TEDDY NOVAK
ONE MONTH AND TWO WEEKS LATER

"So, how are you feeling about going back to school tomorrow?" Dr. Hale asks as he sits across from me in his black, leather chair.

"Fine. It's my third year at Allister, So I'm not overly freaked out about it." I tell him.

He nods and jots something down, "And how long has it been since you spoke to your Mother?"

"Nearly two months."

It's true. I haven't spoken to her since July 5th. It's August 28th. Next week will be the two-month mark. A lot has changed in the last two months. Mostly for the better, but that doesn't mean that life hasn't also been a bitch.

After we left Eldridge Bay, to return to Allister, life got pretty quiet. Allie's parents had become so consumed in fixing the cafe after it was damaged, that it gave Allie and me a lot of alone time.

We spent most of it just lying together, talking. We did eventually go on a real date, a week after we got back to Allister. She planned it all as a surprise. We went down to the lake that sits right at the edge of campus, laid out a picnic blanket and we had lunch together.

That was the day I finally told her what my Mom had said on the phone.

"We're having a baby."

Even replaying the moment in my mind, I feel sick to my stomach. She's going to bring another child into this world after she did *so well* with her first one. The thought makes me feel uncomfortable. I'm going to have a brother or sister and they're going to be brought into my Mom's dramatic life. One where she does irrational, stupid things, without ever considering the feelings of the people around her.

"Teddy? Where'd you go?"

I shake the thought away, "Sorry, I'm just exhausted after moving into the apartment yesterday."

It's not a lie. We spent nearly fourteen hours moving in mine, Logan, Nik and Patrick's things, and setting up. Logan was insistent on the TV sitting in front of the large, three-pane windows. Nik and Patrick shot that down immediately.

Then we had hockey practice from six to eight, only to come back and have to finish setting up and unpacking our shit. I saw Allie for maybe five minutes yesterday. She's busy with doing the same thing. Moving in, practice, setting up with Ana, Jenny and their new roommate Riley.

I don't know anything about her. Allie and I were supposed to meet up for dinner last night to talk about her thoughts, but that didn't happen. Luckily we managed to squeeze in lunch between therapy and practices.

"You live across the hall from your girlfriend, right?"

I nod, "Yep."

"How's that going? Did you guys tell her Dad like we discussed?"

Yeah, no. Why in the fuck would we do that? Coach has been so tense the last few weeks with the cafe repairs, the drama with the rink and its name, and then the team change up yesterday. Three of our players were kicked off the team for being involved in a hazing scandal last fall, with the investigation just finishing up.On top of that, we have no freshman joining the team this year meaning our numbers are low.

On top of low numbers, a shocking article was posted in the Allister Digest that revealed Jim Morrey, the man who started the hockey team back in the sixties, had numerous files unearthed over summer that revealed he was apart of a racist organization back in the sixties. Our team is fucked. The place we play at is nameless. We're short players. Our coach doesn't know I've been dating his daughter for two months now.

Yeah, we're not telling him. Not yet.

I just nod in response to my therapist, lying to him, "He's been giving us both the silent treatment since we told him."

"That sucks, man. Though I'm sure he'll come around." Dr. Hale replies, trying to get on my level.

I don't exactly understand why I got assigned a therapist who is fresh out of college. Apparently, I'm his first fucking patient. Fantastic, right?

I thank every god in the universe when the timer goes off and I part ways with this prying, conniving dickbag.

I can't be mad at him though. It's his job. He's paid to psychoanalyze me.

I exit the office and a black SUV is waiting for me, right where the driver said they would be. I open the passenger door and Allie smiles.

She *fucking* smiles.

And suddenly everything I felt from therapy fades away. Everything feels easy again.

"Hey stud. How was therapy?" Her eyes stuck on me.

I buckle up, "Oh it sucked. But what else is new."

She rolls her eyes, "Teddy. Be for real."

"I'm serious. It was mostly just small-talk about school and my Mom." I reply and sit back in the seat, taking her hand as she begins to drive.

I am so, utterly in love with this girl.

Yet I haven't been able to say it to her again, not since the first time. I haven't been able to just get my shit together and tell Allie that I love her. I can tell it bothers her. She says it every time we see each other. After the first time, she says it every time she sees me. Yet I can't even get three simple words out. Three words I've said already.

Though, she understands why I can't. It's not like I grew up with stable parents, a stable relationship to look up to and say *"I want that one day."*

It's just so fucking hard for me to do.

"Well, what are you thinking for lunch?"

"Want *Q'doba*?" I ask and she nods, content with my choice. It's on campus. Granted, it's on the opposite side of campus than we live on, but with a car, it'll only be a five minute drive.

We have a limited food options on campus, most of which are in the Student Center. The Allister Student Center is pretty much just a one-stop shop for food, merchandise, financial aid, campus jobs and other resources. When we lived in Newman Hall last year, it was just across the quad, but now it's a bit of a walk from the Maplegrove Apartments.

We drive from the business strip of Allister back to our campus.

I usually hate this place. It just feels so confined, but with Allie, it feels like a sprawling kingdom. I've come to appreciate this place more now that I have her in my life.

We still aren't publicly with each other though.

Our friends know, Allie's Mom and my Mom know, but we have to keep it on the low. We don't want Coach finding out yet.

We pick up lunch, then head back to her apartment. She lives in a four-bedroom, two bathroom suite. Same as me. We go into her room and she closes the door.

Her blinds are open, the sun peering in. Her twin-sized bed is elevated on top of her dresser and small bookshelf.

While the apartments are nice, they still come with the unfortunate dorm-room furniture that everyone and their mom despises.

Allie's room feels homey, though. She has a poster of *Taylor Swift*'s new album on one wall, fairy lights frame it. On the other wall is a canvas print of Eldridge Bay. Specifically, the gazebo on the main beach as the sun is setting.

Across the ceiling, LED lights are taped up, following the shape of the room. Her desk is cluttered with school stuff, textbooks and notebooks. The quark-board back has pictured pinned up. Some of her and the dance team, a couple with her and Ana or her and her parents, but there is one right in the middle of it all that sticks out.

It's a picture of us at the sand dunes, after I had made it back up, of course. Ana took it when we weren't looking.

I don't know how she can still be so upbeat and so positive, especially after all the Adam stuff came out.

That's the last picture pinned on the board. It's in the corner, with small athletic and academic pins surrounding it. It's a picture of her and Adam. The summer he had passed.

The other remnant of her brother in her room? The stuffed alligator she packed up before we left. He sits at the food of her bed.

I kick off my shoes and sit next to her on her fuzzy, pink rug.

We sit in silence for a moment, just eating our respective lunches, then she sets her's down.

"We should watch a movie."

She reaches up to her desk and grabs her laptop, setting it down between us on the carpet.

"What kind of movie are you thinking, pretty girl?" I say between bites. I can see her face redden a bit at that remark. I love seeing the effects I have on her. Even calling her pretty makes her get all red.

"Something funny. Lighten the mood before we enter

hell." She says with a quiet laugh and we spend the next half-hour scrolling through various sites, looking for movies. We finally settle on a movie with *Will Farrell*. She sets her lunch aside and scoots closer to me, resting her head on my chest as I lean back into the beanbag chair.

For the first time today, I feel my own body begin to settle and finally feel comfortable in the moment.

The sound of blades cutting into the deep ice is another sound that makes me feel comfortable, but tense at the same time, but it's not the same tense feeling that comes over me when I'm in therapy or dealing with my drama. It's a competitive intensity, one that sends adrenaline pulsing through my veins. I skate past Luke Dermont, who is wearing a red jersey. I'm wearing blue.

Right now, we're just playing against each other. The team is split down the middle. Luke attempts to steal the puck from me, but I juke past him and shoot at the net. The goalie blocks it, shooting it back. Fuck.

Nik would never do me dirty like that, but Sebby would. Coach blows the whistle and I head to the bench to get a drink. Luke approaches, grabbing my shoulder.

"That was a good juke, Novak." He tips back his water bottle and takes a massive swig. I do the same, then nod.

"Thanks man."

I take a seat and he sits next to me, "Heard a rumor you're dating the coach's daughter? That true?"

Well shit.

I forgot to tell Luke.

"We are dating, but keep it on the low. She doesn't want to tell her Dad yet."

Luke nods, mimicking zipping his lips, just like Logan did, "People aren't whispering about it or anything. Nik just mentioned at breakfast we should all do a big date thing together."

"Aren't Nik and Patrick single?"

"Correctemundo, Theodoro," He joking spits back, "But then again, so am I."

This is news to me, but then again, Luke didn't really keep in contact with anyone over summer. He had a fellowship opportunity overseas in some third world country, aiding in disaster relief. I doubt he had an unlimited data plan wherever he was.

"What happened? I thought you and that one guy were doing okay?" I ask, taking a drink from the plastic water bottles that taste like you're drinking chemicals.

"We were, until I left and he ended things over email." *Ouch.*

"You're joking?"

He nods, taking another drink, "Yeah, that was a pleasant thing to wake up to."

"I bet." I reply dryly.

This is one thing I have missed. While Logan and I banter, and so do Allie and me, Luke and I just bounce off-each other's dry sarcasm. He's the same year as the rest of us and is doing a residence hall assistant job this year to pad his resume, or whatever.

I don't see how being in charge of a floor of college students can pertain as relevant experience for a future doctor, but whatever.

It also just so happens that his younger sister, Lauren, has moved to Allister for her first year of college. When I first met Lauren, she was sixteen, quiet, shy. But when she came to help Luke move out back in May, she was a completely different person. She was all grown up. She was snappy, quick-witted, and gorgeous.

I don't see how this is going to go good for Luke. Having such a full plate this semester with hockey, trying to get an internship with the Allister Medical Center, being an R.A. and now watching over his little sister like a hawk?

There's no way he's okay.

But then again, are any of us?

My Mom sucks, Allie discovered she has a dead brother, Luke has whatever the fuck is going on, Nik was nearly busted for having drugs again, and Patrick is inches away from quitting the team to focus on his career.

None of us are doing great anymore.

Well, except for Logan and Ana. The happily engaged couple.

Despite being engaged, they still chose to not live together, which is odd, but whatever. It's not like they live hours apart. It's two steps across the hallway.

Logan saunters over and sits down, pulling off his skates and throwing them to the side.

"My body is screaming right now." He says and both of us look at him as he falls onto his back.

"Oh, poor baby, do you need your fiancé to come take care of you?" I shoot back and he just flips me off.

"Speaking of, fiancé? Really Logan? We're in college still." Luke leans forward, looking past me to Logan, who is rubbing his knuckles up and down against his legs

"And? We're in our twenties. I've known I was in love with Ana since we were five. That's fifteen years, in case you can't do math."

"Hardy har, har. I can do math. I'm not an idiot like this one," and he points to me. Jokingly, I lean forward to bite at his finger. He pulls his hand back quick, "My point proven."

"Just because I barely passed my College Algebra class does not mean I'm an idiot. I deal with financial math all the damn time. Business major, remember?" I reply.

Coach enters the booth, blowing his whistle. Like soldiers going into battle, all of our heads snap up to face him. He goes through his spiel of information, calling out the slackers, pointing out the ones who had good plays. Then, he tells us all to head to the locker room, but he stops me.

I hear Logan mutter a rather loud uh-oh, as the team disperses.

"What's up, Coach?"

"I just wanted to check in. See how things are going. You've seemed a little tense the last few weeks."

Because I have been.

But I won't tell him that.

"It's just life. I guess it's been pretty hard dealing with the stuff with my Mom and everything."

I had also told Martie and Jesse about my phone call with my Mom. About how she's *pregnant*. The look in Martie's eyes after the words left my mouth felt more caring and more motherly, than any look I ever saw in my own mother's eyes.

"I'm sorry, Teddy. Really. I wish there was something we could do to make it easier." He replies, pocketing his whistle and sitting down to put papers into a binder.

"You both have already done so much for me. You pay for me to go to therapy. You housed me over summer and let me continue living with you during breaks. You and Martie and Allie have already done so much." I tell him and his eyes lock on me. He has the same eyes as her. In his eyes, I see her. It's almost unnerving.

"I'm glad you and Allie buried whatever weird hatchet was between the two of you and became friends. It definitely makes this situation easier." He pats my back, then heads back out to the ice to continue coaching, completely oblivious.

Oh, if only you knew, Jesse Hennings. If only you knew.

———

ALLIE HENNINGS

"If only you knew," I tell Ana as I rinse out my water bottle from practice. Ana is sitting on our couch, wrapped in a blanket despite the fact it's ninety degrees outside right now. She's typing away at her computer.

"I have no desire to be at a dance team practice, do you Riley?"

She looks over to the chair in the corner where our new roommate sits, crocheting a hat or a scarf or mittens?

Riley Wright is a freshman, and I dunno how the fuck she got into the apartments as a freshman, but she's pretty chill. She and Jenny seem to really get along.

"God no, I would rather be stabbed in the neck with a pitchfork." She mutters, not looking up from her project. She must register what she said, because her head flits up, "No offense."

"None taken. I've been thinking about quitting anyway. I just don't enjoy it like I used to. And the new captain is an absolute bitch."

"Who is it?" She replies.

"Bella." She stops, eyes looking to me as though I'm joking. I really wish that I was.

"Bella the bitch, Bella?" Ana clarifies, closing her computer.

When we found out our fourth roommate was Riley, we let out a major sigh of relief. We were sitting on pins and needles, hoping and praying that we didn't get roomed with Bella.

She's a fucking bitch. Has been since Freshman year when she put blue hair dye in my shampoo in the communal bath-rooms. That, I don't like to talk about. *Never*. I had been stuck with blue hair for twenty-four hours and it was the worst twenty-four hours of my collegiate life. Or the drama she's tried to stir up with Ana and Logan because she has a big crush on him.

It's like a shitty high school movie.

We're adults.

"Yep!" I reply as I refill my water bottle with ice, cold water and I sit down on the other side of the couch, "While everyone else was just catching up and talking and gossiping, I had to drag out props and equipment. That bin hasn't been touched since April. Those props smell atrocious."

I take a drink and Ana quickly turns her attention back to the computer, "Sorry, I'm listening, I'm just working on something for the paper."

"Already? We just got back?"

She nods, "You know how my Academic Advisor is also the advisor of the paper? Well apparently our Editor in Chief last year transferred out. She was a junior and was supposed to do it again this year. He asked me if I could take a job, so my work load has gotten significantly worse in the span of five hours."

"You got Editor-in-Chief?! Ana! That's so exciting! Why didn't you tell me?" I quickly sit down next to her.

"It is, but it's also terrifying. I'm in charge of the entire paper, the entire website. All of it." She replies, "And I'm working on our storyboard for the first edition right now and I need your opinion-"

She looks to Riley, "You too."

She sets down her project and slides onto the couch between us, "Should we run a piece on the Morrey scandal? Could you get us an interview with your Dad, Als?"

"I can try to."

Riley looks confused, "What's the Morrey Scandal?"

"The original name for the hockey arena was the Morrey Arena, but a report was released by the town's paper that revealed the man it was named after was apparently apart of some shitty hate groups in Allister. The school is scrambling to rename the Arena." I start to explain, but everything freezes. The entry I read this morning.

It was from the month of the charity game last year.

> *Adam,*
>
> *Your father seems to be taking it really hard this year. It's been sixteen or so years now and he managed to find a way to honor you without us outwardly telling Allison. He found a charity that donates to families who lose young children and the Allister Hockey team is raising funds at their next game. We're considering telling Allie before the game, just to let her appreciate it like we do, but at the same time, she's in such a good place. She got Dean's List last semester, she's on track to becoming a captain on the dance team. She's doing so well. I just know that when we tell her, if the timing is even wrong in the slightest of ways, she'll spiral out-*

They have a new name for the Arena right in front of them.

I jump up from the couch, "Where are you going so quickly?"

"I'm getting you that interview!" I take off, not even grabbing my phone before I go.

I don't drive. I fully sprint across campus, dodging past people with the idea sitting fresh in my mind. I burst through the doors of the arena, and rush into the offices. He's not there, but I can hear the boys in the locker room.

So I take a deep breath, close my eyes and enter. I can't see anything, but I sure as hell can smell it. B.O. and sweaty fills the air the moment I cross the threshold. I hear Nik and Patrick, Logan and Luke. But not Teddy. I turn the corner quickly, eyes pinched closed.

"Woah! Allison! What the hell are you doing in here?" Logan shouts, I don't even open my eyes, but I can imagine that they are fully nude or close to it right now. I can practically hear Logan jump up from his locker space, then quickly steps across the room.

"Where's my dad?" I keep my eyes closed, fully aware of the fact my best friend's fiancé could be buck-naked in front of me.

He clears his throat and moves me slightly to the right, "You can open your eyes. I'm not naked, Allie."

I open my eyes and he's moved us around the corner of the locker room. He's wearing sweats and a white tank top, but he conceals my view from his definitely nude teammates, "Where is he?"

"He's on the ice with your boyfriend right now." His voice low, keeping the secret within our circle. Unlike Nik. I'll have to kick his ass for that later.

"What?" Oh *fuck*. Did he find out? Is he grilling into Teddy right now?

I don't say another word as I dart out of the entry way and toward the rink. As I enter, I see them sitting there in the booth. I cut through the bleachers and enter the booth.

"Allison? What are you doing here?" Dad asks. Teddy quickly turns to face me.

"What's going on?" He asks, standing quickly as panic filling his voice.

"I have a solution to your Arena name problem."

Dad looks at me, then Teddy, then back to me.

"What's that?" He sets down his clipboard and turns his full attention to me.

"Adam." I say quickly, still panting to catch my breath. I

can see the gears turning in his head as he processes it, then comes to the idea the same way that I did.

"The Adam Hennings Memorial Arena?" Teddy voices and both of us look to him. His eyes stay locked on me. As if he's saying he's proud of me.

The three of us stand in silence with each, processing this, then small tears form in the corners of his eyes and a small smile comes over his lips. He nods.

"I'll have to talk to your mother, but I think you are a genius, Allison. You too, Teddy. For the quick suggestion." He wraps an arm around me, holding me tightly against him and I lean in, resting my forehead on his shoulder. I wrap both my arms around him and hold him tightly, realizing how much this impacts him. Naming the arena after his son. After my brother. An arena he certainly would've played in, if he hadn't passed.

I pull out of the hug and look to Teddy, he smiles and nods.

"I'll speak to your Mom tonight and if she agrees, I'll bring it up to the Alumni Association at our meeting on Friday. Talk to you later?" Dad replies and I nod.

"I love you. Tell Mom I love her too." I tell him as he grabs his bag, slinging it over his shoulder.

"I will. Call her tonight if you have the chance."

"Will do." I smile, nodding.

He grabs Teddy's shoulder in a fatherly way, "We can continue talking about that play tomorrow, okay kid?"

Teddy nods and Dad leaves the two of us in the booth to go to his office.

"Did you drive over here or walk?"

"Try sprinted."

He laughs as he sits down and unwraps his ankle, "Damn. That's why you're all sweaty."

"No, that would be from practice. I had an epiphany right

after I got back to the apartment and I wanted to tell Dad my idea in person, so I sprinted over here."

"Allie, that's like a mile."

"I know? And?"

He rolls his eyes and he grabs his things and heads to the locker room. I follow him in that direction.

"If you wanna wait ten or so minutes, you can ride back with Nik, Logan and me." He proposes and I nod.

"I'll just sit in my Dad's office." I reply and go to head over to the offices, but his hand grabs mine and he spins me toward him. He's sweaty, still wearing all the padding and the jersey. He smirks as he tilts his head down towards me and presses his lips against mine.

At first, it's a soft kiss, but it quickens into something more as he backs me against the wall, his large hand pressing against the brick, he releases and looks breathlessly into my eyes, "Am I staying with you or are you staying with me tonight?"

"Well, I have an eight a.m."

"My place it is." He replies, "I think I'm finally ready to, y'know?"

Oh-

He *means-*

He means he's ready to have sex with me.

I nod, blushing, wanting the exact same thing.

I feel myself grow tense at the thought of him fucking me. We've made out, we've done some kinky foreplay with each other, and he's fingered me once or twice. But we still haven't done anything past that.

I smile through my blushing, then I nod.

"Okay."

CHAPTER 20
ALLIE HENNINGS

Teddy and I are making out in his bed, atop the forrest green covers. He's shirtless and wearing only his athletic shorts, not even boxers underneath. I'm in a bra and spandex. His hand cups my breast, kneading it. My own hand is grabbing at his growing bulge inside his shorts. It tenses and hardens with every stroke I give it. He lets out a deep groan and I sit up.

"Are you sure you want to do this?"

He nods, "Allie. I've never been more sure of something in my life."

I nod and scoot back, dragging his underwear down with me. I let them rest at the base of his knees and his erection is out and fully on display.

I wrap my hand around it and he lets out a quiet, muffled groan. I drag a finger across the tip, then, I bring my lips to it.

I leave a small kiss right at the top. One hand covers his mouth, the other moves to my head as I slowly take more and more of him in. I continue to tease him, swirling my tongue, grabbing at his balls. He's got to be one of the biggest I've ever saw. Granted, I've only hooked up with three guys total, four now, but Teddy is for sure the biggest. It's not surprising.

The man is built like a tank. My hand moves up and down his stomach, his abs tensing and my nail tracing the rigid lines like it's a maze for me to navigate.

I can't even bring him completely into my mouth. I would suffocate, and I'm not exaggerating.

Before he can even come, he flips me over and presses my hands at the sides of my head, holding my wrists down into the mattress.

"Are you sure?"

"Stop asking or I'll smack you." I look into his eyes with a deep passion. One telling me that he is the one for me.

"That might be hot." He cocks an eyebrow and I roll my eyes as he sits up on his knees, his legs straddling my thighs. He reaches for the condom he put on the nightstand when we entered. Teddy bites the packaging, tearing it open, and he rolls the nearly clear latex over himself.

In one slick motion, his hand moves away from mine and he directs himself into me with a skillful slide. It's a tight feeling, one that I have not felt in almost a year. But it's different. It's way different, because it's with him.

The free-hand that he used to guide himself into me moves to cover my mouth and I do the same thing he did to me at the bookstore. I lick his sweaty palm. He starts laughing and I can't help but laugh too.

He starts off slow, rocking back and forth against me. He moves his hand, pressing his thumb to my lower lip, he slowly opens my mouth and slides his thumb onto my tongue as he takes control of me in two different places. I close my lips around his thumb, the sweaty taste mixed with the faint taste of his hand soap. I suck on it the same way that I was sucking on him a few minutes ago.

"Good girl," He mutters as he continues to rock against me. Fuck. I feel a tingle move down my spine and my legs shake in response. He tears the clasp of my bra, in the front, the one the binds the two parts together in the middle and my

nipples react to the coldness of his bedroom. The air conditioner is pointed down on us, making me feel feverish as he
brings his own lips to my nipple. His tongue circles it, and he
bites hungrily at my breast. Nipping and kissing the skin.

So much has lead us to this point.

I feel my orgasm growing closer and closer as he
continues to take me. As he continues to control my body. I
want him to make me his in this moment. All I want, is for the
world to know, that I am his and he is mine.

———

My alarm goes off at seven in the morning and it takes every
ounce of strength in me to not snooze it. I have to go back to
my apartment, shower, get dressed and eat something before
I have to go to class. I roll out of Teddy's embrace. We make
the twin-bed thing work by spooning. He laid with his back
against the wall and he held me against him the entire night.
My hair sticks to my face. Our skin sticks to each other.

I crawl out of bed and put my bra on. Well, as best as I can
since he ruined it. I steal his hockey hoodie, sliding it on, then
I step into my sandals and creep out of his room.

I can hear talking in the living room. I round the corner
and sitting on the couch, are Logan and Ana. They're eating
breakfast, fully dressed.

"Uh oh, someone's doing the walk of shame." Logan
teases and I grab a pen off the counter and throw it at him in
response. He laughs quietly and I plop down next to Ana.

"Can you come back to the apartment with me? I forgot
my key and I'm ninety percent sure Riley has not left that
door unlocked since we got here." Ana digs out her keys and
hands them to me.

"No, Ana. Can you just come and unlock it for me?"

Logan looks confused, "We're eating here."

"Well I kind of need my girlfriend back now, so come on

Analise." I lift her off the couch. She sets her plate on the table.

"I'll be back in five." She tells her fiancé and follows me out of the boys apartment and into our apartment. Jenny is still sleeping? Or maybe she never came back. I haven't saw her since she finished moving in.

Riley must've left early, because her keys are absent from the key rack.

"What is so important that you had to interrupt my breakfast with my fiancé, Allie?"

She leans against the counter and I take frozen Eggo waffles out of the freezer, throwing two into the toaster.

"Guess who finally had sex last night?" I grab her hands.

Ana nearly screams, "You and Teddy finally hooked up?!"

I nod and jump up and down, "How was it? You haven't hooked up since Joey Dawson, last January, right?"

I nod, "Tiny-Dick Dawson has nothing on my boyfriend is all that I will share."

"No! Really? Like obnoxiously?"

I shrug, "Depends on how you view obnoxiously. In comparison to you, Ms. Five-foot-four, yeah, probably."

"Girl- I'm so happy you finally bagged him. Logan and I have had another bet on when you two would finally have sex-"

Record scratch, wait, what?

"Ana, are you serious?"

"Yeah, I had fifty on first semester, Logan had fifty on second semester. Looks like I'm getting fifty bucks." She says and I stick my tongue out at her.

"You're an ass."

"You know you love me, Allison." She slaps my ass as she heads to the living room, grabbing the last few things she could possibly need for the day.

She's right. I do love her. That's why she's the first person I'm talking to after rolling out of my boyfriend's bed.

"Afterwards, we put on Friends and we fell asleep holding each other. Fully spooning. It was-" I stop and blush, "So good."

The toaster pops and I take out my frozen waffles, throwing them onto a paper plate. I round the counter and go to my bedroom, grabbing my shorts, thin flannel, and brown baby-tee, then socks and underwear and a new bra, because- well-

My boy is a ripper.

"Do you think this fit is cute for the first day?" I shout, then take a bite. She rounds the corner, entering my room and looking at it for a second.

"Wear it with that cute belt you got at H&M last March, and then it's put together nicely."

I nod and grab that out of my dresser.

"Anyway. I'm gonna get ready and I'll see you later, okay? Dinner after practice?"

Ana nods, "Maybe coffee break if we have time. We'll see. Have a good first day, girlfriend!"

She leaves my room and before I hear the front door close, I shout it back to her.

God, life is starting to finally feel good again.

I walk out of the College of Lifespan Sciences and standing there with a brown bag and a plastic cup, is none other than my hot boyfriend. He smiles. He's wearing a light blue t-shirt, one that makes his skin look incredibly tan and incredibly sexy.

I run over to him and throw my arms around him, making him nearly drop the coffee and treat.

"What are you doing here?" I ask.

"I don't have class till 1, so I wanted to surprise you with coffee and a muffin." He holds both out to me and I take the coffee, taking a sip. I read the small sticker on the side. It's my regular order.

"How'd you know my order?"

He smirks and we sit down at a bench near the rock garden, "I may or may not have asked Ana."

I open the bag and it's the muffin I always get: coffee cake.

"This is so sweet, Teddy." I hug him again, food and coffee in hand.

"You deserve it, beautiful." He replies and stretches his arm out on the bench behind me. I throw my backpack to the side of the bench and lean into him.

"Is this about last night?" I ask with muffin in my mouth. He shakes his head.

"No, just to celebrate the first day. Though, last night was fun." He adds and I nod.

"It was," I take a sip to wash down the muffin, "I'm glad we waited before we did anything.

"It's also our two month anniversary next week," He stares at me and his smile is strong. He's happy. I haven't saw him this happy in an incredibly long time. Even last year, when we weren't even friends. I could tell he was confronting something deep and personal. I knew he was struggling with something and his over the top behavior was to compensate for the way he was feeling.

I know he's been taking the drama with his Mom hard and the added stress of hiding a relationship from his coach, aka my Dad.

"After everything we've been through, I'm glad I finally got to make you mine." He says with a smile as his thumb traces circles on my shoulder. I smile, then nod and lean further into his arm and just embrace the moment for what it is. A moment where we're at peace. There's no practice, no roommates or friends or parents. Just me and him.

He smells faintly of the cologne he bought when we went to the mall to get stuff for the apartments. We were smelling perfumes and colognes and there was one that smelt sharp, musky, with a hint of ocean. I told him how good it smelt, and the next morning, he was wearing it.

I didn't even see him buy it, but on him, it's a scent that I've become addicted to. A part of him that I feel incredibly attached to. I finish the muffin and drink most of the coffee, then stand and hold my hand out.

"Want to walk me over to the English building?" He takes my hand and I pull him up off the bench.

"What are you doing taking an English class?" He asks as he takes my hand and walks with me in that general direction. Despite being hundreds of years old, Allister College looks like it's only been here a couple of decades.

Dad told me that right after he graduated, they renovated campus heavily, completely tearing buildings down and rebuilding them to feel more modern. I bet Ana and Logan's mom's would have more information about the renovations.

The only building that remained untouched on campus was the admissions building. The historic, brick building was three stories and had ivy growing up the walls, with a large bell tower on the top.

"I needed to take a three-hundred level writing and composition credit so I signed up for Creative Writing with Ana. It's supposed to be just writing poetry responses and small passages to the different prompts that the professor assigns.

While I did need the credit, I felt like a creative writing class could be a good opportunity to get my feelings about Adam out into the world. Responding to the prompts by writing about him. Or at least what I know about him.

The only memory that has come back to me in the last two months was the one at the zoo. When I went with Ana and my Mom.

Mish is supposed to come visit Allister for thanksgiving break. Thank god. I still feel bad that I didn't get to spend nearly enough time with her this past summer. It all moved by so quickly. My usual time with her was robbed from me. I had already made plans to go to Phoebe's wedding next Spring, but now that that's not happening anymore, I'll just use that opportunity to visit with her. Thank god it lined up perfect with Allister's Spring Break.

I quickly turn to Teddy, stopping him, "Wait, what's your first class today?"

"Economics… again." He grumpily replies. I laugh and nod, continuing walking with him across campus. Luckily for us, we can walk around campus openly as a couple. My dad doesn't come to campus until an hour before practice, so it gives Teddy and me plenty of time.

There's enough students at this stupid school to even register who I am and who Teddy is. The hockey team may be good, but they get nowhere near the crowd that the football team gets.

Football sucks, anyway. The only game I go to is homecoming.

We stop outside the English building and he smirks that boyish grin. My heart does an entire backflip at just the sight of his smile.

God, I'm in love with him.

I am so maddeningly in love with Teddy Novak that I could just spontaneously combust right here, right now.

He tilts my face up and presses his lips to mine.

"See you later, pretty girl." He caresses my chin, then takes off in the direction of the apartment. My heart skips a beat as I watch him pocket his hands. I can hardly turn around and go inside because I just want to be with him.

I want to be with Teddy forever.

CHAPTER 21
ALLIE HENNINGS

We've been back at Allister College for two weeks and I'm already over it.

Today are the auditions for the dance team. Yesterday was the organization fair. It was the chance for new students to learn about the different groups and organizations that they could join on campus.

Bella sat at the booth with another girl who joined last year. She practically acts like Bella's minion, always at her side and defending her as if her life depended on it.

Though, with Bella in her orbit, her life probably did depend on it. With Bella as our new captain, she's the one sitting at the desk with a clipboard in hand. There's a stageful of hopefuls, all of them anxiously waiting for an answer.

I lean towards Melissa, a girl who joined the same year as me. She's taking a drink from her water bottle, "With how long it's taking, you would think she's looking as a drive-thru menu."

Melissa spits the water back into her bottle as she stifles back a laugh. Bella turns to face us, unamused.

I truly don't see a point in all of us being here. Bella and her minion are the ones calling the shots. The rest of the team has no say. Though, if we did, my eyes are locked on someone who did incredibly well.

The short blonde in the far right corner. She's wearing baggy sweatpants and a t-shirt that shows off her belly button, which is pierced. Her hair is tied back by a black hair tie that has a bow on it.

I know her.

Lauren Dermont is the younger sister of Luke. She's a freshman this year and honestly, she is a great dancer. She moves like Mish does, and Mish is one of the best dancers I know.

She auditioned using a song by Tate McRae, which, bonus points to her because Tate McRae's music is awesome.

Bella rises from her seat.

"Alright. First, I'm going to call off the girls who aren't cut, then, I'll pair you with another member." Bella says loudly as she approaches the stage. She calls off four names.

And one of them is Lauren.

Thank god. Before Bella can start assigning, I stand quickly, "Bella! Lauren's mine."

Bella makes a face at me, rolls her eyes, but then nods, "Fine. Lauren, you're with Allison."

I cringe at the use of my full name, at least coming from someone who isn't Teddy.

Speaking of my boyfriend, I have barely saw him this week. Apparently, two new guys were recruited to the team last minute, and they've been having extra long practices to integrate these guys in. They apparently came from the intramural team.

This change has severely effected Ana and me. We've basically saw our men twice this week. Though, it's probably hitting her harder now that they're engaged.

Lauren rushes over to me as Bella continues pairing the girls off. I immediately grab her hands and pull her toward me, "I didn't know you danced!"

"All through elementary, middle and high school. It's the one and only thing I did." She replies excitedly, "I'm so happy right now! I need to text Luke."

I didn't know much about Lauren and Luke's relationship. While Luke and I may be friends, he's always been incredibly private about his life outside Allister. I don't pry. If he wants to share, he'll share.

She quickly goes to the other row of seats and grabs her bag, taking out her phone and texting Luke.

Though, I doubt she'll get a response. Practice is right now, tragically.

"Hey, Lauren," I approach, "Wanna grab something to eat after this?"

She looks up from her phone, thinking for a second, as if her mind is racing a million miles a minute, "Sure!"

The remainder of practice is Bella handing out contracts to the four new girls, then going through and all of us introducing ourselves.

I say a prayer to Adam for prompting an early end of practice. Tragic, I know, but Adam has become almost a spiritual figure for me recently. I've been praying to him as though he's Jesus or something. I wasn't raised religious. Neither of my parents were either. My dad has told me that he and his family only would go to a Midnight Mass or an Easter service to appease his grandparents. My mom has shared the same sentiment.

But without something to speak to or believe in out there, the world can almost feel too quiet. Especially when so much is happening all at once.

So instead of god or Jesus or other spiritual figures, I pray to my brother.

Dad was still waiting to hear back from the alumni association about the Arena's name change. Mom cried when he had told her that I suggested it. She cried tears of joy. I wish I was there to hug her when she found out.

I walk out of the theater with Lauren walking at my side, her bag is slung over her shoulder.

"So, how's your first week been?"

She shrugs, kicking a rock across the sidewalk, "It's been okay. My classes are pretty easy right now."

"What are you taking?"

"College Algebra, English, Yoga, Human Anatomy."

"Yoga? I didn't realize that was a class option?"

"Yeah. It's just a throw-away elective course for my major." Lauren replies. She adjusts her bag on her shoulder, stopping it as it slips down her arm.

"What's your major?"

"Right now, Kinesiology. I dunno if I'm going to keep it though,"

"Why not?"

Lauren just shrugs, "I'm not super passionate about it. I wanted to be an athletic trainer or something, but I also really want to teach younger kids. My Dad said teaching is an impractical career though."

"Okay, and? It's your career, choice Lauren." I tell her and open the door to the dining hall.

We enter Addler Hall. It's where I lived my freshman year with Jenny. It's probably the oldest of the residences halls, as they want it to closely match the other buildings in the College Center, which consists of our admissions building, the performance halls, the Student Center, and the Library.

These buildings all have a similar exterior, the 60's and 70's brick, but the interiors have been completely redone to match something out of the 21st century.

Lauren swipes her ID first, then goes through the turnstiles. I do the same, following her into the best dining hall on campus.

They've always had the best food options, out of both the dining halls on campus. Even last year, Ana and me would walk the two minutes from Newman Hall to the Addler Dining Hall because it was lightyears better.

We get food and take a seat at the booth in the corner. We spend the next hour talking about school and dance and boys. I tell her about my relationship with Teddy and she tells me about a guy she met at a party last Friday.

I bet Luke would blow a fuse if he knew his little sister had met a guy at a frat party her second weekend on campus. I just listen intently. I have no intention of snitching to her brother. She's my dance kid. I can't do that.

Our dinner, is however, interrupted by a text notification on my phone.

Fuck me.

It's our sorority group chat.

> Welcome back, Gamma Girls! We hope your
> moves back to campus have gone smooth
> and you're into the swing of things quickly!
> Our first chapter meeting will be Sunday
> night at 9:00 PM in Beckman Hall. We will be
> discussing our summers, getting ready for
> rush week, and gushing about anything we
> want. The theme is PJ party, so get comfy
> and we'll see you all Sunday!

Sent by our Sorority president herself, Jasmine. Though, I'm supposed to do PR this year, so you'd think that she would've cleared it with me first. Fuck, I'm on the executive committee and didn't hear a word about this until now.

Though, I have a feeling as to why.

The girl who invades my life like a parasitic leech, sucking my blood and doing anything to get under my skin. *Bella.*

I thumbs up react the message, the silence the group chat and turn my attention back to Lauren.

"Did my brother tell you about his celebrity student?" Lauren asks as she twirls her pasta with a fork. I do the same.

"What celebrity?"

"Do you remember the stabbing at Virginia University last fall? Where a college student was stabbed outside of a frat party and nearly died?" Lauren continues and I nod. I remember it too well, unfortunately. It put all of Allister College on high alert. All the news had said, was that it was a random attack and that the student had nearly died. Frat parties were pretty much cancelled the rest of the semester, students no longer traveled alone from place to place after dark.

Ana and Jenny would walk me to dance practice on week-nights and on Friday, I would walk Ana to her meetings for the paper and just sit in the lobby of the Communications building. Paranoia spread like wildfire, though, there was never, ever a second attack. It was an isolated event.

And I wouldn't exactly call this person a celebrity. They're an attack victim who got a bit of press around their story. The name w

"Yeah, why?"

"Well apparently, and you didn't hear this from me, the student who was attacked is one of Luke's students, lives two doors down from him."

"No shit?"

Lauren nods, "Luke's only met him twice and he said he's pretty shy and reserved. I don't blame him though. I would also be incredibly shy and reserved if something like that happened to me."

"I would've dropped out and moved to a remote cabin in Alaska if something like that happened to me, so I don't blame him for being quiet." I reply after taking a bite of pasta. God, this food is so good, but I'm more so focused on the fact that this student who was violently attacked, just returned back to college like it was nothing. I could never, ever have done that, so props to him.

"Same." Lauren says.

We finish our dinner and she heads upstairs to her room,

leaving me outside Addler Hall, all by myself. I send a quick text to Teddy.

> How's your day been going, boyfriend?

There's no instantaneous response, though, I'm ridiculous for expecting one. He's probably still in practice right now.

I pocket my phone into my pocket and walk towards the Maplegrove Apartments, into the darkness, all on my own.

———

After taking a quick shower and chatting with Riley about the new season of *Dancing With The Stars*, I turn in for the night, retreating to my bedroom. I take out the leather bound-journal, and do the only thing I feel like doing right now:

Dear Adam.

I know that mom used to be the one to write to you, hell, she probably still does, but now that I know of you, I want to spend more time writing to you. The same way that she does. Life has been a whirlwind as of late. Teddy and I are officially dating! I bet if you were still here, you'd really like him. He's on the Allister Team and he's really good (I'm not just saying that because he's my boyfriend, I'm saying that because even Dad says he's good). You would probably also grill the shit out of him before we started dating. Or maybe you wouldn't?

It's hard for me to process the fact that you once were physically here. Alive and breathing and moving. It's just crazy that I used to have an older brother. I haven't been able to remember much from when you were alive. Only one memory has fully surfaced over time, and it's when we went to the zoo in Grand Rapids. Shit, you probably don't know where that is. It's just south of Eldridge Bay. Did you even know directions yet? Or were you still blissfully oblivious to the world you only spent six years in? What did you know, Adam? I'm assuming you knew how to speak, how to spell and count?

But what does a person know at six years old? I can barely remember being six years old. It feels like forever ago, because it was, for me. From Mom's entries, from the last seventeen or so years, it seems like you were pretty smart. I read one yesterday that said you started to read short chapter books with Mom before bed. She wrote that your favorite was <u>Magic Tree House</u>, the one with the siblings who travel through time and solve missions from a Tree House? I remember reading those when I was little? Had they just repurposed the copies you had been reading from and gave them to me to read from? All this time, had traces of you been right under my nose and I never ever noticed?

I really wish I could remember you more. Remember your voice. Your laugh. The sparkle of your eyes, the same sparkle that Mom and Dad see in mine. There is so many things that I wish I could remember about you, but I just can't. I can't remember anything about you besides the things that I have already read. Do those things even *count? They aren't my memories. They're Mom's memories. Her memories of you are different than mine. I was your little sister. I should be able to remember parts of it. Any part will do. Please, just let me remember you. I want to remember you-*

I feel warm tears escape my eyes and I rub them away with the back of my hand as I stare down at my handwritten words. I want to remember you, Adam. So deeply and so desperately. I want one memory. That's *it*. Just one, single memory of a time that I got to spend with you in your short lifetime.

This is the hardest part of it all. When I'm all alone, sitting in my dimly-lit room under all my string lights and imagining what life would've been like had Adam not died. My parents aren't here to tell me about him, Teddy isn't here to listen to me talk, Ana isn't here to distract me. Just these quiet, lonely moments where it's just me and my messy mind and aching heart.

I close the journal and throw it to my desk on the other side of the room, listening as it clatters into my things, the roll over, the tears continuing to stream down my face and onto my pillow.

TEDDY NOVAK

Practice ends and I return to the apartment with Logan. After that practice, I want to take a shower, then eat quickly and go see my beautiful girlfriend.

My girlfriend.

The thought of having a girlfriend makes my stomach jump into my chest, and not in an anxious, I'm freaking the fuck out kind of way.

In an incredibly loving, dedicated way.

Logan showers first and I strip down to just my boxers, lying in bed and staring at the ceiling in silence while I wait. The shower on the left side of the apartment, closest to mine and Logan's rooms, is our shower, while the shower on the right side, closest to Nik and Patrick's room, is their shower. We all agreed that if one is occupied, we can use the other, but right now, neither are free. We all just returned from practice.

I got another text from my Mom today. One that is pleading with me to call her back as soon as possible. I instantly deleted the message.

I stare at Allie's message from an hour ago, then quickly type back to her.

> Busy LMAO. What abt you, pretty girl?

> Wyd right now? I'm gonna shower and eat, then I can come over, if you want?

After staring at the screen for a moment with no response, I rest my phone on my chest and feel it slowly rise and fall with my breathing.

Shit, it is nearly ten. She has an early class tomorrow morning, so she's probably sleeping already. I wouldn't be super surprised, honestly.

I hear the shower turn off, then, the song stops playing. Guess Logan's done in the shower. I grab a change of clothes and a towel, then head for the bathroom as he comes out in nothing but a towel, padding the two feet from the bathroom to his bedroom door, closing it silently behind him.

The hot water pelting my skin feels fucking fantastic. The water pressure in the apartments can't even compare to the water pressure in the dorms. It's a jet stream and getting it at just the right spot after practice feels like a fucking blow job.

Heaven.

Allie and I haven't even done anything remotely sexual since the first time, right after we got to campus. We've hardly had time to see each other, classes and practices and organizations immediately consuming our every waking moment.

It kind of sucks, but we both knew that we're very busy people, and that wasn't going to change because we're dating now.

I finish my shower, stepping out and drying off, then I quickly get dressed and head back to my room. There is no response from Allie.

Fuck.

I head out to the living room where Logan now is sitting on the floor, his laptop on his lap with his legs stretched out. There's a bowl of soup to his left, and an open textbook to his right.

I plop down on the couch that he is leaning against and run a hand through my wet hair.

"How do you do it?" I huff. Logan turns, looking at me.

"What?"

"How do you manage to have a relationship if you and Ana hardly get to see each other?" I reply. He turns around and faces me.

Logan shrugs, "We've always just somehow managed. Why?"

"Because I have saw Allie once this week and I feel like broken glass. Like- I'm so fucking down bad for this girl, yet our lives are so busy, that I hardly get to see her."

"Well, you haven't been in a relationship since high school, right?"

I nod, "But neither were you until last fall."

Logan laughs, "Yeah, but it's with the same girl. We skipped all the getting to know each other and the honeymoon phase and jumped right back into what we used to be. It's different, because Ana and I have known each other since we were born. I've saw her in diapers, and she has saw the same of me."

"So you're saying I need to build a Time Machine and go back in time to meet Allie when we're infants?"

"Absolutely not," he laughs, turning to face me, "Look, I'm saying, you need to carve out that time in your schedule. Even if it's ten to thirty minutes a day, you have to make time for her and she needs to do the same."

"I have an idea, but it sounds insane. A year ago, if I said what I'm about to say, you would probably institutionalize me." I tell him and stand up, heading to the kitchen to make something quick to eat. Maybe nachos in the air fryer? Or soup? I don't fucking know.

"And that is?"

"I'm gonna drop the fraternity."

Logan cocks an eyebrow, "Are you sure about that?"

I nod, "I hardly participate now that I'm in a relationship. They had a stop-light party last Friday and I didn't even go. I've gone to one chapter meeting and we've had two now."

"Dude, you're down so fucking bad for her, aren't you?" He's right, I am. If she even brought up the idea of spending forever together, right now, I would say yes.

I nod abruptly, "More than you know."

"Then go over there and tell her how much you love her. Spend time with her. Even if it's the night." He nods to the door, but he can't even finish his sentence. I don't bother putting on shoes, even as I exit our apartment and step into the tiled, dimly lit hallway.

I pound my fist on the door hastily, almost too hastily. It opens and standing there is none other than her new roommate, Riley. She's shorter than Allie, and has an afro that is tied up into a bun on the top of her head.

"Is Allie here?" I ask, looking down to meet her gaze. She just looks bored.

She looks at me silently for a moment, then steps back and holds the door open, "She's in her room."

Weird encounter, but whatever.

I march across the apartment to Allie's bedroom and I don't bother knocking. I just enter the bedroom.

It's dark, being lit up by the soft glow of her string lights that hang from the walls. She's curled into the fetal position, her back moving up and down.

She's crying.

"Allie?" I slowly close the door behind me.

She sits up quickly, startled. Her cheeks are puffy, eyes red and tears soak her pillow. I take two strides from the door to her twin sized bed and I throw my arms around her, tightly. She buries her head into my chest. Her arms wrap around my waist and she doesn't even get out of the bed, but she also doesn't give me the chance to join her. I just hold her against my chest, keeping my breathing slow in an attempt to calm her down.

"Teddy," her voice is hoarse, "I just- I'm- I-"

She stops and attempts to control her breathing as I squeeze her even tighter, "Shhh Allie, it's okay, baby. I've got you."

"Adam. It's about him." Her words are mumbled as she says them into my shirt. But I understand.

I know what she's saying.

I can't even imagine the process of grieving someone you never knew, or at least, someone you can't remember knowing. She was so young when she lost him. She can't even remember anything about her brother.

"What happened?"

I take a step back, but take her hands, tracing a thumb across the tops of hers.

She bites her bottom lip as it quivers, further attempting to control her emotions, "I was writing to him, like Mom does, and suddenly I realized that all this time, traces of him had been right under my nose. My Mom wrote that he used to read this children's book series, and I remember reading the same ones when I was his age. Had my parents just repurposed the copies that once belonged to my brother? Have small glimpses of him been there all-along and I was just oblivious?"

I don't even know what I can do to comfort her in this moment. What the hell can I do to give my girlfriend some kind of comfort in an incredibly raw moment where she is grieving her brother? She leans back towards my chest and just continues to cry. I sit her up, move her over, and pull a blanket over us, wrapping my arms around her until she cries herself to sleep. Our legs tangle together and her head nuzzles into my chest, looking for comfort even in her sleep.

Nearly an hour passes before she cries herself into sleep. And it hurts. It physically hurts me to see her this way.

Her breathing slows until she's softly snoring and I tilt my head down to kiss her forehead. The words just slip out. I don't even think about saying them, I just do.

"I love you, pretty girl."

CHAPTER 22
ALLIE HENNINGS

wake up to my phone ringing from my desk. I'm tangled up with Teddy, who I hardly remember even coming over last night, but I'm glad he did.

I work my way out from his heavy arm, untangling my legs from his. He mumbles something in his sleep and rolls over as I get up and grab my phone. It's Dad.

Quickly, I escape from my room and go to the living room. The apartment is quiet, blinds drawn shut. Everyone must still be asleep.

"Dad? Hey. What's up?" I open the blinds, letting the soft morning sun enter the windows.

"The Alumni Association approved it. I just got the email." He says flatly. I hear mom crying in the background.

Approved.

The dedication was approved.

"What!" I squeal. I can't even contain the excitement in my voice.

"Yeah, and they want the three of us to do speeches to discuss the impact the renaming has at the ribbon cutting ceremony." He replies and I can almost hear the tears of happiness in his voice.

"When is that?" I move to the fridge to check the Academic Calendar for the year.

"Homecoming. That Friday night," He continues, "If you don't want to speak, we will understand."

"No, no, no. I would love to speak. I have to tell-"

I stop myself before I say his name. Fuck.

"Tell who, Hun?"

"Ana and Riley and Jenny. I want them to be there too." I quickly correct my near-mistake. Though I don't know if he is convinced.

"Definitely. I'm going to mention it to Teddy later tonight at practice, unless you see him before me, since he was there when you found out and he has been supportive about it," he stops for a second, "I'm glad you two became friends, Allie."

Oh Dad, we're more than friends. If only he knew that Teddy was currently sleeping in my bed, mumbling and snoring.

"Thank you for calling to let me know, Dad." I can't decide if I want to cry or squeal or do a happy dance right now. *Everything...* I'm feeling everything. All the emotions. Every single one.

"No problem, Allie-cat. Make sure to call your Mom later today, she's a bit of a mess right now." He tells me and we exchange love you's, then end the call. I rush back to my bedroom and quickly close the door, shaking him awake like a kid on Christmas morning.

"Teddy, wake up." I continue shaking him.

Nothing. He just rolls over and grumbles about it being too early.

"Novak!" I shove him hard and he sits up quickly and tiredly, yawning.

"What's wrong? What happened?" He rubs his eyes.

"It got approved." I sit on his lap, grabbing his shoulders and facing him.

"What did?" He asks, and his words are followed by another yawn.

"The name change for the arena. Dad just called and said the name change we proposed got approved. The arena is getting dedicated to Adam during homecoming weekend." I reply, throwing my arms all the way around him and pulling him into an embrace.

He slowly lifts his arms around me and tightly presses me against him, squeezing the air out of my lungs.

He pulls out of the kiss, "I'm glad. You three deserve it."

And we roll over into the bed, continuing to kiss each other deeply, passionately, *happily*.

———

Thank fuck it's Friday. Friday means no classes for me, the same can't be said for Teddy, but y'know what? It gives me time to catch up with Ana and Luke and Logan.

Initially, I wanted to catch up with Jenny, but she's still MIA. Has been since move-in. She's not dead or anything, she still responds to our texts, even if it's with a brief "Okay" or "Not tonight."

Who even knows what she's up.

I sit down next to Ana and across from Luke at the coffee shop on campus. Logan sits across from Ana.

"Where's your dog? Did he break off his leash?" Logan teases. I kick him from under the table.

"That's your best friend. Be nice."

Logan puts his hands up defensively, "Oh, I am being nice. I could've called him much, much worse."

I take a sip of my usual iced coffee order, "So what are we all doing here?"

Luke nods in agreement, "Why was this meeting called, Logan?"

"Well," he reaches down to take his laptop out from his

bag and he quickly logs in, reading something, then turning the screen to face us, "Nik and I have been thinking about throwing an apartment party."

"Do Patrick and Teddy know about this?" Luke asks, somewhat annoyed.

Out of the five boys, he's the hardass. It probably has to do with him being the quote on quote father, of the group, but it's a roll he plays well. That demeanor alone was probably enough for him to get the RA job.

"Yes. They've been informed, *Dad*." Logan bites back and Luke flips him off.

"So why are Allie and me here?" Ana looks between her boyfriend and me.

"We want you girls to cohost the party. Both apartments. We lock the bedroom doors with our keys, and invite whoever the fuck we want. I was thinking of inviting the rest of the team, obviously."

"Absolutely not," Luke replies, "Karter and Carson are not invited."

"Dude, it was almost a year ago!" Logan says with annoyance pricking in his voice, "You gotta let it go."

"Let what go?" Ana asks, eyes frantically darting between the two of them.

Oh, I unfortunately know exactly what it is. I heard it from my Dad. In a post-joining the team hazing stunt, Parker Carson and Julian Carter had been making rounds pulling pranks on everyone.

And the one against Luke was below the belt.

They pretty much outed him to the rest of the hockey team after overhearing him talking about it with Logan.

"It's not important." Luke snaps back, now on edge. Ana takes his tone and realizes to not pry any further.

"Fine, they aren't going to be explicitly invited, but I'm not going to be a dick and kick them out. Team unity, or whatever Jesse preaches." Logan replies, turning his attention away from Luke and back to his computer.

"Anyway. We're gonna clear out the living room and it'll be the main party area, the girl's side, if you're in, will be drinks and snacks and shit." Logan replies and Ana nods slowly, listening. Is he seriously proposing we host a hockey party in campus apartments? We're gonna get fined to hell and back for this stunt.

My dad is going to have all of them on the bench if he finds out.

I look to Ana, waiting for her to approve. She thinks for a minute. A silent minute where the four of us exchange awkward glances.

"What if we have it at the beach instead?"

"Like the campus beach, where they have cameras?" Logan retorts. She shakes her head quickly.

"No, the spot up the coast about a mile. Where we…"

It clicks in his head. Oh my god! She had sex on the beach. I turn to her quickly and slap her arm, "And you didn't tell me!"

"It was before we were even back together. Like in October of last year," She shrugs it off as if it's not a big deal, "Besides, me and you didn't start getting close until home-coming and it was before that."

"Dude, you had sex on the beach? Do you know how gross that is?" Luke adds, "Sand has so many disgusting things in it like fecal contaminants from animals, worms, viruses. That's gross as fuck."

Logan nods, "Oh don't remind me. I showered three times after"

He closes the computer, "Anyway, the beach. Good idea, babe. We can have a bonfire, music, and not worry about housing coming to shut it down."

Ana nods, "And it's like a 'End of Summer' type thing. Temperatures are supposed to start dropping by the end of the month."

The door opens and in enters Teddy. My boyfriend. My eyes lock on him immediately as he approaches and the three others turn to see what my gaze is locked on. Unlike most of campus, he does have class on Friday. A lab for his science credit.

"Uh oh, someone's boyfriend is here." Luke mutters. I hear Ana kick him from under the table. He drops his bag and pulls up a chair next to me. His lips find my forehead.

"Hey, pretty girl."

I take his hand, "Hi boyfriend."

He continues to hold my hand, "So what are you guys talking about?"

"Logan had the grand idea of hosting a party in our apartment. Ana changed the location to the beach though." Luke says before taking a bite of his pastry.

"When?" He asks as he steals a bite from Logan's muffin. Logan rolls his eyes.

"Next weekend. It's supposed to be one of the last warm weekends before temperatures start dropping." I add before Logan or Ana can.

Teddy nods, "Sure. Why not? We all throw money in to get alcohol. I'm sure the guys would be willing to help with set-up."

By the guys, he means Patrick and Nik, whom I've saw for all of five minutes since we got back, and Teddy lives with them. I guess they're like Jenny. Always AWOL. Though, as the boys continue conversing, Ana jumping in every few minutes, my gaze is locked onto Teddy. The way that the sage green t-shirt hugs his muscles. A soft dusting of facial hair is growing in on his cheeks and jawline. There are heavy bags under his eyes, as though he's not sleeping much. I believe it. He's been putting in overtime on the ice, staying late at the library. Tragically, it's been the same for me. It's a hard dynamic. We're both so busy, so distracted, that we've been unable to spend much time with each other.

But even in this disheveled state, I find him incredibly sexy. Every part of him is sexy to me.

It's like he was crafted in a lab, specifically for me. He grabs my hand under the table, squeezing it tightly, then, he slowly moves it to his lap.

My hand is fully on top of his bulge while he's conversing with our friends. He's not even reacting. Not outwardly at least.

Underneath my cold hand, he's growing stiffer.

I gulp back a breath, his eyes quickly darting over to me as a smug smile grows across his lips.

Fucker. Two can play that game.

I slowly guide his arm toward me, pressing his hand against my jean shorts, rubbing it against me silently. His arms tense. I can feel every muscle and nerve in his hand tense. He looks over to me.

"Anyway guys, Allie and me had plans for lunch. We can talk about this later, before practice." He excuses himself, withdrawing his hand from me and grabbing his backpack from the floor.

Yes they can.

We stand quickly, then exit the cafe before anyone even has the chance to say goodbye to us and once we're out of earshot from our friends, he stops and turns to face me, grabbing my face with two hands and pulling it close to his.

"You're getting a little wild, Allison Hennings."

"Says the one who had my hand rubbing his bulge, Teddy Novak." I say quietly. He smirks.

"You know what you do to me."

"I do."

I kiss him once, "And now I want you."

We're back in his room, the curtain peeking open as a soft beam of sunlight spills across the floor, illuminating the space with a warm glow. Teddy lifts his shirt off with such ease that it leaves me breathless—a perfect display of his sculpted torso. My heart races, completely captivated. I can no longer resist; I slide my hand into his jeans, feeling the heat radiating from his body. The moment my palm connects, a shiver runs through me, igniting a fire deep within.

"Do you want to taste it?" he asks, his voice low and teasing as he unzips his jeans, the sound almost electric, making my pulse quicken.

I nod, biting my lip in anticipation, and drop to my knees, dragging his jeans and boxers down to the ground with me. He springs free, fully erect, and I wrap my hand around him, gripping tightly at the base, slowly moving my hand up and down, savoring the sensation of him in my palm.

Teddy presses his hands into the mattress, letting out a deep, guttural groan that sends a thrill through me. I can't help but explore, my fingers gliding down to cup his balls, kneading them gently. The way he pulses in my hand drives me wild, and I can feel the tension building between us.

"Just do it," he murmurs, his voice laced with need. I lean forward, teasingly dragging my tongue across the warm tip, feeling him throb against my mouth, and I can't hold back the smile that spreads across my lips.

I focus on the tip, swirling my tongue while my hand maintains a steady rhythm on the shaft. His large hand finds my hair, tangling in the blonde strands, and he doesn't push me, just holds me there as I take him deeper, relishing the sounds escaping his lips. With each movement, I explore what makes him moan, taking him more fully, and soon a warm liquid beads at the tip. It's intoxicating to see the plea-sure dance across his features.

"Fuck, Allie," he growls, and I can't help but release him from my mouth, springing up to capture his lips in a desperate kiss. Our mouths clash together, urgency boiling over as I trail kisses down his neck, across his collarbone, until I reach his muscular pecs. I tease his nipple with my tongue, the sound he makes is something primal and raw, sending shivers down my spine.

"Again," he gasps, and I oblige, sucking harder, leaving small, purplish marks on his chest. I want him to remember this moment, to remember me. He watches, his eyes dark and pleading, simmering with desire and anticipation.

I smirk up at him, my hand wrapping around him once more, moving back and forth while I pepper kisses along his skin, tasting the sweet, salty taste of him. Each stroke drives him closer to the edge.

Without warning, he releases, his pent-up desire exploding onto me, as it's between the two of us, and before I can fully process what just happened, he flips me over, pinning me back against the bed. The sudden shift leaves me breathless, and in one swift motion, he tears off my shorts, tossing them aside like they're nothing.

"Fuck," I gasp as he rips my panties apart again, his face burying itself between my legs like it was made to rest there, tongue flitting against me like a thirsty animal. I squeeze my thighs around his head, pulling him closer, my legs draping over his shoulders. With every flick of his tongue, he dives deeper into my pleasure, igniting a fire that spreads through me.

"You taste so fucking good, babe. Like drugs, but better," he breathes, his voice muffled against my skin. The moment he dives back in, I can't contain my moan; it escapes my lips uncontrollably, a symphony of pleasure as he licks and sucks, driving me into a euphoric haze.

He drinks me in, slurping up every ounce of pleasure I give him, and I feel my body arch off the bed, teetering on the edge of bliss. Just as I'm about to tumble over into ecstasy, he lowers me back down, my head spinning from the intensity of my orgasm. The world around me fades away, leaving only the warmth of his touch and the pounding of my heart.

Lying next to me, he wraps his arms around me, his body a comforting weight as I come down from the high. "I think I love you, Teddy," I whisper, still buzzing from our connection, the intimacy of the moment wrapping around us like a warm blanket.

"I think I love you too, Allison," he replies softly, pressing a tender kiss to my forehead. I can feel my heart swell, a mix of euphoria and security flooding through me. In this moment, I think I could spend forever in his arms, lost in the warmth of his love, the passion we just shared, and the promise of what's to come.

―――――

TEDDY NOVAK

I cannot get her off my mind. Even hours later, after we just laid together in silence, holding each other, the thought of her lingers in my mind and my dick stirs in my jock at practice.

I skate quickly, shooting the puck to Luke, who then shoots it at the goal. Jesse blows the whistle and we all return.

"That was good guys. You're all looking good out there, but do you think you're good enough to beat Virginia U in two weeks?" He has a stern, serious look in his eyes, though, I can't meet his gaze. His eyes are the same as his daughters, and whenever I stare into them too long, all I see is her looking up at me as she hungrily sucks my-

"Novak, do you think you're ready?" Jesse snaps me out of the thought. I briefly meet his gaze and nod. Jesse's eyes are dark, something is different in them. Something that scares the fuck out of me.

I nod, "Yes, sir."

"Then go sit on the bench." He points to the bench, sliding another player into my place.

What?

I look to Luke, then Logan and Nik. They look equally confused.

"Wait, why?" I ask. He looks to me again.

"Bench. Now." He commands. *Fuck.*

I skate over to the box, stepping in and taking off my helmet and gloves. I tip back my water bottle and Coach blows his whistle, the team returns to skating and going through out plays and Jesse enters the box, closing the glass panel behind him.

Fuck. Did Allie tell him? She wouldn't, right?

He sits down next to me, silent for a moment. His hand rubs at his jaw.

Oh he knows. He totally fucking knows.

He turns to face me, a stern, upset look on his face. It's not filled with anger, just confusion

"Teddy. When I told you that you could stay with us for the summer, what was one of my rules?" A pained look comes across his face.

Oh fuck. He absolutely knows. Why didn't Allie warn me that she was going to tell him? Everything feels hot, as though I'm suffocating in my equipment.

"I told you to play nice," He clarifies, nodding, "And from the sounds of what I've been told, it sounds like you played too nicely with my daughter."

"Listen Coach, I wanted to tell you with her, but I under-stand why she-"

"She didn't. The athletic director saw you two kissing outside the cafe earlier today. He brought up to me this after-noon." He adds, "Allison still has no idea that I know."

"Coach, I'm sorry." I stammer

He holds up a hand, stopping me, "No apologies. Just promise me something."

I nod quickly. He's not mad? This is weird as fuck?

"Anything, Coach." I nod. It's a lie though. If he asked me to break up with her tonight, I don't think I would even consider doing it. I would rather quit the team, if I meant I got to spend the rest of my life with her.

"Don't break her heart. She's gone through a lot this year and the last thing I need is to find out you were just playing her to get something out of it." He adds, a softness in his voice. Something that rocks me to my core.

"Coach, respectfully, I would never, ever intentionally hurt her in anyway. Ever. She has changed my life in so many ways I could never imagine. She's made me feel more loved than I have in my entire life." I confess to him and he processes this for a second.

"You really love her? This isn't just a game?"

I shake my head, "It hasn't ever been a game, Coach. She's always been the one."

"Even when I asked you to move in with us?" The question lingers in a gaze between the two of us.

"Respectfully, again, sir, I think I've had feelings for Allie since the day I met her."

He really sits on this and processes it. I can almost see his mind running a million miles a minute as the information sinks in and he processes this.

"Are you two together, together? Like dating? Or is it just casual."

Without even taking a second to think, "There is nothing casual about the way I feel about Allison."

He nods, "Good. I want you to join us for dinner on Sunday. I'm sure Martie will want to know everything."

"Sir, I think Martie already knows?"

Now that has him really shocked, "What?"

"I think she already knows? I've heard Allie talking to her about us on the phone. I dunno how long she's known, but I think she does." I tell him, attempting to control every emotion in my body as my heartbeat increases and every-thing feels clammy.

"Well, I'll have to talk to her, but I have a feeling she didn't say anything because she wanted you two to tell me," He starts, then sets down his clipboard, "Which I would have appreciated being told by you both and not from the A.D, but I'm glad that you didn't lie to me about it and were honest about the way you feel towards her."

I nod in response, "I'll always be honest about the way I feel towards her. Out of all the fake bullshit in life, Allie is the realest, purest part of my life, and I won't give her up."

I can almost see his eyes swelling as tears brim. I have a feeling that I've brought him to tears. He gives me a soft, fatherly smile.

"Good. Take care of her, Teddy. She deserves it."

"I will always take care of her."

A moment of silence passes before Coach holds out his hand. I shake it firmly.

"Out of everyone, I'm glad it was you." He admits. I nod, looking at him for a second.

"Why?"

"Because you remind me of a younger me." He nods, "And when you finally grow into a fully grown adult, I want you both to have the love that me and her mother have."

Now tears form in the corners of my eyes as I realize the magnitude of it all. He's giving us his blessing to be together. There was no fight, there was no getting kicked off the team or yelled at or losing everything I fought so hard for.

Just a father who wanted to know what my intentions were with his daughter, wanting to know if they are pure, and they are.

Every single thing that I said about Allie is true. Every word that came off my tongue, every held back thought and question. It's true. It's always been Allie.

As if she heard her name, I can see her blonde hair enter

the arena from the other side. Coach sees her and smiles, then waves.

"Look's like it's time for me to have a conversation with her. Get back out there and lead practice until I get back, kid." He rises and walks off, leaving me alone, wonderstruck.

So this is what real love feels like?

It's like a drug.

A pure, all-natural, all-consuming drug that has taken over every bit of my life and leaves me craving more and more. I pull my helmet back on, and head back onto the ice, feeling warmer than ever.

CHAPTER 23
ALLIE HENNINGS

"Allison Hennings, get over here!" Ana shouts, her voice cutting through the salty air as she builds out the fire pit with meticulous care.

With T-Minus two hours until the beach party, my excitement is mingled with anxiety—not a single glimpse of my boyfriend, Teddy, yet. Ana, Logan, Nik, Patrick, and I are busy setting up at the beach while Teddy and Luke are off on some side quest, presumably gathering supplies or plotting mischief somewhere unseen.

Jenny has finally decided to grace us with her presence, unloading supplies from Logan's jeep with Riley by her side. As they work, I can't help but watch her. Jenny is... complicated. When we first met in freshman year, we spent countless hours together, sharing laughs and late-night talks. But after she returned from Christmas break, it was like she transformed. She started going out more, vanishing into the night, and I would be lucky to steal an hour of her time. My heart sinks at the thought of how our friendship has faded; she's barely around since Ana moved in during sophomore year.

Her dark brown hair, nearly black, is pulled back into two tight braids, accentuating her pale skin that seems to glow under the sun. She stands out in her bikini top and worn denim shorts, looking ready for a summer adventure.

As I approach the group, I see Riley and Jenny struggling to set down a laundry basket filled with firewood.

"This thing weighs nine hundred pounds," Jenny complains, massaging her arms after finally dropping it to the sand.

Riley, with an eye-roll, quips back, "Maybe if you lifted more than a seltzer, you could actually carry it."

Jenny shoots her a look that could kill, one that warns her to tread lightly. It reminds me of what Teddy said during move out a few months ago.

Whatever. I turn my attention back to Ana, who is aligning rocks in a circle for the fire pit. I squat down beside her and grab a rock, placing it next to the one she just set down.

"So, Logan told me that your dad found out about you and Teddy?" Ana probes, brushing sand off her hands as she glances at me.

We haven't had much time to catch up this week, what with her new position at the school paper and my own practice schedule.

"Yeah, apparently the AD saw us kissing outside the cafe, and he snitched to Jesse," I reply with a sigh, recalling the awkward conversation that followed.

Ana turns to face me, our knees nearly touching as we crouch by the rocks. "How'd he take it?"

"He wasn't mad, just… disappointed that we didn't tell him ourselves. He said as long as Teddy and I are serious and he makes me happy, that's what really matters."

Ana nods, her brow furrowing in thought. "I would've expected something more cliché, like him forbidding you from seeing Teddy or threatening to kick him off the team if he doesn't break up with you."

Thank God that wasn't the case. Teddy has always

worried about the repercussions of our relationship, fearful of being punished for falling in love. I don't want to be the reason his hockey career suffers. So, I'm grateful my dad isn't the heavy-handed type.

"From my dad? Nah. He can be a hardass, but he's not an asshole. I don't think he'd jeopardize Teddy's career over a relationship, nor would he risk his relationship with me by destroying my happiness," I assure her.

Logan bounds over, cutting into our conversation, "Teddy and Luke just got here with the booze. Need some help?"

Ana stands, nodding in agreement. "Yeah, baby. Just give us a second."

She quickly pecks his lips, and he walks off to help. I rise and face her, a warm smile spreading across my face.

"I'm glad you finally found your person, Allie. You deserve it," she says, taking my hand and squeezing it tightly. I pull her into a hug, feeling grateful for this moment.

"You are my best friend, Ann," I say, squeezing her back tightly. "I don't know if I tell you that enough, but you really are my platonic soulmate."

I'm not sure if she knows it, but Ana is like a sister to me. We've only known each other for a year, yet that time has forged a bond that feels unbreakable.

"Girls!" Logan shouts from a distance, as he and Luke struggle to unload a plastic kiddie pool from the back of Luke's SUV.

We break apart from our embrace and hurry over to join the others in finishing the setup. Teddy is unloading bags of ice from the car, dropping them into the sand. He's only in his shorts, the sun glistening off his toned body, and I can't help but admire the way the light catches on his skin, revealing a thin sheen of sweat.

Damn, my boyfriend is incredibly sexy.

"Allie! We all know Teddy is hot. Stop staring and help

us," Patrick teases, unloading a pack of beer and dropping it next to the kiddie pool.

"Fuck off, Pat," I reply, flipping him off playfully as I side-hug Teddy, trying to steal a moment with him.

Patrick's blonde hair dances in the light breeze as he playfully pretends to be offended, his deep caramel eyes twinkling with mischief. He and Logan really could pass as brothers—they share the same casual charm and nearly identical haircuts.

When I first met this group of boys at the barbecue, I genuinely thought they were twins. Turns out they're just two typical blonde dudes with similar styles.

I grab a smaller bag of ice from Teddy's arms, carrying it over to the growing pile and dropping it on top. The plan, at least what Logan envisioned, is to fill the kiddie pool with ice and toss in our drinks to create an open bar.

Ana and I both agreed the idea is a bit unsanitary, so we brought our own cooler filled with drinks just for us—me, her, Riley, and Lauren.

Luke's sister was supposed to help us, but she got caught up in a lab and won't be out until ten p.m. She promised to make an appearance, but I know the last thing anyone wants to do after a four-hour lab session is party. I spent enough time in the Biology department last year for my natural sciences course to know that it's not worth it.

Once the group finishes unloading everything from the SUV, we quickly set everything up, leaving us with an hour to spare before the party starts. Everyone scatters, and Teddy takes my hand, leading me up the beach.

His grip is calloused yet secure, and I squeeze back with enthusiasm. We find a quiet spot further down the shore, plopping down into the warm sand. I settle between his thighs, leaning back against his chest, feeling the steady rhythm of his heartbeat.

"You're pretty hot, Allison. Even when you're grumpy," he says, a soft laugh escaping his lips. I playfully slap my palm against his chest.

"I'm not grumpy!"

"Sure about that? You've had a resting bitch face since we finished unloading everything," he replies, his teasing tone bringing an eye roll from me.

He's ridiculous sometimes. I can't help but think how lucky I am to have him in my life.

"No, I didn't!" I defend, and he laughs, propping himself on his hands and spinning me to face him.

"Uh, I'm pretty sure you do, babe."

He pulls out his phone, snapping a picture of me. I gasp, attempting to snatch it away.

"I don't!" I protest, but he turns the screen to show me the evidence, and I can't help but frown.

"You're just saying that to get me going, aren't you?" I accuse, seeing the laughter bubbling in his eyes.

He shakes his head, but the mischievous glint in his expression says otherwise. I shove him back playfully, and he falls into the sand, laughing, and I crawl over him, feeling the heat radiating between us. Just from pressing against me, I can feel him harden in his shorts.

"You wanna play that way? Saying I have a resting bitch face?"

"You better choose your next words wisely, pretty girl," he replies, that devilish smirk returning—the same one that ignited my feelings for him last summer.

"Oh yeah? What are you going to do about it, handsome?"

"This," he says, tossing me back into the sand, now mounted over me, laughter spilling from both our lips. He holds my hands down in the warm grains.

"Now what are you going to do about it?" he challenges, teasingly.

I respond by lifting my thighs off the ground and rocking

against him. He tenses, his grip on my wrists tightening in surprise.

"Alright, you're playing unfairly. Someone needs to get punished." He lifts me off the sand and throws me over his shoulder.

Oh, I know exactly what he's doing.

"Teddy! Put me down! Don't you dare! I don't have a change of clothes!" But my protests come too late—he leaps into the water, diving forward and taking me under with him.

We're submerged for only a second before we break the surface, and I shove salty water towards him, splashing him playfully.

He retaliates, splashing me back with a laugh that echoes like a howl through the air.

"You ass!" I shout, sputtering as I get a mouthful of ocean water. He trudges forward, dragging me under again. But before we can break the surface, he glides close and presses his lips against mine, even underwater, finding a way to kiss me.

We break the surface, still connected, and continue to kiss, both of us treading water. It feels like a scene straight out of a movie.

Well, until we're interrupted by the shrill sound of a whistle. We break apart, and Logan stands on the shore, arms crossed.

"Break it up, you two! We don't need you to end up on a list!"

Teddy flips him off, and we both dissolve into laughter.

"Well then, you heard the man. Guess we can't make out in the ocean?" I tease.

"No, but we can at the apartment after I get changed?"

I don't need to say anything more; he throws me over his shoulder once again, carrying me back to the shore.

We're late to our own party, which is embarrassing, but worth it since we spent nearly all that time making out. By the time we return, the sun has set, and the beach is filled with classmates—at least sixty or seventy people here, dancing and chatting. Two massive speakers pump out frat party classics, creating an infectious energy that buzzes in the air.

We find Luke, who is talking to Lauren and a guy I've never seen before.

"There you two are! We thought you bailed on the party," Luke laughs, holding a can of something in his hand. Teddy and Luke dive into conversation about hockey, while I turn to Lauren.

"I thought you had lab?" I ask, curious.

"I rushed through the last part to get out early," she replies quickly, glancing at the new guy beside her. I wonder if he's the one she's mentioned at practice.

He's shorter than me, about five-four or five-five, lanky with curly auburn hair, and wearing a Hozier t-shirt that seems to clash with the tank tops and swim trunks the other guys are sporting.

Lauren must catch me looking at him, because she yanks him toward us. "This is Noah; he's new to Allister and friends with my brother."

The boy smiles shyly and holds out a clammy hand. I shake it, noting the nervousness radiating from him.

"Allie," I introduce myself, trying to put him at ease. "Are you a freshman?"

"No, actually, I'm a junior. I transferred from Virginia University."

Oh.

So this is the—

Okay, that explains the skittishness, the quietness. I glance at Lauren, who gives me a subtle nod of confirmation.

"So, how are you liking Allister so far?" I ask, hoping to make this less awkward for him.

He shrugs, his shoulders relaxing slightly. "It's not bad.

Better than my old school. I actually just got a job at the paper earlier today."

"Oh really? My roommate, Ana, is the editor-in-chief of the paper! Did you meet her?"

He nods, his demeanor softening as he speaks. "I did! She was super sweet. I'm a photographer, so I'll be around campus taking pictures of different events."

"Oh cool!" I reply, glancing at Lauren as excitement bubbles in my chest—Ana will love having someone like him on the team.

"Do you want to go grab a drink quickly? From Ana's cooler?" I suggest.

She nods, "We'll be right back, Noah."

He nods, turning back to Luke, who seems engrossed in his conversation with Teddy.

As we walk off toward Logan's jeep, I lean closer to Lauren. "So, it's a little odd that Luke invited a random student of his, right?"

She nods quickly, glancing back at Noah. "I'm pretty sure Luke is into him, but it's murky territory. Apparently, Luke had to talk him out of a panic attack the other night, and they ended up spending the night together."

"Really?" I ponder aloud, considering the implications. It's not surprising—there aren't many openly gay guys at Allister, and Noah seems to exude that brooding, angsty energy, much like Luke.

But beyond that, I don't see them having much in common. Then again, Teddy and I don't have a lot in common either, and neither do Logan and Ana.

"Do you think Luke even has time for a relationship? Between hockey, lab, and being an R.A.?"

Lauren shrugs, "I doubt it, but you know Luke—always has way too much on his plate for just one person."

She's not wrong.

"Well, I hope he's careful. Someone with immense trauma

is going to be harder to deal with than a regular relationship," I remark, recalling the whispers I've heard about Noah's past.

"You're telling me," Lauren replies, her tone suddenly heavy.

"What?" I ask, sensing an odd shift in her mood.

She shakes it off, taking a sip of her drink. "Just some stuff that happened back home. It's not important."

"Lauren, you know you can tell me anything, right? You're literally my dance daughter." I nudge her gently, hoping to coax her into sharing.

She sighs, glancing around as if assessing who might be listening. "What I'm going to tell you stays between us. It doesn't go beyond either of us, okay?"

"Laur, you're scaring me a bit. Are you okay?" I ask, concern washing over me.

"I'm fine. Luke is fine. Now, at least."

She leans in, and I can feel her hesitance as she tells me a secret that changes my entire perspective on Luke and Lauren. It's heavy, a truth that could alter everything if it ever got out, but I made a promise, and I'm determined to keep it.

Suddenly, everything makes sense.

TEDDY NOVAK

After Luke introduces me to his new friend, Noah, who I'm pretty sure he's into, the three of us walk away to find the other guys. Noah trails a few feet behind us, still seeming a bit shy.

Once he mentioned where he came from, it clicked for me —the skittishness, the quietness, the brooding nature. He's the guy who was attacked last year. I don't bring it up though; I don't want to put him on edge.

"Noah, what are you into?" I ask, turning to face him as we walk.

"Photography, music, writing. The usual artsy-fartsy stuff," he replies, shrugging slightly.

I nod, thinking he would probably get along really well with Ana. She's into similar interests. "You watch hockey?"

He shakes his head quickly, looking almost horrified. "No, no, no. I used to watch football games at Virginia U with my friends, but never hockey. Doesn't Virginia U kind of suck anyway?"

He's not wrong. We usually open the season against them and smoke them. Last year, we were up ten in the third period. It got heated fast, and things turned messy when one of their guys swung on Nik. By the end of the night, Nik had three stitches in his forehead and a busted nose.

Sore fucking losers.

"Yeah, they kinda suck. We've beaten them in all four times we've played against them," I jest, shooting a glance at Luke, who rolls his eyes at my banter.

"Oh, so that's your nickname? Lukey?" Noah teases, a playful smile tugging at his lips, and it feels like he's flirting with him.

Luke sighs, clearly unimpressed. "Look what you started, Theodore."

"Your name is Theodore?" Noah snaps back at me, surprise evident in his expression.

"Just Teddy."

"To everyone except Allison," Luke interjects, and I cock my head at him.

Once we find Logan and Ana, they're dancing near the fire, swaying against each other in a playful rhythm. Luke pulls Logan by the shoulder, his expression serious.

"Dude, seriously?" Logan asks, glancing between us.

"I want to introduce you to someone," Luke says sternly.

Logan looks confused, then his eyes dart to Noah. Ana beams when she sees Noah, her excitement palpable.

"This is Noah Karey. He's a transfer student to Allister from Virginia U. He just started working with your fiancé," Luke introduces them, and Logan awkwardly extends his hand. Noah shakes it quickly, still nervous.

Luke turns to Noah, "You already know Ana, but this is her fiancé, Logan."

"I didn't realize you and Luke were friends!" Ana says, her enthusiasm infectious.

Noah nods, "He lives next door to me. He's my RA."

Ana's eyes dart between Luke and Noah, piecing together what I've already figured out. Luke's got a crush on the new kid.

I don't see that working out very well. Luke doesn't have time for a relationship, and I doubt Noah will be patient enough to wait for the right moment.

A second later, Allie and Lauren return, and Allie jokingly shoves Ana's shoulder. "You bitch! You've been handing out drinks from our secret stash, haven't you?"

Ana shakes her head, a coy smile on her lips. "No?"

"Liar."

"Okay fine, just to a few of my coworkers from the paper. How many do we have left?"

Allie laughs, "Well, once Lauren and I are done, none."

"Fuck," Ana mutters, turning toward her boyfriend. "You haven't drunk anything, right? Can you take me back to the apartment?"

"I drank two. I'm not driving, Ann," Logan replies, his tone firm but light-hearted.

I raise my hand. "I haven't drunk anything yet."

"Can you and Allie drive me back to the apartment?" she asks, looking hopeful. I glance at Allie, who seems to be pondering it.

"Only if we can take the Jeep. We walked over here," Allie says, her eyes sparkling with excitement.

Logan grumbles, reaching into his pocket to pull out his keys. "A scratch and you're dead. You hear me?"

"I got you, Captain," I say with mock formality, earning a laugh as he shoves my shoulder playfully.

Ana leads the way back to Logan's Jeep, her energy infectious as she skips ahead, nearly bouncing with anticipation. Allie takes my hand in hers as we walk, and I can't help but smile at the warmth of her touch.

"What if we just don't come back to the party tonight? I'm just not really feeling it, to be honest," Allie proposes, her expression turning serious.

I shrug, sensing something's on her mind. "Is that what you want to do?"

She nods, her gaze distant. I can see something is bothering her.

"Is everything okay, Allie?" I ask gently, my concern deepening.

"Yeah. I think so," she starts hesitantly. "I can't talk about it because I was sworn to secrecy by Lauren, but she told me something that's just bothering me."

"What was it? You don't have to share details or anything," I reassure her as we reach the Jeep.

"Just something that's super personal, life-altering really. It's about their family," she shares, her brow furrowed.

As she speaks, the gravity of her words sinks in. It sounds serious. I nod slowly, understanding that whatever it is, it's weighing on her.

"Alright, let's drop off Ana and then we can talk more, okay?" I suggest, trying to keep the conversation light.

"Yeah, that sounds good." She smiles, but it doesn't quite reach her eyes.

Ana hops into the backseat, her earlier enthusiasm still

buzzing. "Allie! Come sit with me!" she shouts, her voice playful.

Allie rolls her eyes but laughs. "Alright, Ann." She turns to me before we get in. "We can drop her off and just go back to the apartment if that's okay with you."

"Whatever you want to do, pretty girl," I reply, caressing her cheek and leaning in to give her a quick kiss before we all pile into the Jeep.

The air is warm, and the hum of the engine fills the silence as I drive under the darkening sky. My palms wrap around the steering wheel, and I feel a sense of ease wash over me, mixed with a hint of anxiety about the conversation ahead.

I've driven Logan's Jeep before, mostly after practices or games when he's been injured, so the handling isn't new to me. But tonight, the atmosphere feels different, almost charged.

I slow down at a stop sign, pressing my sandal down firmly on the brake pedal, but it feels loose—too loose. My foot sinks all the way to the floor, and panic races through me as the Jeep doesn't slow.

"Teddy, why aren't you stopping?" Ana asks, her voice filled with concern as she notices the speed we're carrying.

"I'm trying to," I reply, my heart beginning to pound.

I push down with every muscle in my leg, nearly standing up to apply more pressure on the brake pedal, but the Jeep continues to roll forward, completely unresponsive.

"Allie, call 911. Tell them the brakes seem to be broken in the Jeep," I instruct her, my voice steady but urgent.

"What?" Both girls shout in unison from the backseat, their expressions shifting from playful to alarmed. Allie pulls out her phone, and I see Ana doing the same, presumably to call Logan.

As the lapse in time stretches on, I glance at the intersection, my heart racing. A car speeds through the stop sign, barreling toward us. There's no time to react, no time for anything but sheer instinct. I attempt to swerve, but it's too late.

The collision is sudden and jarring, metal crunching as the other vehicle slams into the side of Logan's Jeep. A blinding flash of pain shoots through my body as the world around me erupts in chaos.

The impact sends us spinning, and the last thing I remember is the sound of glass shattering and the sensation of everything tumbling in slow motion.

CHAPTER 24
ALLIE HENNINGS

open my eyes and my parents are standing at my side. Tears are in my mom's eyes and my dad wears a look of concern. There's a tight pressure against my head.

"What happened?" My voice comes out groggy.

"You were in a car accident, Als." Dad tells me with a sullen look on his face. The small reminder takes me back to the jeep.

It happened to quickly, like a blink, quickly. Another guy sped through the stop sign. The feeling of being thrown about the jeep felt like being thrown into a free-fall. I remember the shattering of the glass, the sound of Ana screaming.

"What happened? Where's Ana and Teddy?" I asks shakily and my mom takes my hand in her's, squeezing it tightly.

"Ana is next door. She just has a concussion. Teddy is in the intensive care unit," My heart drops at those words. A chill comes over my body and I feel sick to my stomach. I sit up quickly, but my Dad puts his hands out to press me slowly back down onto the bed, "Allie, honey, no. You broke your ribcage. Don't get up."

A sharp pain shoots through the left side of my chest and

my eyes move down. I'm in a hospital gown. I lift it up, the blanket covering my lower half. There's a tight wrapping around my chest.

"I broke my ribs?"

"Just a few of them, hun. On the left side, from the seatbelt. You and Ana are lucky to walk away with minor injuries." Mom says, moving closer to me and tucking a strand of hair behind my ear.

"What happened to Teddy? Why's he in the ICU? Isn't that bad?"

They look between each other, "He has a few injuries, but he's in the ICU for a small puncture in his lung. He'll be okay."

What? A few?

"What else?"

They say nothing, "What other injuries does he have?"

Dad sighs, looking hurt by this, "He has an ACL and meniscus tear. A severe one. He might never get back to playing the way that he used to."

Everything feels like it's spinning. He just got over the anxiety that came from our relationship in relation to his career in hockey and now this? He may never be able to play like he used to? His entire career could've just ended because of an accident. Something completely out of his control, but I know it's something he's going to blame himself for.

It was not his fault at all. He couldn't have known.

"What happened with the jeep? The breaks weren't working and we couldn't stop."

"The break line had ruptured from debris. The jeep was older, as you know and apparently something had clipping the break line, causing it to leak fluid. The police department said it could've been something as insignificant as a pothole or a bigger rock in the road." Mom adds and Dad nods softly.

They both take a hand in theirs, "Are you okay?"

"I'm sore, and a little confused, but I'm more so worried

about Teddy? Is he awake? Does he know yet? How did he take it?" The words come out quickly and my side aches again. It's a burning, stinging pain. One similar to the feeling as when I broke my arm as a little kid, except it's my fucking ribcage.

"He hasn't woken up yet, but he's stable. They have him out for the pain." Dad replies, "His Mom is in the lobby, though. I almost told her to fuck off."

I don't blame him. After everything Teddy has told me about her, she is the last person he's going to want to see when he wakes up.

"Was she alone?"

Mom shakes her head, "She has a newborn and a man with her."

"She had her baby." I mutter. They look at me.

"What?"

"Fourth of July weekend, she told Teddy she was pregnant. She wanted him to give her another chance and he said no. When he told me, I didn't think she was THAT pregnant. She has to be freshly postpartum." I reply and they listen. My Mom's eyes rise in shock and my Dad looks fucking pissed off.

"I'm going to tell her to leave. She doesn't get to just waltz back into his life like this." He rises from sitting on the foot of my bed. My mom grabs him by the arm, stopping him.

"Jesse Adam Hennings, sit down right now."

And it reminds me that my parents were so close to losing their other kid tonight. I could have died. My parents would've lost me, seventeen years after losing Adam. Tears swell and burn in the corners of my eyes and they both look to me.

"Allie? What's wrong?" Mom asks, rushing closer and wiping my tears with the sleeve of her grey hoodie.

"I just," I pause, attempting to control my emotions, "I

was just thinking about how freaked out you two were. You could've lost your other kid tonight. I could have died."

My Dad leans toward me and presses himself against me in an embrace and my Mom holds my shoulder tightly, rubbing her thumb up and down against it.

"But you didn't die, Allison. You're here. We're all here." He says and I can hear the emotions breaking through, he slowly releases and sets me back down against the bed.

"The only thing that died tonight, was Logan's shitty jeep, which everyone has been telling him to get rid of for years now."

I stifle back a pained laugh, "Yeah. The first time I rode in his jeep freshman year, I told him he needs to get rid of it."

They both nod, then there's a knock on the door. It's Logan, Luke and Lauren.

"Looks like you have visitors," Mom smiles, "Your father and I are going to check on Ana and Teddy."

They rise and head toward the door, opening it and my three friends enter. My parents quickly exit and slowly the door behind themselves. Lauren's eyes are red and puffy. Logan laughs quietly, holding a bottle of water. He sets it on the small table next to the bed.

"Thought I told you guys to not leave a scratch?" He jokes and slowly hugs me, being careful to not hurt me. I smile back at him. Even though he's telling jokes, I can see a haunted look in his eyes. One that is blaming himself for this.

"Well, it's not our fault your jeep was a piece of shit."

He grabs at his chest, "Wow, rude."

I do a half shrug, not moving my left side, "It's the truth. How's Ana?"

"She's kinda loopy and only has the concussion," Logan replies. Lauren nods.

"I'm so glad you're all okay though." She squeezes me tightly into a hug and I wince. Luke clears his throat and she quickly releases, "Shit, I'm sorry."

"It's okay, Laur."

She nods, "So, has anyone checked on Teddy?"

"They won't let anyone see him. He's out of it in the ICU right now," Luke starts, pulling up a chair, "But it's not good, not for his career, at least. He'll live a normal life, it just might be one without hockey."

That's what I feared. Teddy losing hockey is like a bird losing wings. I don't know how he could possibly function without that aspect of his life. It's so important to him, that I fear how it'll affect him if he loses it.

"How do you think he'll handle it?"

Luke shrugs, "Well, before you, I would've said that it would wreck him. But I dunno, since you two have been together, he seems to be taking it less seriously."

Logan cuts in, "Not as though he's not putting in effort, just that, it doesn't seem like he sees hockey as the be all, end all anymore. I don't know what he's thinking, but that's just the way he has seemed to all of us."

I process this information. I hadn't even noticed a change in him. Has he even noticed it? He had to of, if all of his team-mates have noticed it. Right?

It's all so confusing and makes me feel dizzy. How long has he been changing like this? Is it because of me? I spend the next half-hour chatting with my friends. Talking about the rest of the party. About Ana.

And Teddy.

They eventually leave and I'm left alone. Just me and my thoughts in the bleak hospital grey.

The soft sound of the heart monitor beeps, the soft hum of the air conditioner groans. I slowly reach my arm over to the table where my bag of belongings sits and I grab my phone. It's been nearly twenty-four hours since the party. It's eight p.m. the following day. Teddy still, as far as I know, hasn't woken up. Ana and me, according to Luke, are supposed to be released tomorrow morning.

I open the notes app on my phone and my fingers press at the buttons as I type out everything swirling in my messy, overwhelmed mind.

> *Dear Adam,*
> *Last night, Mom and Dad almost lost their second child.*
> *Me.*
> *I was in a pretty bad car accident with Teddy and my roommate Ana. Apparently the breaks were bad in Logan, Ana's fiancé's, Jeep and we were hit by a car and thrown into a ditch.*
> *I was inches away from meeting a similar fate as you. Gone. My mind is really struggling to comprehend it. The fact that I was inches away from knocking on death's door. I was so close to meeting the same fate as you and making our parents childless. The concept that I could have died and left them with nothing... it hurts. It reminds me that we've lost you and puts that loss into a perspective I didn't truly understand before. I knew about you. I knew you were my brother and I grieved you, but I don't think I necessarily understood the impact your death had on Mom and Dad until today. I can't even imagine the pain that they're feeling. The anxiety and the hurt and the grief that they nearly lost me, too.*
> *On top of that, I'm struggling with the fact that my boyfriend is about to find out that his dream has been taken away from him because of one*

accident that was nobodies fault in the first place. It makes me feel physically sick, realizing that everything he has worked so hard to achieve, through all the blood, sweat and tears. Even through his anxiety disorder and the panic attacks. He has gone through so much. But then again, we all have. We all have gone through so, so much in our lives. I lost you, I forgot about you, then I found you again and this time, I won't forget. I won't forget you again, Adam. Just like how I will be there to support Teddy through whatever life throws at him, even if that means helping him craft a future that doesn't include playing hockey. What would you have done, Adam? If you had someone you really cared about who had to give up something they loved because of something that happened? Hypothetically speaking, as you are eternally six, but how would you, as an adult, have reacted to something like this? I'd like to think you would react like Dad. You would acknowledge that it sucks, but you wouldn't give up with them. You would help them fight for the future that they deserve.

So that's what I'm going to do. I'm going to help Teddy craft the future that he deserves. Even if that doesn't include hockey.

Love,

Allie <3

I stare at the words typed on my screen, reading them back and realizing the absolute ramble I wrote out. I bite my lip to stop the tears from falling once again and I throw my head back into my pillow, closing my eyes and allowing myself to drown in the moment.

———

TEDDY NOVAK

Everything hurts.

Every bone in my body is burning and screaming in agony. I feel like *Doctor Strange* after he was in a car accident and nearly died. My eyes slowly move down my bed, my knee propped up in a brace. I attempt to wiggle my toes, trying to gauge what happened. A stinging feeling moves up my leg and into my thigh. I wince in pain. I'm wearing nothing but the same boxer briefs I was wearing to the party. A tube sticks out of my side, connected to a machine.

What the fuck happened to me? I remember everything up until the other car struck Logan's jeep. Everything after that was dark.

I slowly reach my arm for the small remote attached to the bed and page a nurse. I need a drink. I need answers.

My mouth feels like sand paper, my body feels like I've been repeatedly body checked on the ice. I definitely have some kind of break or tear, if I'm in a brace.

A second later, a nurse rushes into the room and sees me, "Welcome back, Mr. Novak."

"What…" my voice trails, "What happened?"

"You were in an accident with some friends. Is there anything I can get for you while you wait for the doctor?" She asks, coming over and checking the monitor. She quickly writes down information I don't understand onto an iPad.

"Water. Please."

She nods, "Right away. The doctor will be here momentarily."

"Wait-"

She stops as she grabs the handle, turning to face me, "Where's Allie? Where's my Allie?"

She leaves the door closed, coming over to me, "I can't give you information, but I will tell you that she is awake and okay. Is there anyone you would like to see, besides her."

"Is her father here? Jesse Hennings? He's my coach." I mumble and she nods.

"I'll send him right in."

She leaves and the silence is piercing. It's deafening. It hurts.

Well, technically, everything hurts. Every bone in my body hurts. My head is pounding. My leg feels fucked. Everything is completely fucked.

I know that they have me doped up on pills right now, because if they didn't, I would be on the verge of having an anxiety attack right about now.

I attempt to take a deep breath to calm my mind, but even that hurts. The door opens and Jesse enters. He looks disheveled. His grayish hair a mess, his blue eyes tired. He's wearing a t-shirt and sweatpants. I don't think I've ever saw him like this. Even the night that they told Allie about Adam, he looked more put together.

"Hey kiddo." He mutters quietly as he approaches, "How are you doing?"

"Everything hurts." I reply flatly. He smiles tiredly and nods, sitting on the edge of my bed.

"I bet. You got the worst of it."

I did?

"What happened to Allie? Ana?"

"Allie just has a couple of broken ribs and bruises. She'll be okay. Ana has a concussion and some scratches. Had to get stitches in her eyebrow, but they said it'll heal quickly."

A glum silence lingers between me and my coach as we process what happened. I don't want to ask the question about what happened to my knee, because I fear I know the answer.

"And me?"

"Teddy, uh-" He's interrupted by the doctor entering the room. He's an older gentlemen, older than Jesse, at least. He's bald and tall, not much muscle on him.

"Glad to see you're awake Mr. Novak, and Hello Mr. Hennings."

Jesse nods a polite hello and I look between them, "What's the diagnosis?"

The doctor swipes on the iPad a few times, then looks up, "You have a torn ACL and meniscus. A severe tear. You also have a small puncture in your lung."

"So what does that mean?" My eyes dart between the two men in front of me. Jesse understands what it means. A frown fills his face.

The doctor looks to Jesse, wanting him to break the news for him. Fuck me. I know exactly what it means from the silence. His silence tells me everything that I need to know.

"I won't be able to play again, will I?"

Jesse sighs, "You could heal and be able to play, but you'll never play the way that you used to. This injury means, less playing time, and playing in a less intense position."

"So going pro is over for me?"

Jesse frowns, "Not completely over, but with this injury, your chances of being drafted are slim."

Everything else that the doctor says is in stereo. I feel as though a sledgehammer has been taken to the glass that has been posted around me and it has shattered to pieces at my feet.

My future in hockey is gone.

Getting to play. The opportunity to spend the next two years on the ice with my closest friends has ended. Will I get kicked off the team and lose my scholarship because of this?

Am I going to get kicked out of Allister because of one, small moment where the brakes of Logan's jeep betrayed us.

I can't imagine the way he feels right now. He's probably blaming himself for all of this. For the accident. For me not being able to play anymore. For whatever the fuck happened to Allie and Ana. I know Logan enough to know that he will be carrying this moment on his shoulders for the rest of his life. This is going to be a moment that he never lets go of.

The idea makes me feel absolutely sick to my stomach. This isn't his fault.

It's not my fault. It's not Allie or Ana's fault. It was an accident.

An accident took away the one thing that I have cared so much about.

But in a way, it makes the love I feel to my other love, feel ten-times stronger.

My love for Allison Hennings has grown in this moment. We went through hell together, and now we are going to recover from this moment together. We're going to carry this night forever. This moment.

Every ounce of pain and hurt we felt will stick inside our souls like paper and glue.

Logan mentioned something to me this morning or the morning before today. I don't remember what day it is. It was that he had noticed something change in me. He had noticed that the number one thing in my life wasn't hockey anymore. That I had pushed it back to make room for something else.

The new number one thing is Allie. My love for her.

As long as I have her, I could be without everything else in my life and feel complete. I could not go pro, I could throw away everything I've worked for and genuinely? I think I would be okay.

The only concern I have with hockey right now, is how will losing it affect me in finishing college. My schooling is paid for because I am on the team, so if I'm not playing on the team, then how am I going to afford school? How I am I going to continue going to Allister?

The thought makes me feel sick. It's not the losing hockey itself as a game, but it's the benefits that playing has given me. It's given me free room and board and tuition for the last three years. I'm closer to being done with college than I am starting it. I want to finish it. I want to get my degree and get the fuck out of here. Start a future.

With her.

With my girl.

Because at the end of the day, all that I need to keep going, is her. It's always been her.

The door opens again and every thought that was rushing through my head turns to dust as I see the figure standing in the doorway, holding a bundle close to her chest.

It's my mother. And she's carrying a baby.

Jesse freezes. The doctor stops speaking.

"Teddy, baby." She says quietly as she rushes over to my side, the silent baby not even making a peep.

My breath catches in my throat as she hugs me, pressing the infant between us.

"Mom. What-"

Jesse turns to her, "Samantha. Now is not a good time to drop this on him."

"Drop what on me?" I ask as a tight feeling grows in my chest. A fire has formed inside me and I feel like I could snap at any moment.

"Teddy, this is your brother."

You've gotta be fucking kidding me. When she said she was pregnant on the phone during the Fourth of July weekend, she was really pregnant. Not just a few weeks.

A few months.

"Mom. What?"

"His name is Alex, he's a month old." She attempts to hold him out to me, but I turn my head away from her.

"Get out." Is all that I can manage to say.

She looks confused, the baby stirring, "Get out!"

There is a pained look on Jesse's face. He looks to me, as if he's asking what I want him to do.

"Teddy, you don't mean that. That's just the meds talking." She stammers and the baby begins to cry, loudly.

"Get the fuck out or I'll have the doctor escort you out of here. As far as I am concerned, I never, ever want to see your face again." I snap. I can't even meet her gaze.

She slowly backs up, towards the door, as though she's been shot in the heart.

"You don't mean that, baby. I'm your Mom." Tears form in her tired eyes. The baby is crying.

I shake my head stiffly, "You haven't been my Mom in an incredibly long time. You don't get to just step in now that you're starting over. The time for you to be my mother has passed, and I sure as hell hope you act more like a mother to that kid than you ever did to me."

I feel a shortness of breath, my chest pinching and aching. Stupid fucking lung.

Her eyes are glassy with tears, yet I feel no pity for her. She was hardly around in my life when I was a kid. She barely around when I was a teenager. Then she completely ditched me for a dude when I turned twenty.

The only person I feel pity for in this situation, is that baby. Is she finally going to step up and be a mother, or is she going to become so flighty, so enthralled by the different men coming and going from her life to even remember she has a kid?

She hesitates to leave. Until Jesse turns to face her, "Get out. He asked for you to leave, so leave."

Saying nothing else, she exits the room, crying.

The doctor follows behind her, realizing the intensity of the moment. Jesse turns to me the minute the doctor exits.

"I'm sorry, kid."

I shake my head, "Don't be."

He grips my shoulder, trying to keep me calm I look up towards him, meeting his tired gaze.

"So, when am I getting out of here?" I break the silence and Jesse lets out a quiet chuckle, wiping his eyes with his sleeve.

"Anywhere between Monday and next Friday." He tells me. My brow furrows? Seven whole days here? You've gotta be kidding me.

"Why?" I shake my head. Why am I going to be here for so long?

"Well, they're monitoring your punctured lung. If it heals the way it should, you should be able to go home Monday."

I nod, processing this information.

"Can I see her?"

Jesse rises, then shakes his head, "She's out right now. Maybe later, okay?"

I just nod and watch as he leaves and the nurse returns with a small plastic cup of water. I sip from the small straw and feel the dryness of my tongue melt away at the liquid touches it.

Eventually she leaves, and I'm left in the crippling silence.

———

When I wake up, it's dark out, but the sun is rising. I still have no idea what day it is? How long I've been trapped in my prison cell? But I feel a set of eyes locked on me from the corner. I slowly raise my bed.

Sitting in the corner, looking tired, is Logan Finlay. The room I'm in is different before. It's less bleak. It feels more like a suite than a hospital room.

He stands quickly when he sees me rise, "Teddy. Man, fuck."

He comes over to my side, dragging the chair and sitting down.

"You look worse than the jeep."

I roll my eyes at him, not saying anything.

"No quip back?"

I shake my head. My voice is caught in my throat and it's hard for me to speak. I point to the stack of sticky notes, and the pen with the hospital information engraved on it.

He watches as I write out the words *FUCK YOU*

He laughs, "So you can't talk?"

"I can. Not much." The words finally escape my throat. I must've fucked myself up when my Mom showed up. Logan nods, reaching into his hoodie pocket and taking out a phone. My phone.

"This is pretty much all that was left of your personal belongings. Your clothes were destroyed by the paramedics. I charged it the last few days, so it should have a full battery.

I click the screen to life and it's filled with notifications. Hundreds of them.

One message from Allie.

> I got released. I'll come see you Monday, handsome. I love you.

A bunch of random messages from other guys on the team and classmates occupy the rest of my lock screen.

I click on Logan's contact and I point to my phone screen, motioning for him to turn it on

> I think i fucked myself up from speaking when my mom showed up

> Coach told us about that. Said she had a baby with her

> She did. My brother.

No shit????

Yea.

Dude, I'm sorry.

It's fine. What day is it anyway, I didn't check.

It's Monday.

And I get released today?

Nah dude. The doctor came in just before you woke up and told me that the healing it taking a lot longer than expected. He said latest you'll get out is Thursday

Motherfucker.

Don't shoot the messenger.

Friday is homecoming... I'm gonna be on fucking bedrest and miss the naming ceremony and the first game.

Do you want to miss these things?

No fucking chance.

Then we'll make it work. Even if I have to push your ass in a wheelchair.

I snicker, attempting to not laugh at that because laughing will only make me ache more, and I turn my attention back to my phone screen.

Did coach tell you about my injuries?

Yeah man, I'm sorry.

It's fine. I just don't want to lose my scholarship and get kicked out of Allister. Hockey, I can learn to move away from, but getting my degree when I'm so close to being done? I can't.

That's funny.

Wow, thanks asshole.

No, just that the Teddy I knew a year ago would've never said any of the things you're saying now.

Well, I've changed since then. Did I tell you I dropped my letters for the frat?

You mentioned it a few weeks ago, but I didn't think you actually did it. The frat you practically were begging me to join last year?

Yep. That one.

Shit, dude. You really are whipped.

Not the word I would use, but sure.

Our conversation is abruptly ended by the large, wood panel door opening and I see her standing there. She only has some scratches on her beautiful face. Her hair is tied into a ponytail and she wears a long-sleeve t-shirt. One that is incredibly baggy on her.

It's mine.

She walks over to me slowly and sits down on the side of my bed, taking one of my hands in both of hers. She holds it tightly. So fucking tightly.

"I've been so worried about you." She say quietly and I nod. Tears in my eyes and moving down my cheeks. She wipes them with the sleeve of the shirt. Logan steps forward.

"He said it's hard for him to talk right now-"

But I cut him off, "But I'll do it for you."

She breaks down in tears, lying down at my side and throwing an arm around me, she presses her forehead against my cheek, holding me tightly against her.

Logan nods, then slowly backs up, "I'm gonna call coach. Let him know how you're doing."

I nod and I don't even watch him leave. Despite my shortness of breath, I press my lips to her's and kiss her deeply. She moves further into the kiss. Deeper.

Her hand cups my cheek, thumb moving up and down my face.

She lets go and I slowly breath to catch my breath, "I love you Teddy Novak."

"I love you Allison Hennings." I reply weakly and she presses our foreheads together in a moment that we both drown in. The feeling of her here, with me, makes me feel way better than any drug they've given me here.

We're young and we're in love.

We're here, in the present moment.

And it's in this moment that I realize I want to spend every waking moment of my life with her.

CHAPTER 25
ALLIE HENNINGS

"We are gathered here today for an incredibly important reason," dad starts from the podium set up in front of the arena. The sign is behind us, concealed by a sheet, "Today, I have the honor of re-dedicating the Allister Ice Hockey Arena to someone who means the world to me."

Mom stands to his left, I stand at his right, "I've never spoken openly about it, but seventeen years ago, my family experienced a painful loss. Our son, Adam Scott Hennings, passed away at age six after experiencing a seizure while swimming with our daughter, Allie."

The crowd in front of us is in the hundreds. Hundreds of former players, of other athletic teams, of current players.

Specifically, in the front row.

Sitting right in front of us, are my closest friends. Logan, Luke, Patrick, Nik.

Teddy.

My Teddy.

He gives us a small, somber smile and even from a wheelchair, leg in a brace, he still looks the same as he did. Incredibly, undeniably hot.

Behind the boys stand Ana and Lauren and Riley and Jenny, and shockingly, something I hadn't known about until this morning, Mish and Phoebe.

All of the people I care the most about are right here.

"Adam Scott was many things, even at six years old. He was smart, he was determined, he was careful with his baby sister, and he wanted nothing more than to play hockey." Dad continues, choking on his words as he grows emotional.

He's wearing a suit, a rare occurrence for my father. My mom is wearing a dress, one that goes to her knees and covers her shoulders. It's Allister maroon.

And I'm wearing a suit. It's too cold today to be wearing a dress.

Despite it being fifty degrees out, the sun is high in the sky, the sky is blue and the clouds are minimal.

It's a perfect day.

"So, we're happy to announce that the arena has been renamed to the Adam Scott Memorial Arena. With this change, we will now be able to publicly honor our son and give him the remembrance and respect that he deserves."

The guys behind us pull down the sheet over the main doors, exposing the sign. His name is on the side of the building and my heart thumps in my chest, heavy.

Dad steps away from the podium and Mom steps forward, reading out of the leather-bound journal. It's her memory of Adam playing hockey with Dad while she held me on the sidelines when I was little.

Then, it's my turn. I step forward and gulp back the fear bubbling up my throat, "My name is Allie Hennings. I'm currently a student here at Allister, and I'm proud to dedicate the arena to my brother, Adam."

I start, hands shaking. Everything feels intense in the moment. Hundreds of people are watching. Journalists are recording it from the side. This is something everyone is going to see.

My eyes lock on Teddy and he nods an encouraging nod, giving me that small smile that I've come to love so so much.

"You've got this." He mouths silently and I nod, wiping a stray tear from my cheek.

"Until this summer, my memory of Adam was non-existent," I start, taking a breath, "As a three-year-old, watching your sibling pass, can be something that is incredibly traumatic, and as a response, my mind erased it happening in the first place to protect myself and my peace. My parents painfully had made the decision to tell me when they felt like I was ready, and I unfortunately made the mistake of finding out before they could tell me. I stumbled into what was his bedroom and my entire world shifted. All the bitterness, all the anger, all the painful emotions inside me dissipated and I was left realizing how short life can be."

Teddy nods, I turn to look to my parents who are giving me small, pain-filled smiles, "Life is short, tomorrow is something that is never guaranteed, and the past is something we will never forget. From this moment forward, this arena, this place where my father goes to work day-in and day-out, will be a reminder of the son that my parents lost, of the brother I was never given the chance to grow up with. Hug the people you love, tell them that you love them, because you never know when it will be the last time. You never know what will happen after you step out that front door, or what will happen when you get behind the wheel. You truly never know."

I take a shaking breath, the tears fighting to come out, but my mind is fighting against them. Keep your composure, Allison.

"So take the moment. Take the extra second to hug that person. Take an extra second to tell them how much you love them, how much you appreciate them," I turn to look to the sign, "And for my closing remarks, I would like to say something to Adam."

My mom comes closer and takes my hand in hers as I lift the paper with my other hand and read the words that I wrote last night.

"Adam, I will love you forever. I will carry you with me until the day I eventually pass and join you in whatever afterlife may bring. I promise and I swear upon everything in my life, that I will never forget you again. I will never let my mind trick me into believing you never existed, and I will never ever take the life I've been given for granted. Part of me wishes that you could be here with me in this moment, going to college and experiencing the highs and lows of it. I like to imagine that you would've played hockey and you would've went to every party that I went to just to watch over me. You would've grilled the crap out of the guy that I now am so grateful to call my boyfriend before you even let me go on a date with him. You would've done the things that all older brothers do. In that moment, I look to the men in my life who are older brothers, and who are so fiercely protective of their younger brothers or sisters," My eyes look to Luke and Logan knowingly, they nod, "I look to all the little sisters I know, to see what my life would've been like had you still been here."

My eyes flit to Lauren and Ana and Riley, all of whom are younger sisters, "And in these people, I see a vision, albeit hazy, of what our life would've looked like if you had still been here."

I crumple the letter up in my hands, fidgeting with the paper, "I'll love you forever and I'll love you always, and as long as I'm living, you will be my big brother. Thank you."

I step away from the podium and the three of us turn to face the sign with his name on it. Dad is in the middle of us, both me and mom leaning into his side with his arms around each of us, and in this moment, my life has never felt so complete, so whole.

I have never ever felt so damn loved as I do right now.

TEDDY NOVAK

We all head inside after the Hennings gave their beautiful speeches, the rest of the team going to get ready for the four'o clock game. I wheel my way over to Allie as she chats with Mish and Phoebe near the snack table.

"Eldridge Girls." I say as a greeting and both of them look to me.

"How's is hanging, hunk?" Mish asks, holding a small flask in her hand. I shrug.

"I've been better." I reply with a shrug and Allie giggles like a kid.

"She's so down bad for him," Phoebe turns to Mish, as though we're both not standing right here.

"Damn straight." Mish replies after taking a swig. She holds it out to me and I shake my head.

"Can't. I'm on pain killers right now."

She nods understandingly, "Alright, more for us."

She passes it to Allie, who takes a small swig, then turns to me with a smile.

"Excuse me girls, I have a small surprise for my boyfriend." I like the way that sounds coming from her pretty mouth. Boyfriend. I am her boyfriend.

She grabs the handles of the wheelchair and walks us away from Mish and Phoebe, "A surprise, eh? What trick are you hiding up your sleeve, beautiful?"

She shrugs as she stops us in front of an elevator, "You'll see." We step into the elevator and go down to the floor where the locker room and offices are and she stops us at a small office right next door to her Dad's. There's a piece of white paper hanging over the plaque on the door.

"So, I know you've been worried about losing your scholarship since you won't be able to play anymore, so I spoke with my dad," she peels back the white paper and my name is on the plaque, "And he worked out a deal with the college, that as long as your grades stay up, you can serve as the assistant coach to the team and keep your scholarship until you graduate."

There's a feeling in my chest, but it's not anxiety. It's a warmth. A reminder of how much she and her parents love me and care about me.

"I've seen fifteen years of players come and go. You boys are like my own kids after everything we go through together." Jesse's words from the beginning of summer ring through my head at this moment. I turn to her, feeling so incredibly loved by her in this moment.

"Really? I get to stay at Allister?"

She nods, big smile on her face, and her eyes glassy, "Until we graduate, baby."

I reach out and pull her down onto my lap, she yelps and I quickly press my lips to hers, kissing her and taking in every single moment of this with her.

"Whatever happens, I'm always on your team, Teddy Steven." She says lovingly.

"And I'll always be on yours, Allison Marie."

And I kiss her again, "I'm so glad that I get to call you mine."

She smiles against my lips, hand resting on my chest, "And you are mine."

She gets up and opens the door to the office and I roll in. She closes the door behind us and I revel in every kiss that we get to share beyond that door.

Even though I may never be able to play again and I have a lot of personal stuff to work through, I got the girl that I've always fucking wanted.

And no one will ever take her from me.

ALLIE HENNINGS

Dear Adam,

It's been four years on the dot since I found out about you in the middle of the night. Four years since I stumbled into what was your childhood bedroom and found all of your belongings, left behind and collecting dust, but preserving the memory of you for our family. I'd like to think that overtime, I've begun to remember you more and more. Sometimes, I just see glimpses of memories of you. Other times, I get the full memory of you. One of my favorites so far, was, according to mom, from the same summer you passed. She recounted it to me, to confirm the memory.

It was a warm, sunny day in Eldridge Bay and you had been playing with a friend. I don't know or remember his name, but he was a friend for sure. Mom also doesn't remember much about this friend, just that you two played together all the time. I was the fairy princess, at only three years old. You and your friend were knights, and Dad was a dragon. You and your friend had been using pool noodles as swords and you had been fighting against Dad to free me from my tower, a treehouse, which I also don't remember very well. Eventually, you two had "defeated" the dragon and saved me, the princess from my tower.

This memory is one of my favorites, because it makes me realize how our relationship would've been, had you not passed away. You would've protected me, done anything for me. You would have watched over me fiercely and saved me from any hurt, any grief, any pain that I had experienced in my life without you. You would not have let anyone ever hurt me.

A boy broke my heart? You would've taught him a lesson. A bully was harassing me? You would've set them straight.

I imagine that our relationship would've been similar to Luke and Lauren's. They have a similar age gap and I imagine you would react in a similar way to how he does whenever something has happened to her. Would we have been them? Both ended up at Allister College, living so close together. You watching over me at parties, or social functions, but still supporting me with the activities that I do. Speaking of Lauren, she just graduated back in May. Seeing Luke celebrate that moment with her definitely made me imagine that it was me and you.

Dad is sure that you would've played hockey all

through childhood and through the angsty teen years and into college, though, he doesn't think you would go pro. He thinks you would get a degree in some noble profession like a doctor or a teacher or a zookeeper. Mom agrees. I imagine you being a firefighter, saving people from burning buildings. Putting yourself at risk to save others. I graduated with my master's degree in May and start a job as a child psychologist.

I also imagine that you would be here today, on this very special day in Eldridge Bay.

Adam, today, I am getting married.

It's insane to even comprehend that I am getting the chance to marry my best friend in life. He's staying with Dad, Logan, Luke, Nik and Patrick at a small boutique hotel while I'm at the house with Mom, Ana, Lauren, Mish, Phoebe and a few other friends.

If you were still here, I wouldn't want you at the hotel with Dad and the guys. I would want you here, with me and Mom. I would want you to be the first man to see me in this beautiful dress.

I would also want you to be the man to walk me down the aisle. I know that a job like that usually goes to the father of the bride, but I'd like to think me and you would be close enough to where you would walk me down the isle and give me away to my future husband.

God. Teddy Novak is going to become Teddy Hennings in one hour.

Also incredibly untraditional, but Teddy has decided that he wants to take our last name. He's been distancing himself further and further from his past to grow as an individual. He hasn't spoken to his Mom since Junior Year of College. They had a big fight around Christmas, which was a follow-up to the conversation they had after the naming ceremony, and it ended with Teddy telling her he no longer wanted her in his life at all. He cut her off. Blocked her on everything and they haven't spoken since.

He's spent every holiday with us. He's become apart of the family, even before we got engaged last Christmas. Mom and Dad decided to change things up and the four of us, plus Logan and Ana, spent Christmas in Hawaii. Teddy proposed to me on the beach at sunrise. He had gotten flowers to spell it out for me across the sand. Ana, using the photography skills she picked up from Noah, was hiding out, taking pictures and not revealing herself until afterwards. It was so so so romantic.

Teddy is now doing Financial work for a big NHL team, leading them to victory after victory. Although he can't play like he used to, he is still able to skate around, even if he's only a financial manager. It's incredible.

There are so many stories that I want to tell you Adam. Maybe one day, I will, but for now, I want to be here. Be in this moment.

We have a chair set up, right in the front row,

next to Mom and Dad with your picture. It's a picture of me and you from that summer. It's a picture that was taken a month before you passed.

I wish you were physically here for this, Adam, but honestly? I think you've always been with me. Through every good moment and every bad moment.

I have carried you with me, even when I couldn't remember you.

You have always been in my heart Adam Scott Hennings.

You always will be.

- Allison Marie Hennings.

Return to Allister College in Summer of 2026 with Told You Things, Noah Karey and Luke Dermont's romance; Continue reading for a preview!

Told You Things

STARTING OVER HAS BEEN HARD, UNTIL I MET YOU.

KC MATTHEWS

CHAPTER ONE

NOAH KAREY

The smell of my dorm is stale, even three days after I initially moved in. I've had my windows open with a fan pushing the dusty, smelly air out of the room but it has not been working the way that I want to. Shit, I've even been lighting candles, which is a big no-no, but I'm desperate to make my room a bit more comfortable.

I've lived in two other dorm rooms before, this is my third, but it's my first time not having a roommate. My former school, Virginia University, had way too many students to even allow single room accommodations, unless they were absolutely forced to by doctors or medical professionals or something. But at Allister College? All I had to do was tell them my name and where I came from and they immediately gave me an exemption.

Guess that's what happens when your story goes public. Incredibly public. As in, they talked about it on every major news outlet. Or at least, only a few details. Even with all the attention, it never gave me proper closure. He got to walk away scot-free, and I'm the one left with all the baggage.

I have a large, pink tinted American flag hung up on one wall with Jonathan Bailey's *PEOPLE magazine* photo on it. String lights with fake leaves line the ceiling, making their way across the room, tucked into the corners where my prison cell ceiling meets the plaster walls.

The floor is completely tile, a faded grey with hints of blues and reds. There's a massive stain in the tile near the window, which based on its look, I guess is from nail polish remover.

This is good for me. This a good, fresh start, and I desperately needed it.

College has always been the goal, and just because of what happened, I had every intention of continuing my bachelor's degree in Photojournalism. At Allister, the major is broad, and named Media Studies. Broad, but you pick a pathway and go down in. The three most popular pathways apparently are cinematic arts, journalism, and photography.

The day I was gifted a small camera for my birthday when I was six, was the day that I fell in love with photography.

My camera is sitting on the bookshelf next to my twin-sized bed, the lens covered by the cap and my faded, leather strap hangs haphazardly, nearly reaching the floor.

For the first time in the last year, I feel like I can finally breathe.

I finally feel at peace.

Kind of.

Falling onto my bed, I stare at the ceiling, where posters are tacked into the quark-board tiles, but not blocking the fire alarm, I'm not an idiot.

Today is the first day there is no orientation events or presentations. Today, we just are supposed to meet our RA's, find our classes, or hang out.

Well, I'm not going to the RA meeting to hear the same spiel I always do. I'm sure I can find my classes, they're all in one building, and I have no one to hang out with because I don't know anyone.

My mom told me that starting at a new school was a good chance for me to re-learn how to build connections with real people. People I'm not related to at least. I spent way too much time hanging out with my grandma or my younger brothers these last six months.

Sure, I'll join a few organizations, go to some events, but I don't want to put myself in the situation that I was in. A back-stabbing friend who knew every detail about my life. A guy she was obsessed with in our friend group. No thanks, never happening again.

I would rather be stabbed again.

There's a knock at my door and I shoot up quickly. Who the fuck is at my door right now? I don't really know anyone yet. There was the blonde girl from orientation who only decided to sit with me because I was wearing a Noah Kahn hoodie.

Lauren Dermont. She's a freshman, I don't see us actually being friends. She's a freshman and I'm technically a junior.

But she doesn't know where I live. I've already been very careful with that information. I took the fucking name tag off my door and put it on the inside. I don't need my name being openly advertised to everyone else.

I look through the peephole and standing on the other side is a tall, curly-haired blonde guy. He's well built and is wearing a tight-fitting t-shirt and athletic shorts. Do I hide? Do I just open the door? Who the fuck is this guy at my door?

As I look, he knocks again and I suck in a breath, freaked out. Part of me really wants to hide right now. What if he knows?

What if he knows Jack? He looked built enough to be a football player, like Jack. Did he send one of his goons to Allister College to keep me quiet?

"Noah? Noah Karey? My name is Luke. I'm your Residence Hall Assistant-"

Before he finishes speaking, I quickly open the door.

"Sorry, um-" I rub the back of my neck nervously, "I was taking a nap."

He nods slowly, holding out a folder, "I just am going around and introducing myself to everyone before the meeting later."

I take the folder, tucking it under my arm, "Well, it's nice to meet you, Luke."

My eyes quickly scan over his body. He has to be a foot taller than me. His bicep is bigger than my neck. *Shit*, he's built like a giant in comparison to me. He's got a boyish charm, but there's also a pain in his eyes. *That pain*? I recognize it. I saw a lot of it through the months of therapy I went through.

He gives me a half-smile, "I'll have a meeting tonight in the lobby. Will you be there?"

I stare at him for an awkward amount of time. Enough to where his face reddens. Oh fuck, I made him uncomfortable.

"Sorry-" I shake my head quickly, "I'm sorry, really, I just-"

"See you later, Karey." He winks and heads to the next room.

What the fuck was that?

I close my door and lock it. The minute my back hits the door, a tremble roars through my body, and I shake. My heart begins to race. My palms begin to sweat and I feel sick to my stomach.

"You are a worthless piece of shit!"

Kick.

"No one is ever going to be into a fucking loser like you."

Kick.

Even a year later, that night is still as clear as day in my mind. Every single second of it. Even the parts where I blacked out. Even the part where I was pronounced dead for two minutes.

It's all like a vivid movie, stuck in my brain and playing on repeat and no matter what, I can't turn it off. There is no off-switch. There is nothing in the world that made that movie leave my brain.

I slide down the door to the floor and bring my knees up to my chest. My forehead presses into my knees and the tears escape my eyes as the sobs ripple through my throat.

Just the idea of someone who looks like he would've been friends with Jack scares the fuck out of me. He probably doesn't even know him. Virginia U. is two hours away from Allister College. There is no possible way your RA personally knows the fucking loser who did this to you, Noah.

The loser who not only physically broke you down, but the fucking loser who took away your innocence. The loser who took everything that made you, you, and he smashed it on the ground. Kicked the shit out of it until your ribs had cracked and black and blue bruises covered your chest.

Two months had passed before I was even able to leave the hospital. In those two months, I had barely been able to speak. Yet he walked free, as if it never happened. If we had been thirty feet to the left, there would've been security footage.

He walked away free of any punishment. I walked away with months of therapy, scars that will forever be embedded in my skin, and the feeling that I can trust no one other than myself and my family.

I quickly and shakily stand up, pulling on my over the ear headphones and turning them on. I grab my phone and curl up on top of my comforter and turn on the only music that can calm me down.

Hozier.

Music has been incredibly beneficial in my healing journey, but there's no other artist that I connect to like him. His music quickly became my therapy. While I still see my therapist once a week over a FaceTime call, I've become less dependent on Debra. She agrees that it's part of the healing process. Sometimes I need to let myself have moments like this.

Moments where I curl into a ball and listen to my loud music and just *cry*.

So that's what I do. I allow myself to drown in the moment, becoming full consumed by the dark cloud that has lingered over my life for the last ten months, two weeks, six days, four hours and twenty-seven minutes.

———

It's seven p.m. when I enter the lobby of Buchanan Hall. Luke is sitting on a table, chatting with two other guys and there's a small smile on his face as he talks to them. I take a seat in the corner, one of the free ones, next to a short-haired girl with her eyes glued to her phone. She's tan, with reddish-brown hair. She's also wearing concert merch. From Sabrina Carpenter's last tour, I think?

So I speak up, "Cool shirt."

She looks up from her phone, looking to me, and my own shirt, "You too. I'm Gwen."

"Noah."

She smiles, "So where'd you transfer from?"

Under other circumstances, I would've asked how she knew that, but I live on a floor made up entirely of transfer students. Everyone at this meeting transferred from somewhere.

"Virginia University, you?"

"Cape Cod Community College. I had to get out of my hometown and Allister offered me a good scholarship," she replies, "Wait, Virginia U, that's where that kid got-"

Fuck.

I've gotta start saying I'm from somewhere else because if this is how it's going to be for me at Allister, I'm screwed.

"Yeah, uh. I didn't know him." The lie just slips right through my teeth, "I was at the party though it happened outside of."

"Wow. That must've been scary."

I shake my head, my heart already racing in my chest as the lie effortlessly comes out, "It wasn't super scary, to be honest. I didn't personally see anything. From the sounds of it, the attack was personal and not just random."

She nods as she processes this, "Makes sense. There are 800,000 aggravated assaults in the United States every year, most of them aren't just random attacks."

That is an… odd fact?

"Oh?"

She laughs quietly, shaking her head, "Sorry, Forensic Sciences major. I want to work for the FBI one day."

"Wow. That's a big goal."

"What's your major?"

I shrug, "Nowhere near as cool, photojournalism major and writing minor."

Her eyes widen, "Shut up! Photography was my second choice. You prefer taking pictures of-"

She's interrupted by Luke silencing the herd of students.

"Alright, I met most of you earlier, but just to introduce myself again, my name is Luke. I'm a junior, forward on the hockey team, and this is my second year as an RA," my full attention turns to him. I watch every muscle in his arms, the way his lips move, the slow rise and fall of his chest as he talks, "Essentially, for those of you who haven't had an RA before, my entire job is to keep you all out of shit with the higher-ups of the college. I'm pretty lax when it comes to rules, unless they are repeatedly broken, then we will have a problem. Now do you have any questions before we go over the rules?"

A few of the people closest to him raise their hands, asking random questions I already know the answers to. Like no, you cannot light candles. No you can nail things into the walls. Just the same boring bullshit as always.

I turn back to Gwen, "I prefer taking portraits of people, or at least photos with people in them."

She nods, listening intently, "I prefer taking pictures of nature, like flowers, trees, you know?"

I nod understandingly.

Luke clears his throat and Gwen and I both turn quickly. His eyes lock on me, though.

"Are you two listening or no?"

"Sorry," Gwen stammers, "Just chatting. We'll listen now."

He nods, but even as he speaks to someone in the front, his eyes continue to flit to me in the back row. Every so often, they lock on me like lasers.

I would say like daggers, though, that might be bad wording

My stomach feels empty, even though I just had microwave pasta about thirty minutes ago.

I see a glimpse of something makes me feel really sick to my stomach.

It's me. *Kissing Luke.*

I don't even know this guy, yet I can't stop myself from imagining him bowing his head down to me to press his lips to mine. His tongue sinking into my mouth.

Stop.

He's probably not even gay. He's probably got a girlfriend who he's going to sleep with after this meeting and then cuddle with her afterwards while they fall asleep to *The Office.* You know nothing about him Noah Colin Karey.

The meeting ends after he goes over all the bullshit rules, and Gwen and I exchange social media handles, then I attempt to sneak my way through the crowd, to go back to my room, but a hand stops me. I turn and look up to meet eyes with him.

"Noah. You okay?"

I nod quickly, "I'm fine. I just want to go back to my room."

"Okay. Just wanted to check." His voice is calm. Not angry. As if he's genuinely concerned that something's wrong. Was it that obvious that something was bothering me? Do I need to work on my poker face?

I feel as though he is reading my like an open book and I'm just letting him do it. I slam the book shut.

"Can I go now?"

He stops, looking down and deep into my eyes, looking for answers, but I turn my head to the side, not being able to make eye contact with him.

"Yeah. You can go."

I walk off quickly. I don't bother turning around, because even if I do, I know that his eyes will be locked on me, watching me as I go back to my room and slam the door closed behind me.

———

ACKNOWLEDGMENTS

The first time I started creating Allister, I was a sophomore in college. I was struggling with a lot of emotions and feelings and needed to manifest them somewhere, and that just so happened to be here: In Teddy, Allie, Logan, Ana, Luke, Lauren, Patrick, and Mish.

To start off: Thank you to all my friends from *instagram*. Your support for me and this book has been unprecedented and I love and appreciate you so much! To Sarah, Ash, McKayla, Assunta, Alliah, Maria, Lex, Sam, Nora, Mars, Em, Gigi, Syd, Bre, Lila, Emily, Priyanka and so so so many of you. I can't possibly list all of your names into one acknowledgements page, but for all the love so so many of you have shown to this book... I couldn't do this without you all.

To my family; there's so many of you I want to thank. My parents, my brother, my grandparents, my aunts and uncles, my cousins, my soon to be step siblings, and my godsister. You are all the reason why I am where I am today. Without you, I wouldn't be here, writing the acknowledgments to my first ever novel. Teddy and Allie would not exists if it wasn't for all of you.

Extra thank you to my Aunt Cyndi for being my first beta reader of this book and reading it as I wrote it. You have been the number one cheerleader for Allie and Teddy since day one and I appreciate you so much.

To my best friend Zoe, I have been changed for good, having you in my life. To my other friends: Olivia, Jayden,

Alivia, Alexandrea and Will; thank you for making college bearable and worth the journey.

Also, to my favorite authors, Krista and Becca! Thank you for giving me advice on the self-publishing industry at a time when I realllllyyyy needed it.

And I want to give Sam another round of applause for the beautiful character art of Allie and Teddy that is present on the title page and I have used in literally every instagram post to promote this book <3

I would like to end off by saying thank you to you, dear reader. Without you, this book would not be where it is today and I appreciate you so so so so so much for giving my debut novel a chance!

- KC, 2025

ABOUT THE AUTHOR

KC Matthews is an emerging author of College Romance and Poetry. KC is currently a College student studying English and Creative Writing. In their free time, they are reading romance novels, running their fan-instagram page, and watching trashy dramas.

instagram.com/@authorkcmatt
facebook.com/kcmatthewsauthor